THREE-DAY TOWN

THREE-DAY TOWN

MARGARET MARON

THORNDIKE
CHIVERS

GALE
CENGAGE Learning

This Large Print edition is published by Thorndike Press, Waterville, Maine USA and by AudioGo Ltd, Bath, England.
Copyright © 2011 by Margaret Maron.
The moral right of the author has been asserted.
A Deborah Knott Mystery.
All epigraphs taken from *The New New York,* by John C. Van Dyke, Macmillan Company, 1909.
Thorndike Press, a part of Gale, Cengage Learning.

ALL RIGHTS RESERVED

Thorndike Press® Large Print Mystery.
The text of this Large Print edition is unabridged.
Other aspects of the book may vary from the original edition.
Set in 16 pt. Plantin.

LIBRARY OF CONGRESS CATALOGING-IN-PUBLICATION DATA

Maron, Margaret.
    Three-day town / by Margaret Maron.
      p. cm. — (Thorndike Press large print mystery)
    ISBN-13: 978-1-4104-4144-7 (hardcover)
    ISBN-10: 1-4104-4144-X (hardcover)
    1. Knott, Deborah (Fictitious character)—Fiction. 2. Women judges—Fiction. 3. New York (N.Y.)—Fiction. 4. Large type books. I. Title.
PS3563.A679T47 2011b
813'.54—dc22   2011038784

BRITISH LIBRARY CATALOGUING-IN-PUBLICATION DATA AVAILABLE
Published in the U.S. in 2011 by arrangement with Grand Central Publishing, a division of Hachette Book Group, Inc.
Published in the U.K. in 2012 by arrangement with the author.
U.K. Hardcover: 978 1 445 88626 8 (Chivers Large Print)
U.K. Softcover: 978 1 445 88627 5 (Camden Large Print)

Printed in the United States of America
1 2 3 4 5 6 7 15 14 13 12 11

This one is for the *Weymouth 7* —
Diane Chamberlain, Katy
Munger, Sarah Shaber, Alexandra
Sokoloff, Kathy Trocheck, and
Bren Bonner Witchger — who were
there at the conception and
cheered me on to the delivery.

Thanks, ladies!

I love short trips to New York; to me it is the finest three-day town on earth.

— James Cameron

DEBORAH KNOTT'S FAMILY TREE

Annie Ruth
Langdon
(1)

m.

(stillborn son)

(1) Robert   m.
- 1) Ina Faye
- 2) Doris > Betsy, Robert, Jr. (Bobby) > grandchildren

(2) Franklin   m.
- Mae > children > grandchildren

(3) Andrew   m.
- 1) Carol > Olivia > Braz, Val
- 2) Lois
- 3) April > A.K., Ruth

(4) Herman*   m.
- Nadine > *Reese, *Denise, Edward, Annie Sue

(5) Haywood*   m.
- Isabel > Valerie, Steven, Jane Ann > grandchildren

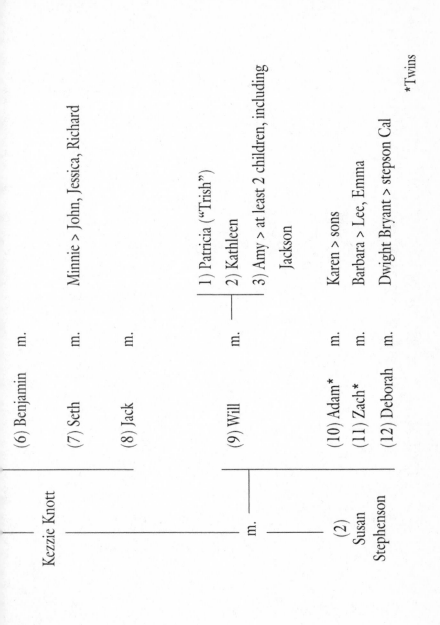

Kezzie Knott

(6) Benjamin m.

(7) Seth m. Minnie > John, Jessica, Richard

(8) Jack m.

(9) Will m. 1) Patricia ("Trish")
2) Kathleen
3) Amy > at least 2 children, including Jackson

m.
(2)
Susan
Stephenson

(10) Adam* m. Karen > sons

(11) Zach* m. Barbara > Lee, Emma

(12) Deborah m. Dwight Bryant > stepson Cal

*Twins

1940

With flirtatious ceremony, Associate Professor Steinberg, Art History, lifts the heavy silver table lighter from the coffee table in front of his brown leather couch and clicks it two or three times till the wick catches fire before holding it out to Miss Barclay, who teaches Modern Poetry. Two of their students roll their eyes at each other when Miss Barclay cups her slender hands around his, as if the flame might be blown out by a strong wind before her cigarette is fully lit.

Professor Abernathy, Modern American History, watches, too, but her steely blue eyes are narrowed in disapproval. In her opinion, a lady does not smoke — not that Miss Barclay is a lady if she lets herself be wooed by the first Jew in the long (and previously all-Protestant) history of Stillwater College. And what the dean was thinking of, she could not fathom. "A modern liberal education should include exposure to other races and other cultures," he had told the faculty search committee, but *really!*

Poor Miss Barclay, thinks one of the watching girls, the only sophomore in this interdisciplinary seminar. While not yet a completely dried-up old prune like Professor Abernathy, Miss Barclay has to be at least thirty-five, if not close on to forty; and although Professor Ronald Steinberg may look like the answer to a maiden's prayer with his manly pipe, graying temples, and cleft chin, she knows for a fact that he is queer, having seen him kissing a younger man on the lips a few weeks earlier. Fortunately, he had not seen her.

Had she reported him, he would have been summarily fired. Not that she ever would. In the first place, she would have to admit that she had sneaked off campus after hours to meet a boy and had wound up in a part of town strictly forbidden to Stillwater students even in broad daylight. Too, she has always enjoyed knowing things that no one else knows, and this is a particularly delicious secret. That this oh-so-proper girls' school has not only hired a Jew but a fairy as well?

On the other hand, it would serve him right if she exposed him. Of all the teachers at this small New England college, he alone mocks her accent and acts as if a Southern drawl automatically deducts ten points from her IQ. Only this morning when she correctly answered a question about Picasso, he had stared at her in exaggerated surprise and said, "Well, hush my mouth! Is the South finally dipping its toes into the twentieth century?"

It's bad enough that half the class has a crush on Professor Steinberg, something that he does nothing to discourage, but to lead poor Miss Barclay on as if he really does have a sexual interest in her? Although the sophomore considers Miss Barclay naïve and too carried away by poets who burn their candles at both ends, she likes the woman and thinks it's rotten of Professor Steinberg to toy with her emotions.

Discovering that he is a phony in one area has made her question everything else about him. He claims to have had drinks with Joan Miró and Max Ernst in Paris before the invasion and to have played chess with Marcel Duchamp when he was working on his doctorate at Columbia University. The paintings on his walls, the framed photographs, the bits and pieces of artwork scattered around the public rooms of this house — are they by important artists or merely pale imitations he has picked up down in

13

New York?

Two senior girls arrive as Miss Barclay and Professor Abernathy take their places on the couch and prepare to lead the afternoon's discussion of how their three disciplines overlap and enhance each other.

While Professor Steinberg helps the latecomers off with their coats and scarves, the sophomore goes upstairs as if to use the bathroom. Once out of sight of the others below, she opens the door opposite the bathroom and steps into the professor's private office. The door was slightly ajar when she was up here last week. Amid the jumble of artifacts on a chest near the door, a small object had piqued her curiosity.

No chance last week to examine it closely. Now she quickly enters the room and is delighted to realize that it is even more vulgar than her original impression. Without really considering, she hastily jams it to the bottom of her capacious bookbag, shifts the items atop the chest to disguise the gap, and returns to the living room. Another girl passes her on the stairs as she descends. Before today's session ends, she knows that at least three or four others will have visited the bathroom. Even if Professor Steinberg realizes tonight that something is missing, he will have no idea which of them took it.

14

Or why.

As she sinks onto a cushion on the floor she recognizes why this theft is doubly satisfying. He will not be able to report his loss or even accuse one of them. The piece is modern and much too crude to be valuable, but even if it were, he cannot risk the questions a description of the piece might raise with both the police and the dean.

The South may be mired in the nineteenth century, she thinks, *but Stillwater's dean is a direct descendant of seventeenth-century Puritans.*

CHAPTER 1

Neither is it the place to get the best cab accommodations. The horses are street-car derelicts, the harness gives evidence of disintegration, the carriage and the shabby unshaven driver are usually the worse for wear. One resolves not to be bothered by such small matters.
— *The New New York,* John C. Van Dyke, 1909

Dwight paced the kitchen, muttering about school buses that clog our morning roads and how we were going to miss our train if I didn't quit dawdling and what the hell was taking me so long, but I had a mental list of what had to be done before we could leave and I was determined to check every item twice even though we were a couple of weeks past Christmas and I wasn't Santa Claus.

- Cal and a week's worth of clean clothes over to Kate and Rob's. *Check.*
- Bandit and a week's worth of terrier chow to Daddy. *Check.*
- Amtrak tickets in Dwight's jacket pocket. *Check.*
- Keys to Kate's Manhattan apartment on both our keychains. *Check.*
- Cosmetics and warm clothes packed. *Check.*

(*"One new wool hat. Check,"* whispered the preacher, who lurks on the edge of my subconscious and approves of all things useful.)

(*"And one new black negligee,"* chortled the pragmatist, who shares the space and has his own opinion as to what is useful.)

- All perishables out of the refrigerator. *Check.*
- Gas turned off at the tank. *Check.*
- Thermostat —

"Let's go, shug."

"One more minute," I pleaded. "I know we're forgetting something important."

"That's what phones are for. Anything we forget to do, we can call Mama or one of the boys and they'll come take care of it."

True. My brothers and I do have keys to each other's houses. Nevertheless . . .

"Dammit, Deborah!"

Reluctantly, I let Dwight herd me out into the frigid winter air.

After a full year of marriage, we were finally going to have a honeymoon. His sister-in-law Kate's first husband had been a successful investment banker on Wall Street. After Jake's death, she had moved down to his family farm here in our neighborhood, where she met and married Dwight's younger brother Rob, a Raleigh attorney. She had kept the apartment in Manhattan, though, and rented it furnished to a Frenchman whose business interests took him to Europe several times a year. Part of the rental agreement was that Kate would have the use of the apartment whenever he was away, which was how she could give us a week in New York as a Christmas present.

"January may not be the best time of year," Rob had teased us, "but you'll have your love to keep you warm."

We were in Dwight's pickup and halfway down our long driveway before I finally remembered.

"That package!" I cried. "We have to go back! I forgot Mrs. Lattimore's package."

He kept his foot on the gas. "No, you didn't. Your suitcase looked pretty full, so I stuck it in mine."

Relieved, I leaned back in my seat and watched the sun edge up over the horizon. It sparkled on frost-covered fields planted in winter rye and turned bare oak branches into lacy Victorian silhouettes against the early morning sky as Dwight pointed the truck toward Raleigh. He glanced over at me and smiled.

"You look like a kid on her way to a party."

I smiled back at him. "That's exactly how I feel."

Most of the time I love my life, but a whole week with no work and no family? Just Dwight and me alone together in New York? A long-bed Chevy pickup is nothing like a pumpkin coach, but I really did feel like Cinderella on her way to a ball.

Best of all, my happily-ever-after Prince Charming was driving the horses.

The Amtrak station lies on the south side of Raleigh and it was crowded with passengers waiting for the Silver Star. Although today would be my very first train trip, I had already decided it was better than flying.

Dwight found a space for the truck just a few steps from the station door. No parking decks or fees. No security lines, no taking off our shoes, no X-raying of luggage, although I wouldn't have minded seeing what was inside the small package we were taking to New York for Jane Lattimore, one of Kate's elderly connections.

She had handed it to me at Kate and Rob's Christmas dinner party and asked me to carry it up to her daughter in New York. No hint as to what it could be and too securely wrapped in heavy brown paper and tied with carpenter's string for me to sneak a look. Longer than it was wide and surprisingly heavy, the package could have held a tall can of beer or a jar of the white lightning my daddy used to make, except that it didn't gurgle.

Or rattle either, for that matter.

Okay, yeah, I *did* shake it. Hey, if they're strip-searching little old ladies at the airports, who's not to say a strong-willed old lady couldn't be sending a bomb north?

Mrs. Lattimore is rather wealthy and had once been a very large fish in our small-pond end of the county. She and my Stephenson grandfather were second or third cousins, once removed — a kinship so tenuous as to be meaningless anywhere except in the South. My mother had used that kinship to get Mrs. Lattimore's support

21

for enriched school programs, but there was no social interaction. The Lattimores were connected by wealth and marriage to some of the leading families in the mid-Atlantic states, while Mother had forfeited any Junior League aspirations when she married the area's biggest bootlegger. Growing up, she may have known the three Lattimore daughters, but they had scattered as soon as they reached college age and began impressive careers in other states. Some of the grandchildren used to come for a week or two in the summer, but they kept to themselves behind the iron railings that surrounded the large Queen Anne–style house.

I had briefly met the daughter I was supposed to give the package to. Anne Lattimore Harald is a Pulitzer Prize–winning photojournalist, and the museum in Raleigh exhibited her work a few years ago. Kate introduced me at the opening reception, but there's no way she would have remembered me among so many that night.

Kate's first husband had been more closely related to the Lattimores than my weak link, and Kate kept a sort of a watching brief on Mrs. Lattimore, a thankless task since the elderly autocrat had sworn her to secrecy as her physical condition deteriorated. "She knows her daughters would try to bully her into more chemotherapy," Kate said, when I told her that I'd been commissioned to take something to New York because Dwight is a deputy sheriff.

"Aunt Jane's been sorting through the house and labeling everything so that they will know who's to get what when the time comes. Even her jewelry and her silver and her antique furniture. What could be so valuable that she'd risk letting Anne know how sick she is just so she could be sure it got to her safely?"

That Christmas dinner was the first time I'd seen Mrs. Lattimore in months and I'd been shocked by her fragility.

According to Kate, Mrs. Lattimore was convinced that chemo would only give her a few extra months. Miserable months at that. With no desire to prolong the inevitable, she intended to wait until it was clearly too late before telling her children.

"She doesn't want to spend the last year of her life bald and wretched," said Kate, "and the older I get, the more I think she has a right to make that decision for herself."

Chemotherapy has probably advanced tremendously in the twenty-one years since Mother died, but remembering how nauseated, weak, and physically depleted she was by the end of that summer, I could understand Mrs. Lattimore's reasoning. All the same, difficult as it had been for me to watch Mother struggle and suffer, the memory of that summer is precious to me, and I thought it was unfair of Mrs. Lattimore not to give her daughters the choice of being there with her while she was still able to enjoy them.

Not my decision, though. Unless I was asked a direct question by Mrs. Harald, I didn't plan to say a word.

From far down the track, the train's airhorn sounded absurdly like the whistle of the toy train Cal and I had given Dwight for Christmas. My stepson wasn't unhappy about spending the week with Kate and Rob's three children, but he *was* wistful about missing a train ride. At its approach, I was swept up in the same happy anticipation as the other passengers who watched the huge engine ease to a stop. No puffs of steam like the toy train, but the brakes did make a satisfactory squeal.

Soon we were wheeling our suitcases down the aisle to a pair of comfortable seats beside wide windows. Dwight stowed our things on the capacious overhead rack and snagged a couple of pillows for our necks.

Legroom was at least half again what you get on a plane and there were even adjustable leg- and footrests. I know it wasn't the Polar Express, but I could have sworn that the conductor who came around to punch our tickets looked a bit like a black Tom Hanks.

As we pulled out of Raleigh, the last call for breakfast came over the intercom and Dwight and I lurched down to the dining car, where we shared a table with a couple who had celebrated their thirtieth anniversary with a week in Florida and were now on their way back to Brooklyn. Over scrambled eggs and French toast, they gave us a list of must-do things while we were in New York. We added their suggestions to the list we'd drawn up, then they headed back to the sleeper cars and we returned to our coach.

When Dwight insisted that I take the window, I didn't argue. I put my seat back, adjusted the pillow, and watched the landscape roll past till I fell asleep to the rhythm of the wheels. When I woke, we had stopped in Rocky Mount. Dwight's own seat was as far back as it would go, his eyes were closed, and his long body was almost a straight line. Neither of us had slept more than four hours the night before. I'm a district court judge and my calendar had been jammed as we played catch-up after the holidays. Dwight is second in command at the Colleton County Sheriff's Department and he, too, had put in extra hours so that he could take this week off with a clear conscience.

Carefully, so as not to wake him, I turned my head on the pillow and studied his face, a face I had known since infancy. Indeed, he was there the day I was born. Daddy had rounded up all the boys in the yard that hot August day, packed them in the back of his pickup, and hauled them over to the hospital. After eleven sons, he was so tickled to have a daughter that he'd been sure the boys would want to see me, too, whether they were his sons or friends of his sons. Dwight swears he remembers seeing me held up to the nursery window. My twin brothers don't. "All I recall is that Daddy stopped on the way home and bought everybody ice cream cones to celebrate," says Zach.

"First time we ever had pistachio," says Adam.

"And it's not like babies were real rare in our family," Will says when the subject comes up. "But pistachio ice cream cones? Now *they* were few and far between."

"Only reason I remember," says Dwight with a teasing grin, "is that I'd tasted pistachio ice cream before, so you were the only thing new to me that day."

Except for his height, nothing about him is particularly memorable — ordinary nose, strong jawline, clear brown eyes, straight brown hair with an obstinate cowlick at the crown.

For years, he was just good ol' dependable Dwight, a handy escort when I was between men, a convenient shoulder to cry on when a love affair went sour, and certainly not someone who had ever made my heart flutter. Then, out of the blue, he proposed to me last year. I thought it would be a marriage of convenience for both of us, but to my complete and utter surprise, after a lifetime of taking him for granted, I found myself falling wildly in love. It was like taking a second look at a chunk of glass and discovering a diamond.

"Do I pass inspection?" he asked in a lazy voice with his eyes still closed.

"Absolutely," I said and tucked myself under his arm. With my head nestled on his chest, we both fell asleep again.

When we finally awoke for good, we were well into Virginia. In Washington, our diesel engine was changed over for an electric one, which gave us enough time to go up into Union Station and grab sandwiches to take back to our seats.

While Dwight worked on a proposal the Colleton County Sheriff's Department planned to present to the county commissioners at their February meeting, I took out my laptop to review some of the work that would be waiting for me when I got back. Most of the cases were routine, but I was truly conflicted about a custody battle that loomed on my calendar. Jenny and Max Benton are both casual friends, which is the trouble with living and working your whole life in a small town that's also the county seat. All my judicial colleagues know the Bentons one way or another and several are related through blood or marriage. I tried to recuse myself from their case when it was first assigned, but they both wanted me and they both swore they would abide by whatever ruling I made without bitching about it afterwards.

I'm cynical enough to know that won't happen. Jenny's probably counting on the fact that we serve on a charitable board together and often have lunch with some of the other members after the meetings. Max, on the other hand, has been my insurance agent ever since I had anything worth insuring. When my car was totaled last year, he got me the maximum from the underwriter and expedited the process.

Both work full-time, but Jenny's a control freak and a micromanager, who would drive me crazy if she had any say in my life. She's devoted to Jamie, the sixteen-year-old in dispute. Very conscientious about his well-being. Too conscientious, say some. She never gives him a chance to fail, and he would probably be a neurotic mess without the leavening influence of his dad.

Max is more laid-back. An ad hoc guy, he takes life as it comes and each day is filled with mostly happy surprises for him, thanks to an efficient secretary who keeps his workday on track. He loves the outdoors and takes the boy fishing and camping whenever they can sneak away — activities too unstructured for Jenny to join them.

On the face of it, Max would be the better custodial parent of a teenage boy, but Max is also a high-functioning alcoholic who has no desire to exchange malt liquor for Adam's ale. I'm told that he usually limits himself to a single shot of scotch every evening, but once or twice a year he goes on monumental benders that can last a week.

Overprotective mother or unpredictable father?

I'm sure their lawyers will present both

arguments and everyone will expect the wisdom of Solomon. I just hope I don't have to get out my sword.

Our train pulled into New York right on schedule, a little after seven. Here at the tail end of rush hour, Penn Station was a confusion of shops and exits, and the space swarmed with people who all seemed to know exactly where they were going. I hadn't been there in several years and would have stopped to savor the scene if Dwight hadn't already been heading toward the Eighth Avenue escalator for a cab going uptown.

A short and skinny teenage boy might have fit into the backseat of the first taxi, but there was no way Dwight's long legs would. The second one was only marginally better, so Dwight slid into the front seat, which left me in possession of all the windows in the rear. Rather dirty windows actually, but I didn't care. By the time we got up to Kate's apartment in the West Seventies, I almost had whiplash from trying not to miss a single neon sign.

The cab let us out in front of the building's nondescript brick exterior, a block off Broadway, and we stepped into a frigid wind straight off the Hudson River. It stung our cheeks and almost blew Dwight's hat off. The inner door was locked, but before we could ring, an elderly gentleman was leaving and he courteously held the door open for us. Inside the lobby, the elevator man watched as we approached, trailing our roller bags behind us across a floor tiled in earth-tone ceramic squares. A hair or two taller than me and trim in a dark brown uniform, he had skin the color of weak tea, his dark hair was going gray, and he wore a pencil-thin gray mustache above narrow lips that pursed in disapproval. A brass name tag identified him as Sidney.

"Does Mr. Gorman know you?"

"The man who just left?" asked Dwight. "No."

"He should not have let you in." He spoke sternly in an accent that sounded slightly Asian to me. "No one is supposed to enter this building without proper identification."

I tried not to smile. This Sidney had a wiry, muscular build as if he worked out regularly, but unless he had a black belt in martial arts, no way could he have physically stopped someone Dwight's size once he was inside the lobby.

Instead of arguing, Dwight simply flipped open his wallet and held out his driver's license. "I believe Kate Bryant, the owner of

6-A, notified the super that we were coming?"

"Mrs. Bryant? Oh. You mean Mrs. Honeycutt that was." He squinted at Dwight's ID, then reluctantly stepped aside so we could enter the elevator.

Almost immediately, five more people pushed through the outer lobby door, two women and three men. Like us they were muffled and hatted against the icy wind. Laughing and chattering, they greeted Sidney by name as they converged on the elevator. The alpha female pushed back the fur-lined hood of her black parka and let a cascade of blonde hair swing free. Her face was too long and thin and her chin a bit too pointed for conventional beauty, but from the indulgent smile she was getting from ol' Sidney, she could have been a glamorous A-list movie star. There was a familiar lilt to her voice, and for a moment I wondered if I had indeed seen her before. If not on the big screen, maybe television?

Dwight and I stepped back and pushed our bags closer together. Even so, there was no room for all of them.

"Sorry, boys. You'll have to wait," the blonde said as she pulled the other woman, a small brunette, into the car with her. One of them wore a delicate spicy scent that contrasted pleasantly with the smell of cold wool.

The blonde gave us a friendly smile and then read the tag on my suitcase with blatant curiosity. "Cotton Grove, North Carolina? Where's that? Anywhere near Charlotte?"

"A few miles south of Raleigh," I said.

"Cam's from North Carolina," she said. "Do you know him?"

"Who?"

"Cameron Broughton. One of the left-behinds in the lobby."

I hadn't looked closely at any of the men although Cameron and Broughton are both prominent names in the state. I glanced up at Dwight, who gave a negative shrug.

"Sorry," I said.

"It's a big state, Luna," said the other woman with an amused shake of her head. "You'll have to excuse her. Cam's got her thinking that everybody in the South knows everyone else. Or is related if you go back far enough."

"Well, just look at yesterday," the blonde said as if scoring a definite point. She turned back to us. "Two couples came out of the hotel down the block, and just as we were passing, they realized that they were all from North Carolina and that one of them was the sister-in-law to the other woman's cousin. Cam says it happens anytime four Southerners get together. There's never the full six degrees of separation."

In keeping with the Arts and Crafts ambiance of the lobby, the small elevator was probably original to the building. Sidney had manually closed the brass accordion-type gate before turning a thick brass lever that let us rise. Once we left the lobby's fixed door, there was nothing between the gate and the ugly concrete shaft. We passed the numbered floors and stopped in front of the door marked with a large black 6.

The two women exited and Sidney unbent enough to tell us that 6-A was on the right, which made the blonde called Luna turn back with renewed interest.

"You're staying in Jordy Lacour's place? Cool! We're neighbors. How long will you be here?"

"Just a week," I told her.

"Then we'll be seeing you again," she said.

They went on down the hall to the apartment at the other end and Sidney did not linger to watch us open the door, which was just as well, given how long it would have taken us to figure out which key turned which of the two locks. I had forgotten how most city dwellers have more than one on their doors and I had a sudden flashback to the law student I'd lived with after Mother died when I dropped out of school and ran away from home. The door of Lev Schuster's West Village efficiency had three locks and a deadbolt and his jaw used to tighten if I left any of them unlocked.

In the end it didn't matter, because Dwight had barely inserted the first key before the knob turned and a stocky man filled the open doorway. His dark brown coveralls were the same shade as Sidney's uniform and his own brass name tag read PHIL. Unlike Sidney, who was so sleek and trim he could have stepped off a wedding cake, this middle-aged man filled his coveralls to the bursting point with lumpy bulges. His hair was a tangle of salt-and-ginger curls that probably sneered at combs. His square face was clean-shaven, but his bushy eyebrows more than made up for it. Like the hair on his head, his brows were so thick and wiry they reminded me of woolly bear caterpillars foretelling a hard winter. His nose looked as if it'd been broken at least once, but his smile was welcoming.

"You the people Miz Bryant said was coming?" He had a smoker's gravelly voice but no smoky odor emanated from his coveralls.

"That's right," said Dwight. "And you are?"

"Phil Lundigren. I'm the super here. There was a leak in 7-A and I was checking to make sure it didn't come through the ceiling." He reached for the handle of my suitcase. "Here, let me give you a hand with that."

He led us through the vestibule and down a short hall into the master bedroom, switching on more lights as we went. He wasn't particularly tall, but there was strength in his bulky frame, for he carried my heavy bag as if it were a feather and gently deposited it inside the door.

"My wife cleans for some of the owners and she came in yesterday after Mr. Lacour left and changed the sheets and towels. I didn't find any water damage, but you folks might want to keep an eye out and call me if you see any damp spots on the ceilings, okay? My number's there by the house phone and my apartment's on the ground floor around from the elevator."

He explained how to adjust the radiators and opened a service door off the kitchen to show us where to leave our garbage after we had separated out the paper, glass, and

36

tins. He told us how the keys worked and how to buzz someone in, and warned us not to let anyone in that we didn't know. After saying there was a grocery around the corner on Broadway, he finally took himself off so that we could explore the apartment for ourselves.

There were two bedrooms, two baths, full kitchen, separate dining room, and, unexpectedly, French doors that opened off the living room onto a tiny balcony. Two chairs might fit out there in nice weather, but they'd have to be awfully small ones. Leaning over the iron railing, we could make out the upper end of Broadway, half a block over. Knots of people passed on the sidewalks while yellow cabs weaved in and out of the lanes, missing each other by inches. The horns, the lights, the wail of a fire truck — all added to the exhilaration of being in one of the world's great cities.

"It's freezing out here," Dwight said and we stepped back into the warmth of the apartment.

"First things first," I said as I slung my coat and scarf on the back of the black leather couch. "I'll call Mrs. Lattimore's daughter and —"

"No," said Dwight, taking me into his arms. "First thing is to remember that this is our honeymoon."

It was after 9:30 before we were ready to think about food. The refrigerator was empty except for a stick of butter, a bottle of salad dressing, and six different kinds of mustard. Rather than go out for supper, we bundled up and headed around to Broadway to find the grocery store the super had described.

Here on a freezing Friday night, Fairway's aisles were as crowded as our local grocery would have been on a warm Saturday morning. Of course, these aisles and carts were only half as wide as ours, but the shelves and cases were piled high with exotic delicacies of every description. One corner was filled by a dozen different varieties of olives in open barrels, hundreds of cheeses were stacked in another section. Hot foods, cold cuts, salads, baked goods, custards — we hardly knew where to begin. Every turning brought unfamiliar smells and entrancing temptations.

In the end, our eyes were limited by how much we thought we could carry, and we went back to the apartment with eggplant parmigiana, ravioli, artichoke salad, a small packet of bruschetta, and a Washington State merlot.

"We can come back tomorrow for milk and juice," Dwight said, happily taking it all in. I tried not to roll my eyes. This was his honeymoon, too, and if he finds grocery stores more entertaining than I do, who am I to complain? Especially since Kate had given me the addresses of a few specialty shops more to my own liking.

By the time we finished eating and stashed the remains in the refrigerator, I decided it was too late to call Anne Harald.

"I'll do it first thing in the morning," I said through a barely suppressed yawn, and we were soon back in bed.

This time to sleep.

And the evening and the morning were the first day.

CHAPTER 2

Among the detached sculpture in the parks and streets, bad as much of it always was . . . there are still some notable examples which people do not care to forget.

— *The New New York,* 1909

We slept till after eight the next morning, and while Dwight went out for coffee and breakfast rolls, I checked my email.

Cal wrote that he and Mary Pat had made 100s on their end-of-the-week spelling test and that he was now one level higher than she on one of their long-running computer games. Both of them were going to a class-mate's birthday party the next day.

My friend Portland had finally uploaded some of the pictures she'd taken of her year-old daughter at Christmas. She and Avery named her Carolyn Deborah, and one of the pictures showed her wearing the red plaid dress I'd given her.

Minnie, the sister-in-law who is my campaign advisor, wrote that barring a last-minute surprise, I wasn't going to have to run an all-out campaign for reelection.

"She says that Paul Archdale's decided not to run for my seat after all," I told Dwight when he returned.

"Probably knows he'd be wasting his time and money," said my loyal spouse, busily unloading plastic bags from Fairway Market onto the kitchen counter.

The smell of freshly ground coffee and warm bagels made my mouth water. Dwight set out milk, orange juice, a block of cream cheese, several slices of smoked salmon, and a small jar of wild strawberry jam. I opened another bag to see an applesauce muffin, a turnover oozing with blackberries, and a little wedge of Brie. A third bag held more packets of deli items.

I shook my head. "All this for breakfast? I'm not letting you go back to that store."

He laughed. "Try and stop me. You call Mrs. Lattimore's daughter yet?"

"I'll do it right now," I said and scrolled through the list of names on my cell phone's contact list till I came to *Anne Harald.*

There were the usual chirps and blips and then four long rings before I heard a woman's voice say, "You've reached Anne and Mac's answering machine. If you need to reach Anne or Mac before February, find a pencil. Got it? Okay, listen up, 'cause here comes the number to call."

By then I had grabbed a pen from Dwight's shirt pocket and scribbled the number on my hand, a 212 area code, which meant it was right here in Manhattan.

A few minutes later, I was listening to a second answering machine message. A different woman's voice crisply instructed me to leave a short message and a callback number. There was no promise that she would actually call back, but I dutifully gave my number and explained that I was trying to deliver a package to Anne Harald from her mother in North Carolina, but —

At that point the answering machine cut off and left me with nothing but a dial tone.

Exasperated, I ended the connection and helped Dwight finish putting our breakfast together.

The coffee was even better than the aroma promised, and I'd forgotten how delicious toasted onion bagels are with a thick *schmeer* of cream cheese. I couldn't decide whether to top mine off with smoked salmon or the wild strawberry jam, so what the hell? I cut it in half and had some of each. Yum!

I told myself I didn't need to worry about waddling onto the train home, because the city encourages walking. All the New Yorkers I've ever known walk miles more than country people, who tend to jump into a car or truck if it's more than a few hundred feet. Once again, memory stretched back across the years to the winter I spent here with Lev Schuster. A penniless law student, I knew he couldn't afford cabs, but "Can't we at least take a bus?" I would whine, only to have him look at me in surprise that I would waste money on a bus when the restaurant or museum or library was only fifteen or twenty blocks away. I grew to hate crosstown blocks, which are two to four times longer than the north–south blocks, and I planned to reacquaint myself with the bus and subway systems as soon as possible.

"What do you want to do first?" Dwight asked me when I emerged from the bedroom warmly dressed in wool slacks, sweater, and sturdy shoes made for walking.

We both had lists of things to do, restaurants to try, and exhibits to see. He wanted to reconnect with an old Army buddy who taught at John Jay College of Criminal Justice and had promised to give Dwight a tour of the place next time he was up.

I had already decided that would be a good time to check out some of the stores along Fifth Avenue. But for today?

"Let's take a bus down to Columbus Circle. I want to see that exhibit of Madeleine Albright's pins."

"Pens?"

"Pins," I said firmly. "Brooches. They're not just girly stuff. I've read that when she was secretary of state, she used her pins to set the mood for some of her negotiations. We don't have to stay long if you get bored, I promise."

Bundled up against the cold, we were waiting for the elevator when the door at the end of the hallway opened and the blonde from the night before appeared. She wore a fuzzy pink sweater over flannel pajama bottoms and her bedroom slippers were stitched with pink rhinestones.

"Oh, good!" she said in her maddeningly familiar gurgling voice. "I was going to slip this under your door but now I can just hand it to you. I'm having a party tonight and I'd adore for you to come." As the elevator door opened, she gave that impish, slightly conspiratorial smile we were coming to know. "If you're part of the party, you won't complain about the noise."

"You'll get enough complaints from five and seven," today's young elevator man warned her.

"Oh, pooh, Antoine! Who cares about them?" She turned back to us. "Things should get under way around nine-ish and I won't take no for an answer."

"We'd love to," I said before Dwight could think of an excuse to decline.

"That one and her parties," Antoine said with a grin as he pulled the cage closed. He didn't look much older than the girl. Of medium height with a reedy build, he had honey brown skin, a very short Afro, and what the kids at home call a chinstrap beard, a narrow line of facial hair that followed the contour of his jaw. "They'll have her up before the board again, you mark my words." Those words carried a faint Jamaican accent.

"A New York party!" I told Dwight as we stepped out into the frigid morning sunlight. "A rowdy New York party. It'll be fun."

He gave me a jaundiced look, finished reading the invitation, and stuck it in an inner pocket of his parka before pulling on his gloves. "Luna DiSimone. Why does that name sound familiar?"

It did, but I couldn't place the name

45

either. "We'll Google her when we get back," I said.

We hurried down Broadway to the nearest subway station so that we could buy fare cards for the bus and trains. From behind, a sharp wind pushed us along, and I would have moaned about it except that I noticed that the people we passed who were heading into the wind all seemed to have their hats pulled low and their scarves high. The wind whipped tears into their eyes and gave everyone red noses. I turned up the collar on my coat, rewrapped my scarf an extra turn around the back of my neck, and tried to match Dwight's long strides. No sauntering for him either.

The exhibit of Madeleine Albright's pins at the Museum of Arts and Design had so much historical documentation that Dwight almost forgot that they were costume jewelry and enjoyed the witty symbolism. Who knew that woman had such a sense of humor?

From there, we rode a bus down to Chinatown, where we turned into full-out gawking tourists. We bought toys for Cal and his cousins and lengths of exquisite red-and-gold silk for Kate and for Dwight's mother, who both like to sew. I saw a charming tea set that was almost beautiful enough to convert me from iced tea, but reason prevailed, to Dwight's relief. Both of us were already loaded down.

Lunch was dim sum at a place that wasn't much bigger than a broom closet, but the shrimp dumplings were perfection. When we came out of the restaurant, the temperature had dropped even further, although the wind had died down a bit. The sky clouded over and a light rain began to fall. Mindful of our heavy paper shopping bags, we headed for the subway and arrived at our stop on the Upper West Side minutes before the rain began in earnest.

"As long as it's not snow," we told each other as we rode up in the elevator.

"Eighty-five percent chance of snow before midnight," Antoine told us cheerfully. "Hope the weather doesn't spoil your visit."

Back in the apartment, I realized I had left my phone on the kitchen counter and discovered I had a voice message from that 212 number: "This is Sigrid Harald. I believe you have something of my grandmother's for my mother? Please call me before four o'clock."

I glanced at my watch. Ten till four. I hastily punched in the numbers and this time was answered on the first ring.

"Ms. Harald?"

"Yes?"

I explained who I was and that Mrs. Lattimore had sent something to her daughter.

"What is it?"

"I have no idea. It's a small but rather heavy little box."

Sounding clearly puzzled, Ms. Harald said, "I wonder why she sent it up now when she knew my mother was going to be away for six weeks?"

"I gather she didn't want to trust FedEx or UPS and she knows my husband is a sheriff's deputy."

"Really?"

"Really."

"And you know my grandmother how?"

"I think we're distantly related through her Stephenson kin," I said, realizing how stereotypically Southern I must sound to this no-nonsense voice. "But we're staying for a week in Kate Bryant's apartment because she's married to my husband's brother and —"

"Oh yes. Now I remember. Kate said you're a judge, right?"

"Right." Jake Honeycutt, Kate's first husband, was Mrs. Lattimore's nephew, and Kate had kept in touch with his people for her young Jake's sake.

"Look, my mother's in New Zealand and I have an appointment down here in the Village in a half hour. Would you mind opening the package and telling me what it is?"

"No problem," I assured her, happy to have permission to satisfy my own curiosity. "Hang on a minute."

There were scissors in a pencil jar on the kitchen counter and a few snips revealed a sturdy cardboard box. Inside, something was swaddled in newsprint and bubble wrap, and inside that —

"Dear Lord in the morning!" I said before I could stop myself. I'm not a prude. I've leafed through the Kama Sutra and I've seen my share of naked men, but this was not something I would ever have expected from someone as proper as Mrs. Lattimore.

It was a bronze statuette, about six or seven inches tall, roughly cylindrical, and so intricately modeled that it took me a minute to sort out the intertwined arms and legs and other bodily appendages and to decide exactly where those appendages were and what they were doing. Dwight glanced up from our digital camera, where he was reviewing the pictures we'd taken that day, did a double take, and then grinned broadly as he snapped several shots of me turning that thing in my hand.

"What is it?" I heard Ms. Harald ask.

"Um . . . uh . . ." I examined it up, down, and sideways, and each view was more lascivious than the last.

Dwight took it from my hand and pointed out a particularly inventive position. "We should try that one," he murmured with an exaggerated leer.

I put my hand over the mouthpiece to hide my laughter. "In your dreams."

"Mrs. Bryant?" The woman's voice was becoming impatient.

"It's a little statuette," I said. "Looks like bronze."

"A statuette? Of what?"

"Well, I think it's three men." Even as I spoke, I discovered at least two more faces and another penis amid the tangle of arms and legs.

"You *'think'*? Is it abstract?"

"Oh, no," I assured her. "It's realistic. *Very* realistic. It appears to be several naked men who are" — I searched for an appropriate word — "who are . . . um . . . *pleasuring* each other."

Dwight chuckled, but there was blank silence from the other end.

"Ms. Harald?"

"And my grandmother sent this to my mother? Perhaps I should come up this evening after all. Would ten or ten-thirty be too late?"

"Not at all," I assured her. "But someone down the hall has invited us to a party at nine. You might ought to follow the noise and check for us there first. I'll be wearing a red sweater."

"Then I will see you at ten-thirty," said Ms. Harald.

CHAPTER 3

They make quite an animated throng as
they enter the vestibules or crowd the
staircase, or foyer, bowing and chatting to
each other, all smiling, all newly garbed,
all on pleasure bent.
                    — *The New New York,* 1909

Despite all the jokes about Chinese food
never filling you up, I wasn't hungry enough
to go splashing out in the rain for dinner. It
was coming down quite hard now, but
Dwight volunteered to go get us something
light from the market's deli section and said
that as long as he was going, he'd pick up a
bottle of wine to take over to the party.

We had Googled Luna DiSimone and
found some YouTube videos. In the first
batch, she and three other kids sang along
with Big Bird about the letter J and the
number 6. (It was probably catty of me to
notice that her hair was a rabbity brown

back then.) After leaving *Sesame Street,* she had played bit parts in several short-lived television series, and three years ago had starred in a bad movie that went straight to DVD. There was a mention of voice-over commercials for a hotel chain and I realized that's why her lilting voice sounded so familiar.

Kate had given me a key to her owner's closet and told me to help myself to any of the clothes or supplies I found there. Most days, I just hop in and out of the shower, but with almost four hours till party time, I filled the tub, dumped in some of Kate's bubble bath for a good long soak, then wrapped myself in her fleecy robe and took a short nap.

Luna DiSimone's party was well cranked up by nine o'clock and even before we opened our door to join them, we heard laughter and loud talk. Two long metal coat racks now lined the hallway and people were chatting to each other as they hung up their outdoor winter wear. Most of them seemed to be wearing khaki shorts, short-sleeved Hawaiian print shirts, or, in the case of several women, brightly printed sarongs. I watched one woman kick off her boots and slip her bare feet into a pair of orange rubber flip-flops. The door to the third apartment on this floor stood open, too, and as we passed the elevator, it disgorged three ukulele players who strummed a corny Hawaiian tune. They were dressed in frayed straw hats and raggedy jeans.

I clutched Dwight's arm. "Aren't they with the Steffingtons?"

Dwight shrugged. He's not into rock bands, but I'd gone to a Steffingtons concert last summer with some of my nieces and nephews and I was pretty certain that at least two of the ukulele players usually played guitars with that band.

"Keep an eye on them, and I'll get the camera," I said and darted back inside the apartment. Dwight had left it on the kitchen counter next to that obscene little statue, and a moment later I was following the flow on down to the end apartment.

Here in dreary, cold, and wet January, it was like stepping into a beach house, a very crowded beach house, even though I later learned that two walls had been knocked out to create the large main room. White rattan chairs and couches were piled deep with coral, hot pink, and lime green cushions. Airy white sheers fell to a whitewashed plank floor bare of rugs. A huge seascape, framed in what looked like bleached driftwood, hung over a white brick fireplace that was filled with a rainbow assortment of candles. Their citronella smell evoked summer evenings on a patio. The ukulele players had staked out that corner. One had a sandaled foot propped on a green Adirondack chair as he strummed and sang in a sweet tenor voice. I wasn't the only one taking pictures. Several other people had their phones aimed at the group, too.

Dwight and I edged our way through animated clusters of guests and eventually found our hostess and two men lounging amid colorful soft cushions in an old-fashioned white wicker porch swing suspended from ceiling hooks. She was barefooted and wore a necklace of bright plastic flowers, a black bikini, and a soft pink terry beach jacket that swung open to reveal a well-toned body. A pink hibiscus was tangled in her long blonde hair. As soon as she saw us, she jumped up with happy little cries.

"I didn't realize it was a beach party," I said, feeling more than a little overdressed.

She laughed. "And I didn't think you'd come if I asked you to wear a bathing suit in January. This is my To Hell With Winter party." She pulled one of the men to his feet beside her. "And this is Cam. Cameron

Broughton. Now tell me your names so we can start figuring out if you're kin to each other."

"Don't be tiresome, Luna," the man said.

He appeared to be about thirty. Black hair curled around his ears and halfway down his neck. He wore baggy red-plaid shorts, red flip-flops, a green tank top, and blue swim goggles around his neck. Gold wire-rimmed glasses with round lenses of pale blue made him seem young and vulnerable despite the light age lines around his eyes. I always notice eyes and there was something slightly familiar about his, but I couldn't quite place him.

Dwight and I introduced ourselves.

"Sorry, Luna," he said. "No Bryants or Knotts in my family tree."

"And no Broughtons in mine," said Dwight.

"Mine either," I said. "Are you related to the Raleigh Broughtons?"

"Not that I know of," he said, looking down into his empty glass. "All of my people come from Wilmington."

Before we could pursue it, he excused himself and melted into the crowd. Luna accepted the wine we'd brought and escorted us to the bar, where she left us in the hands of a hired bartender while she went to see what was holding up the caterers and the hors d'oeuvres.

Neither Dwight nor I have ever had trouble talking to strangers, and soon he was in a deep discussion with two bearded men about brewing one's own beer, while I found myself discussing Madeleine Albright's pins with two white-haired women, old-line feminists who, after all this time, were still disappointed that Hillary Clinton had wound up as secretary of state instead of president. "I mean, I like the man we got, but damn it all, this was probably our best chance to see a woman president before we die."

"Speak for yourself, Celia," said the older of the two. "I'm good for another three election cycles."

"And you never know but what a woman may head up the other ticket," I said.

"Oh please!" she exclaimed.

A waiter in a starched white jacket and red-striped bathing trunks offered a tray of shrimp and pineapple chunks on skewers. I took one and moved on, overhearing snatches of conversation I would never hear back in Colleton County.

"— almost landed the role of the roommate in that new ABC sitcom."

"Forget about getting an eight o'clock

reservation before April."

"He'll be curating the show at the Arnheim but —"

"— looked all over the Biennale for you. Where the hell did you go?"

"— three bedrooms and still rent-controlled!"

"When she was on *Sixty Minutes* last week —"

"— paid three million and will be lucky to get a million-five unless —"

Our fellow guests were an eclectic assortment of old and young and most appeared to be connected to the arts. Although Dwight and I were not the only ones wearing seasonally appropriate wool and fleece, most were dressed as if this were indeed a beach house in the middle of summer.

A girl who turned out to be in the chorus of *Mamma Mia!* suggested that I get tickets for an off-Broadway show that was getting a good buzz, and when a pleasant-faced man heard that Dwight and I were here on our honeymoon, he produced a pair of tickets to a Wednesday matinee of a Gilbert and Sullivan show that he couldn't attend and insisted that we use them.

Another tray passed by loaded with colorful fruit. I put a toothpick into a cube of melon that was at its peak of sweetness.

By 10:30, the spacious apartment was so crowded that I had lost sight of Dwight altogether. I had also lost count of how many glasses of wine I'd plucked from various passing trays when I found myself shoved into a trio of art enthusiasts who were trashing a new exhibit at the Museum of Modern Art. I apologized for the bump, but one of the men gave me a friendly smile and moved over so I could join them. Late forties, he was tall and angular and wore hiking shoes, pipestem jeans, and a gray tweed jacket over a blue sweatshirt that advertised Yamaha motorcycles.

Before we could introduce ourselves, his eyes lit up and his smile broadened for someone behind me. "Sigrid? What the hell are you doing here?"

"Hello, Elliott. I could ask you the same thing. Actually I'm looking for —"

I turned and there was a tall thin woman, perhaps three or four years older than me, with soft dark curls and wide eyes that were an unusual smoky gray. She smiled as she took in my red cowl-neck sweater. "Judge Bryant?"

"Knott," I said, holding out my hand. "Deborah Knott. And you must be Sigrid Harald."

"Sigrid Harald?" There was almost a

reverent tone in the voice of a nearby man who had turned around eagerly upon hearing her name. He had a shaved head and wore yellow-rimmed trifocals. "*The* Sigrid Harald? I'm Charles Rathmann. I've been dying to interview you about Oscar Nauman's last —"

Her gray eyes immediately turned to chips of ice.

"No," she said before the man could complete his sentence.

The chilly finality of her tone, coupled with the glares he was getting from the storklike man she'd called Elliott, left Rathmann red-faced and defensive. Even the top of his head turned red.

"I do assure you, Ms. Harald —"

"Not now, Rathmann," the first man said. His tone was mild, but Rathmann must have heard something more, for he muttered a truculent apology to Ms. Harald and melted back into the crowd.

"Elliott Buntrock," the man said, offering me a firm handshake, "and I gather from your drawl that you're not from around here."

I smiled but didn't answer, because I didn't know what their relationship was. Kate had told me that Mrs. Lattimore's granddaughter, a homicide detective with the NYPD, had inherited the large estate of one of the leading artists of the twentieth century. I could imagine just how many Rathmanns must be buzzing around her like a swarm of mosquitoes. Was Buntrock another bloodsucker or a flyswatter?

"Thanks, Elliott." Her half smile reached her eyes and melted those chips of ice.

Flyswatter, then.

"Actually, I'm glad you're here," she said. "This is Judge Knott, a friend of my grandmother, who seems to have sent my mother a very odd piece of art. Would you take a look at it?"

"Sure. When?"

"Now?" She looked at me. "I'm sorry to take you away from the party, but —"

"No problem," I assured her.

Easier said than done for three people to move through that crush of people. Near the doorway, Dwight was in animated conversation with two men — one an African-American, the other of Asian descent — and he brightened when he saw me. "Deb'rah! Look who's here! This is my old friend Josh Cho."

"From John Jay College?" I asked, taking the hand of the short, slender man whose military posture and immediate appraisal of me would have ID'd him as former Army

Intelligence even if I hadn't known.

He nodded, but his words were lost beneath all the talk and laughter going on around us. I did make out that the second man was with the New York Police Department and that both of them had worked as consultants on an abortive police drama that was to have starred Luna. When I introduced Elliott Buntrock and Sigrid Harald to Dwight, the second man said, "I've had the pleasure of working with Lieutenant Harald before."

She smiled at the tall black officer with what was clearly genuine pleasure. "Sergeant Vaughn. You still with the Six-Four over in Brooklyn?"

He nodded. "But it's lieutenant now, ma'am."

"Congratulations."

"I heard you took early retirement?"

"A premature rumor," she said as she gave me an inquiring look that reminded me that she was not here to socialize.

I explained to Dwight that we were going over to the apartment to get Mrs. Lattimore's package. He grinned and said he'd see me when I got back.

We murmured the usual pleasantries to the others and eventually worked our way out into the hall, past the coat racks and the open doorway, where the party seemed to have spilled into the other apartment. The hall was blocked by people waiting for the elevator, and we had to step back as more partygoers arrived.

I had my keys in hand as we edged past the revelers toward Kate's apartment. Once there, though, I was surprised to see that the door was ajar. In my hurry to get back to the party with the camera, I hadn't thought to check that it was firmly latched.

Out in the kitchen, surprise was soon followed by dismay. "I left it right here on this counter," I told the other two. "And a pair of gold earrings, too."

The countertop was now bare except for the box and the wrappings that had swaddled that bronze sculpture.

I hurried into the master bedroom and was relieved to see no sign that the drawers had been opened and rifled. The little silk travel bag with the rest of my jewelry still lay atop the dresser, exposing the gold-and-blue-enamel bracelet I'd brought with me. A posthumous gift sent down through the years from my mother, its value to me was above rubies.

"Anything else missing?" Lieutenant Harald asked.

"My laptop?"

I darted into the dining room, shivering at the thought of all the lost data. Happily, it was still there on the table.

An instant later, I realized I was shivering as much from cold as from dismay.

"Where's that draft coming from?" I wondered aloud.

We followed the icy air into the dimly lit living room, where one of the French doors was ajar. Elliott Buntrock crossed the room in long strides and tried to close it.

"Something's caught in the hinge," he said and pulled the door toward him to see what it was.

A shoe.

With a foot in it.

Connected to the leg of someone slumped against the railing of the icy marble balcony.

CHAPTER 4

It is useless to discuss [it], whether in brass or iron or gold, as either an ornament or an excrescence.
— *The New New York,* 1909

Reacting automatically, Sigrid Harald warned us not to touch anything. She stooped over the figure and pressed her fingers against a pressure point on his ankle before moving onto the balcony to check the side of his neck.

"No pulse," she said.

Rain had saturated his hair and run down the side of his face, and when her fingers came away, they were not only wet but tinged with blood. Buntrock handed her his clean handkerchief. She wiped her hand dry, then pulled out her cell phone.

When someone answered on the other end, she said, "Hentz? Lieutenant Harald. I didn't realize you were on call tonight."

She described the situation and gave him the address. "Lieutenant Vaughn of the Six-Four is here, but we need extra uniforms immediately. There's a big party on this floor so there should be possible witnesses to whoever entered this apartment. I want everyone detained till we get all their names."

While she talked, Elliott Buntrock wandered over to look at the signatures of several paintings grouped on a wall.

Dwight and I had not used this room except to check out the balcony when we first arrived, and I hadn't paid much attention to the furnishings. A little wooden cat — Mexican? — painted in lavender, turquoise, and pink stripes sat on a table beneath the pictures beside two small, brightly enameled cloisonné pillboxes. The pointed face had blue eyes, a knowing grin, and yellow whiskers and it was utterly charming. I was surprised that I hadn't noticed it before. Such whimsicality didn't really go with either the pillboxes or the rest of the apartment, which had been stripped of Kate's personality and replaced by what I presumed was her tenant's more conservative taste in décor. The more I thought about it, the more certain I became that there had been several of those boxes and that the cat hadn't been there earlier.

"Would you mind getting Lieutenant Vaughn?" Harald asked me. "And maybe your husband, too. He's a sworn law officer, isn't he?"

I nodded and hurried toward the door.

"Try not to let any of the others know," she called after me.

Moments later, Dwight and Vaughn were following me back into the apartment. Josh Cho had tagged along, too. I hadn't been able to keep him from hearing and I figured it didn't matter. Anyone who teaches at John Jay would surely be professional enough to help, not hinder.

I hadn't tried to see the dead man's face, but Dwight took one look and said, "It's the building's super. Phil Something."

"Phil Lundigren," I reminded him. "He told us he and his wife live on the ground floor." I was still feeling guilty about the open door. "Maybe he's the one who left the door open."

Dwight frowned. "The door was open?"

I nodded. "Remember when I came back for our camera? I thought I closed it, but when we got here just now it was standing open a crack."

"Which opens it up to everyone out there in the hall," Lieutenant Harald told Jarvis

Vaughn. "So if you would . . . ?"

She didn't have to say more. He immediately headed for the door. "I'll tell the elevator operator not to take anyone else down."

"What about stairs?" Dwight asked her.

"Yes, please."

"There's bound to be a service elevator, too," said Josh Cho, trailing after the other two. "I'll go secure it."

When it was just the three of us again, Lieutenant Harald questioned me more closely as to our interaction with the building's dead super, then asked, "How much time elapsed between your coming back for the camera and when we discovered the body?"

"About eighty-five or ninety minutes tops," I told her. "We came out into the hall around nine. The hall was jammed with people, and when I saw some guys from the Steffingtons —"

"The *who?*" she asked.

"Not the Who," I said. "The Steffingtons."

Buntrock grinned. "Who's on first?"

She frowned at him. "Not a game, Elliott."

"Sorry. The Steffingtons are a bubblegum rock group, not Daltrey and Townshend."

"My nieces like them," I said defensively.

"And being a good aunt?" he asked.

"Exactly."

Harald was unamused. "The time?"

"Not more than eight or ten minutes past nine," I said meekly.

"And the hall was crowded?"

I nodded.

"Can you describe anyone in particular when you came back for the camera?"

"Not really. I was more intent on getting past them. And besides, the elevator kept bringing up more people. I do remember a woman in a hot pink tank top and white jeans, and there was a man with a blue Mohawk, but dye his Mohawk red and put her in something that didn't scream triple-D cup and I couldn't give you an honest ID. I'm afraid I'm a typical eyewitness — blind in one eye, didn't see out the other." I was hoping to foster a little collegiality. After all, we were fellow officers of the court, weren't we? She didn't smile. "Anyhow, we both know how inaccurate such accounts are unless the witness knows the person."

She gave a curt nod and wanted to see specifically where I had left my earrings. "Is anything else missing or disturbed?"

"I can't be sure. We only arrived last night, but I'm fairly certain that painted cat wasn't there and that there were more of those little boxes." I realized anew how chilly the apartment was now and moved over to the radiator, which was hot to the touch but ineffectual with the French door opened so wide.

"Can't we at least close the door?" I asked. "His foot's barely blocking it and surely it won't matter if we nudge it over a couple of inches." I offered her my camera. "You can even take pictures if you're worried about disturbing a crime scene."

She pushed the door to until it was in the same position as we'd found it, but an inch-wide crack remained. At least the icy rain wasn't coming from that direction.

"Sorry," she said, not sounding sorry at all as she pulled on leather gloves from the deep pockets of the parka she was wearing. Even her friend was wearing at least two layers, while I had only my red cashmere sweater.

Resigned, I said, "Then you won't mind if I get my coat."

She followed me back into the bedroom. "In the closet?"

I nodded and she used her gloved hand to carefully turn the knob on the closet door.

Dismayed, I said, "You're not going to have your people dust for prints in here, are you? Do you know how hard that stuff is to clean up? Worse than cigarette ashes."

She eyed my exposed jewelry and conceded that it would probably be pointless.

Once I was zipped into my own parka, I could satisfy my curiosity about Mrs. Lattimore's by-the-book granddaughter. Other than her changeable gray eyes and her height, I couldn't see much family resemblance. Even in sickness and old age, Jane Lattimore retained remnants of great beauty, and this woman was striking without being beautiful as the world usually defines it. Thin nose and high cheekbones, yes, but her neck was a little too long, her mouth too wide, her chin too strong. She certainly had the Lattimore reserve in spades, although it seemed tinged by sadness. Or maybe that was only my imagination, because Kate had told me how that artist had died in a car crash a few short months after they became lovers. If there was any chemistry between her and this Buntrock, I couldn't see it. Not on her part, anyhow.

On his?

Hard to say. Certainly he seemed very much attuned to her restless pacing as we waited for the troops to arrive. "Rathmann?" he asked.

She gave an impatient twitch of her thin shoulders. "I should be used to the Rathmanns by now."

"I was sorry to hear about your loss," I said inanely even though her lover's death must have happened at least two or three years ago. Her face froze and I instantly wished I could take back the words.

Buntrock cocked his bony head like an intelligent bird on the alert and rescued me. "About that object that's missing . . ."

As if grateful to change the subject, she said, "Yes, my grandmother gave it to Judge Knott and —"

"Oh please," I interrupted. "Call me Deborah. We may not be kissing cousins, but we *are* kin. Somewhere back in the family tree."

Diverted, Elliott Buntrock said, "What's a kissing cousin?"

For the first time since finding Phil Lundigren's body, I laughed. "All cousins are blood kin, but a kissing cousin is one closely enough related that you automatically hug and kiss going or coming."

A slightly horrified look crossed the other woman's face, and when she visibly drew back, I almost laughed again. "Don't worry, Sigrid. I'm not going to hug you."

Once again, I did not get the smile I'd hoped for.

"That thing my grandmother sent. Did she include a note?"

"I didn't notice," I said. "Not after I saw what it was."

"But what *was* it?" Buntrock asked again.

"Well . . . it was rather intricate and — Oh wait! I can show you." I set the camera to display, and when I found a close-up that Dwight had taken, I zoomed in and handed it to him.

Both were too sophisticated to make the obvious lewd remarks, and Buntrock's brow furrowed as he concentrated. "God! What a racist bit of obscenity. The hooked noses. The exaggerated lips. And yet it reminds me of — Oh, Lord! Could this be one of those Streichert maquettes?"

"A what?" Sigrid and I both asked.

"There was an article in the *Smithsonian* magazine last month on Al Streichert and his early works. Did you see it?"

I shook my head. I'd never heard of an Al Streichert, but Sigrid was nodding slowly. "I didn't read the article, but someone mentioned it."

"Who's Al Streichert?" I asked.

"Albrecht Streichert. Sculptor. Worked mostly in stainless steel."

I rummaged through old memories of the one art history course I had taken in college. "Like Henry Moore?"

Buntrock nodded. "Only less abstract and

not quite as famous. He left Germany in the mid-thirties, but not before he'd bought into all that Aryan garbage about the need for racial cleansing. Once he got to New York, though, and saw how thoroughly integral to the artistic culture Jews and blacks were, he was so conflicted — at least that's what he later said in his autobiography — that he made a few small bronzes like this thing for his own pathetic amusement."

He handed the camera to Sigrid, who frowned as she studied it closely. "How on earth did my grandmother come by something so odious?"

"I don't suppose she was part of the New York art scene in her youth?"

"Not that I'm aware of. Mother might know. On the other hand, Grandmother's taste in art has always been American landscapes like the Hudson River School."

I peered into the camera when she handed it back to me. "If he made a bunch of these —"

"But he didn't," said Buntrock. "And he never showed them to anyone except like-minded bigots. That's what makes this so curious. We know about them solely by hearsay and a single photograph which was taken by one of those friends. According to the *Smithsonian* article, he only made three or four, and he melted those down and donated the bronze to the war effort when he fell in love and married his wife. She was Jewish and he was utterly devoted to her. According to the granddaughter — she's the one who gave the interview — he never got over being ashamed of that part of his past."

"Maybe this one's not by him after all," I suggested.

"I don't suppose you checked to see if it was signed?" asked Buntrock.

"Sorry."

Sigrid was still puzzled. "I wonder why Grandmother sent this to Mother. Why didn't she just destroy it if she read the article?"

Buntrock shrugged. "Would you destroy a Henry Moore?"

Before she could answer, the front door opened and a man and a younger woman entered. I didn't need to be told that they were homicide detectives.

CHAPTER 5

New York is proud of its police force and keeps reiterating that it is the very "finest" in the world — a statement that is not modest but has a good deal of truth in it.

— *The New New York*, 1909

Sigrid Harald — Saturday night

Had Sigrid realized that Sam Hentz was on call that evening, she would have pulled in Sergeant Tildon, with whom she was more at ease even though Hentz was the best on the squad and the one who had taken over for her when she fell apart after Oscar Nauman's death. Despite her slight seniority and better fitness reports, he was a year older and had resented her from the first because he had expected to get that promotion. He had not bothered to hide his resentment, but she had let it ride until he goaded her into losing her habitual cool. Out of the hearing of others, her normally

76

calm gray eyes shooting sparks of ice, she got in his face and in a low cold voice said, "That's the last time you question my authority, Hentz. I got the promotion, you didn't. Deal with it or put in for a transfer."

After that, they had developed a modus vivendi that allowed them to work together with grudging respect, which was all that Sigrid required, especially when the job became awkward on a personal level. Part of it was inheriting artworks worth millions; the other part was discovering that her boss had once been her father's partner and her mother's lover. Within the department, it was like the shifting of tectonic plates. Even those who managed to take her new wealth relatively in stride and who knew that she was good at her work could not help wondering if she had made lieutenant because Captain McKinnon had smoothed the way.

After Mac retired and married her mother, things should have been easier. Instead, his replacement was a woman who alternated between sucking up to her and making digs at what was presumed to have been Sigrid's protected position. She was aware that most of her colleagues wondered why she continued to stick it out when she no longer needed the pension and budgetary constraints had frozen promotions, but no one had the nerve to ask her why, not even Til-don, the detective who was most comfort-able with her.

Social ease had never been one of her strengths and she had struggled hard to mimic it after Nauman died. Feeling that she owed it to the artist's memory to be-come the woman he had thought she was, she styled her hair, learned how to dress, and mastered the intricacies of makeup. Ac-cepting that she had become a public figure was a different matter. When her housemate sat her down in front of his computer and Googled her name, she had been appalled to see over a hundred thousand citations. Nevertheless and against all reason, she still hoped the job would eventually let her become anonymous again.

From Hentz, sleek and urbane in a well-cut topcoat and dark fedora, she got a neutral, level-eyed nod, but the others gave her respectful smiles as they crossed the room to join her by the French doors. Lieutenant Vaughn entered, too, followed by Kate's brother-in-law and the John Jay professor. Close on their heels were the crime scene team and an ME. Beyond them, she saw several uniforms from the local house trying to placate the noisy and curious crowd of party guests who objected to being kept there against their will.

She was pleased to see her team immediately note and document the smear of blood and scuffing on the hardwood floor, two indicators that Lundigren had been killed there in the living room near the coffee table and then dragged onto the balcony. One of them scraped up some of the blood smear and bagged it for the lab. Yes, it was probably the victim's blood, but assuming the obvious was how cases got lost.

After setting up floodlights to facilitate their camera work, they opened the French doors wide. Rain had changed to sleet mixed with snow and the room's temperature quickly dropped.

"Rigor's starting, so go ahead and get him on the gurney before he stiffens up," the ME said.

As they shifted the body to zip it into a bag, Sigrid leaned forward and said, "What's that in his hand?"

More clicks of the camera and Hentz opened the dead man's callused fingers, tipped his find into a plastic evidence bag, then turned to hold it up so the others could see. A small object gleamed golden in the floodlights.

"That's mine," said Sigrid's newly met

cousin who had left Buntrock in the dining room to come stand next to Major Bryant. "Where's the other one?"

She reached for the bag, but Hentz drew back. "Sorry, ma'am. I'll have to give you a receipt for it."

"Evidence, shug," murmured Deborah's husband, a ruggedly attractive man.

By the time the gurney was on its way through the suddenly subdued crowd out in the hall and down to the service elevator that was accessed by a door next to the front elevator, Deborah and Buntrock had each described to the detectives how they left the party with Sigrid, how crowded the hall was, how they had noticed the open door and then discovered the disappearance of a small heavy piece of bronze.

Sigrid had not looked too closely at the head wound, but upon reflection she realized that the piece could have made a handy weapon.

The three of them and Dwight Bryant were fingerprinted so that they could be eliminated from the prints found on the balcony doors, the inside knob of the door into the hall, and the kitchen counter where that little bronze had stood. Wiping the ink from his fingers, Bryant said, "Lundigren told us that his wife cleaned here this week, so you'll probably see her prints here, too."

One of the techs had found what looked like a clear thumbprint on the mirror of the medicine cabinet in the master bath, and she had lifted several from the flush handles and raised seats on both toilets as well as the faucets.

Sigrid heard Deborah say, "I was the last one out of our bathroom, and I did *not* leave the seat up."

"Maybe we'll get lucky," said the tech.

"What about that painted cat?" the judge said. "I'm about ninety percent sure it wasn't here when we left tonight, so where did it come from?"

"Print the cat," Sigrid said.

In the dining room, the room closest to the front door, Sam Hentz pulled out a digital camcorder and began to take brief statements from some of the party guests that the uniforms had sent in.

"Look, the line was five deep around the other bathrooms and you know how long women can take," said a young man in a Hawaiian shirt, yellow clamdiggers, and purple sneakers. "I saw the door here wasn't locked so I came in and took a quick leak. That's all I did."

"You didn't check out the kitchen or

bedrooms?" asked Hentz as a crime scene tech inked the young man's fingertips and rolled them onto a card.

"Absolutely not."

"Or notice a draft of cold air?"

The man shook his head.

"What time was this?"

"Around nine-thirty, I guess, give or take a few minutes."

"See anybody else in here?"

"Guy with a blue Mohawk? He came in as I was leaving."

The uniformed officer standing nearby nodded when Hentz shot him an inquiring look. By the time Hawaiian shirt had given his name, address, fingerprints, and held his ID up to the camera, the officer was back with a very tall and very thin man whose stiff blue Mohawk added a good four inches to his height. He was dressed like a beach-comber, and his unbuttoned vest hung on a bare torso so skinny they could count his ribs.

"He was right outside the door when I left with our camera," Deborah said.

"Quite right," said the man in an impeccable British accent. "Sorry, m'dear, but I was in urgent need of a loo and when I saw that you hadn't latched the door and that another chap had gone inside uninvited, I'm afraid I took advantage of your unintended hospitality."

"And it didn't occur to you to latch the door when you left?" Deborah asked sharply.

"Actually, it did," he said in an Oxbridge drawl. "And I did."

"You left the door locked?" asked Hentz.

The blue Mohawk nodded in affirmation. "I think so. To be precise, I didn't push any buttons or turn any knobs, but I did pull it shut and felt it click. I assumed it locked automatically."

"Which bathroom did you use?"

"The one through there." He gestured toward the master bedroom.

"Was anyone in the apartment when you left?"

"I suppose there could have been," he said, sounding dubious. "But I didn't see or hear anyone. I must admit that my tummy kept me in the loo for quite some time and I did hear the other toilet flush at least twice before I emerged."

"And what time was it when you think you locked the door?"

He pursed his lips in concentration. "Bang on twenty till ten. I looked at my watch because I was supposed to meet someone at ten."

"Did the apartment seem chilly to you when you were here?"

"No, but you Americans keep your buildings so bloody hot." The front of his open vest swung back across his scrawny bare chest. "I was quite grateful to Luna for an excuse to dress comfortably."

"I don't suppose you glanced into the living room?"

"Sorry, mate."

They checked his ID, then sent him over to be fingerprinted.

"Did you notice the chill when you got here?" Hentz asked.

Sigrid nodded. "And I was wearing a coat."

"So if they're both telling the truth," said Hentz, "the murder probably took place between nine-forty and eleven."

Sigrid glanced at her watch. Almost one. By now, the hallway was nearly empty except for a small cluster of guests who lingered down by Luna DiSimone's doorway and four uniformed police officers who were ready to turn over the lists of names they had collected.

"I think we got them all, ma'am."

"Anyone see the victim enter the apartment?"

"Not that they said. Before we let people

leave, we asked them for as many names of the other guests as they could remember," said a veteran patrolman who seemed to have taken the initiative. "I figure you guys can cross-match and probably come up with the names of everybody that was here tonight. I also had them send the pictures they'd taken with their cell phones to the address I got from Detective Hentz."

"Good thinking, Officer" — Sigrid leaned in to read his nameplate — "Huppert. Nice work."

She passed the yellow legal pads over to another detective and asked him to finish talking to the remaining guests Officer Ted Huppert had seen fit to send in for extra questioning.

"If you don't need me anymore, Lieutenant, I'm going to shove off before the snow gets too deep," said Jarvis Vaughn.

They all glanced toward the balcony and saw that snow had indeed begun to accumulate.

"Don't you want someone to drive you home?" she asked.

"All the way to Sheepshead Bay?" He grinned. "Thanks, but the subway's quicker and I'm only two blocks from the station. Good seeing you again. Just sorry it couldn't have stayed social."

"I'll walk with you," said Josh Cho. "Call me, Dwight, if you or Deborah change your mind. Friends tell us it's a comfortable couch."

Dwight Bryant had put his arm around Deborah and Sigrid heard him say, "We'll be fine. Right, Deb'rah?"

By which Sigrid gathered that they meant to go on staying in this apartment. For some reason she had thought that this Southern woman would be too squeamish to sleep here tonight, but the judge shrugged and said, "This building must be close to a hundred years old. I'm sure he's not the first person to die in it."

Knowing this would be their last chance at the apartment before it was thoroughly contaminated by the Bryants, Sigrid instructed her team to give the room a final examination.

Her dread of emotional confrontations made this next part of the job difficult for her, but knowing it could not be put off any longer, she signaled to Sam Hentz and said to Vaughn and Cho, "We'll ride down with you."

On the ground floor, Lieutenant Vaughn and Dr. Cho headed out into the falling snow. The elevator man on duty earlier had been relieved by the night operator, one Jani Horvath. He was big and beefy, with a snowy white walrus mustache. When Hentz asked him when he'd last seen Lundigren, the man seemed genuinely surprised. "Phil? That was *Phil* that got killed? I thought it was somebody from Luna's party."

"Did you see him tonight?" they asked.

He shook his head and his mustache seemed to droop mournfully. "No. I came in early on account of the snow. The weather channel said we were gonna get at least twelve inches. I sacked out for a few hours downstairs and relieved Sidney early so he could get home before it got too deep. I heard somebody got killed, but I never thought it was Phil. Poor bastard. You coming to tell Denise?"

"Is that his wife?"

Horvath nodded. "You'll go easy on her, right? She's real shy. I forget what they call it — where somebody can't stand to be around new people?"

"Social anxiety disorder?"

"Yeah, that's what Phil called it. There was a time that he was the only one she could talk to or relax with, but then a psychiatrist bought into the building and he helped her a lot. She's okay with people she knows good or in a crowd that's not paying her

87

any attention, but she still has a little trouble with new people where she has to talk or answer questions, so —"

A loud buzz from someone on the sixth floor interrupted him and he stepped back into the cage.

"Right around the corner," he told them. "First door on the right."

They rang the doorbell twice and knocked loudly, but no one came.

"If she's a nutcase, we may be wasting our time," said Hentz.

Sigrid held her finger on the doorbell until the door, secured by two safety chains, finally opened a narrow crack.

The woman who peered out at them had a thin drawn face and sleep-rumpled coal black hair that needed a touch-up at the gray roots. Incongruously, her eyes were sooty with heavy black mascara, blusher pinked her cheeks, and her lips were freshly painted a bright red that matched her quilted satin robe.

Sigrid tried to remember what she had read about social anxiety disorder and wondered if putting on makeup was part of this woman's coping technique.

"Phil's not here," the woman said. "Come back later."

Hentz blocked the door with his foot before she could close it, and they held up their badges.

"Police, Mrs. Lundigren," Sigrid said. "May we come in?"

"Phil's not here," the woman said again.

"We know. That's why we have to talk to you."

Grudgingly, the woman removed the chain, then quickly retreated to the far doorway of this small room to watch them uneasily as they entered her home. The moment their eyes met hers, she instantly looked away.

Having seen the body of the dead man, bulky and coarse-looking in his dark brown coveralls, and having heard that his wife supplemented their income by cleaning, Sigrid had subconsciously expected an equally bulky woman and a drab apartment, perhaps furnished with castoffs from the building's residents.

Instead, the wife was slender and pretty and this tiny room was nicely furnished. The walls were painted a deep red with white enamel trim. The single window was draped in white linen over white sheers. Red-and-white floral cushions softened the clean lines of an off-white loveseat, and two wingchairs were upholstered in white velvet. Several dainty crystal cats sat atop a gleaming end table that also held a lamp with a cut-glass base and white silk shade. A modern oriental-style rug lay on the dark oak floor. The whole effect was crisply feminine.

Mrs. Lundigren's arms tightened across her thin chest. "Where's Phil?"

"Excuse me?" Sigrid said.

"You said you know he's not here, so where is he?" Her eyes flickered over to them and then dropped to the floor.

"When did you last see him?" Sam Hentz countered.

"After supper. There was a party up on six. Loud people coming and going through the lobby. He said he was going up to check on things."

"What time would that be, Mrs. Lundigren?"

"Maybe ten o'clock? I don't know." Her fingers brushed her wrist absentmindedly. "I don't have a watch."

They glanced around the small room. There was no clock in sight. No television either. In fact, now that Sigrid looked more closely, this room did not seem to be used at all. Nothing out of place.

"Is this where you were when he left?" she asked.

Mrs. Lundigren studied the floor and

shook her head. "In the den."

Without really knowing why she cared, Sigrid took a step forward and said, "May we see?"

"No!"

The force of her refusal surprised the two officers.

Trembling now, she edged behind a wingback chair and moaned, "Please. Go away now. And tell Phil to come home. *Please!*"

Sigrid looked helplessly at Hentz, who made soothing noises. "It's okay, Mrs. Lundigren. We're going to stay over here. Why don't you take a seat and let us tell you why we came?"

He continued to reassure her with soft words, and eventually she forced herself to come out from behind the chair and sit down in it. Once she had stopped trembling, Hentz stepped aside for Sigrid, who took a deep breath and said, "I'm really sorry, Mrs. Lundigren, but Phil is dead."

"What?"

"Up in 6-A. Someone —"

"No," said Denise Lundigren. "No, no, *no!* He can't be dead."

When they did not reassure her, she looked around in wild agitation as if her husband might suddenly appear. "Who's going to look after me?"

"Is there someone we can call?" asked Hentz.

She shook her head, then, almost meeting his eyes, she said, "Are you sure he's really dead? Not just hurt?"

"I'm very sorry, ma'am."

Wrapping her arms even tighter, the woman began to rock back and forth, keening in a high shrill wordless scream that seemed to go on and on forever.

Hentz started to reach out to her to offer comfort, but she recoiled, screaming even louder.

"Bellevue?" Hentz asked Sigrid in a low voice.

She nodded.

CHAPTER 6

Eating and drinking, instead of being the satisfaction of a physical need, is here a social function.

— *The New New York,* 1909

When I looked out, I saw that the snow was falling more fiercely than ever, driven by a sharp wind that had already piled several inches against the French doors where we'd found Phil Lundigren a few hours earlier.

Although Dwight had taken a professional interest in the proceedings and was now in deep conversation with the detectives Sigrid and her colleague had left to finish up, I was too tired and hungry to listen. Supper had been a few glasses of wine, two bites of cheese, and a cube of melon, and that was over three hours ago.

I stifled a yawn and Elliott Buntrock said, "Tired?"

"Not at all," I lied.

"If you prefer, I can wait for Sigrid down-stairs."

"Don't be silly," I said, knowing that it would probably be at least another hour before everyone cleared out and left Dwight and me alone. "I *am* hungry, though. Can I get you something, too?"

His bony face brightened. "What do you have?"

I laughed. "I'm not sure. The last time I looked, though, the refrigerator was stuffed. My husband's absolutely besotted with the grocery store around the corner."

"Fairway Market, right? It's a madhouse, but people come from all over town to shop there. Have you tried their café upstairs? They do a great breakfast."

Without actually being invited, he followed me into the kitchen. While I wiped fingerprint powder off the countertops, he murmured approval of the high ceilings and period woodwork, then held the refrigerator door open so I could rummage through the little plastic boxes and bags.

"Artichoke salad? Mixed olives? Bruschetta?" I asked. "Sliced rare tenderloin? Smoked salmon?"

"Yes, please," he said. "And is that a pack of oatmeal stout hiding in the back?"

It was.

94

"I must say that I rather like your husband's taste."

We dumped everything on the kitchen counter and pulled out two of the four stools. Picnicking at a murder scene might be considered a little bizarre, but if Dwight and I were going to stay here, we needed food and drink, and I was ready for both. Besides, the crime scene team seemed to be through with the kitchen.

"Plates in here?" Elliott asked, reaching for a cupboard door.

"Glasses there. Plates one door over," I told him.

As he assembled dishes and utensils, I moved the cardboard box that had held that chunky bronze thing that Mrs. Lattimore had sent and started to wad up the paper that had cushioned it.

"Wait a minute," Elliott said, rescuing one of the sheets of paper. "Look at this."

When I unpacked that miniature piece of sculpture earlier, I assumed Mrs. Lattimore had just used whatever was at hand. Now I saw that they were pages torn from a magazine.

"It's the interview with Streichert's granddaughter." He smoothed them out and showed me a black-and-white photo. "That's Albrecht Streichert."

The sculptor had possessed a pumpkin-shaped head, broad and quite rounded, wider at the brow than in the jaw. A receding hairline emphasized the bulging brow. Ordinary eyes and nose and thin lips that were tightly closed in what looked like a habitual frown. Further down the page was a picture of a sculpted steel cylinder that could have been a larger-than-life version of the one that had been stolen. Instead of Jews and blacks, this one was a writhing mass of generic Caucasian male and female nudes. Although slightly cleaner, it, too, was a depiction of carnal sensuality and . . . um . . . agility. Both were bounded by the cylinder shape and both had clearly sprung from the same artistic mindset.

"Let's save this for Sigrid."

"Have you known her long?" I asked, curious about their relationship.

"We met about three or four months before Oscar died." A shadow passed across his avian face. "Hard to think he's been gone so long."

"What was he like?" I asked softly, hoping to encourage his reminiscence.

"A brilliant artist. What he knew about color and —"

"I meant as a man."

"As a man? Funny. Intelligent. Generous.

Opinionated as hell and not shy about voicing those opinions." He gave a wry smile. "He didn't suffer fools, but he had the widest circle of friends of anyone I've ever met. From garbage men to governors." He cocked his head at me like an egret examining a dubious minnow. "But that's not what you're asking, is it? You want to know about his affair with your not-kissing cousin, right?"

"Guilty," I admitted sheepishly. "And way out of line. Sorry."

"Don't be. You're not the first. He could have had almost any woman in the city, while Sigrid . . ." He hesitated. "Well, let's just say she was no Lady Francesca Leeds when they first met."

"Francesca Leeds?" A mental image of that red-haired Irish beauty flashed through my head. She often appeared on the talk show circuit. A stunning and witty woman. "She was on the red carpet at the last Tony Awards, wasn't she? On the arm of some gorgeous man?"

"Probably." He lifted the lid on the olives and popped one in his mouth. "She usually is."

I was impressed. "And Oscar Nauman knew her?"

Elliott nodded. "They were together for

several months before Sigrid came along."

I was moving from impressed to incredulous. "She took him away from Francesca Leeds?"

"He wouldn't have put it like that, but in essence, yes. You want to put all this out on a platter or shall we just serve ourselves from the boxes?"

"In other words, you don't want to talk about it anymore?"

"Talk about what?" asked Dwight as he rounded the corner.

"The murder," I said. "Pick up any tips from those detectives in there?"

"Nope. Everything's standard procedure and their funding's even worse than ours. They do a lot of their own preliminary lab work, too." He held out his hand to Elliott. "We didn't really get a chance to talk before. I'm Dwight Bryant."

"Elliott Buntrock. Hope you don't mind that I've helped myself to one of your beers."

"Not a bit. In fact, I'll join you."

"So what brings Southerners to New York in January?" Elliott asked when we had filled our plates and Dwight had poured part of his ale into my glass.

"It's supposed to be our honeymoon," I said.

He lifted his glass in toast. "Congratulations!"

"Thanks," said Dwight, "but the wedding was a year ago."

Elliott grinned. "I thought you people only talked slow."

Dwight laughed and cut himself a piece of some smelly cheese that was pockmarked with flecks of blue mold. "Things kept coming up."

"I gather you're a police officer, too?"

"Sheriff's deputy. Pass the mustard?"

Elliott put a dab of dill mustard on his salmon, then passed the little jar on to Dwight. "So you catch them and Deborah sentences them?"

"If I find them guilty," I said mildly.

"She keeps us honest. Won't let us get by with sloppy work even if the guy's guilty as sin and she knows it."

I ignored the bait and said, "And what do you do, Elliott?"

"I'm a freelance curator."

"A curator? Does that mean you put on exhibits?"

"That's part of the job description."

"What's the rest?"

"I'm on retainer at a few galleries and museums. Say a venue wants to have a special showing of an artist or a period. Take

Oscar Nauman. He finally agreed to let the Arnheim give him a retrospective, but he died before any real planning got under way. I had to contact collectors all over the country and in Europe and Japan and arrange to borrow some key works. You can imagine the paperwork — insurance, customs forms, shipping. Then I had to go through the paintings that were still in his possession and come up with a theme that would tie his different periods together. Finally, I had to put together a full-color *catalogue raisonné* with essays by some of his contemporaries and fellow artists."

He pulled off a piece of the bruschetta and smeared a little mustard on it. "If a client wants me to, I'll research, acquire, and authenticate certain works of modern art. I also do a little writing for various art journals."

"And run interference for Sigrid? Like with that Rathmann guy who wanted to interview her?"

"When she lets me." He gave a shrug and hunched into his gray tweed jacket like one of Aunt Sister's guinea hens hunching into its gray feathers. Maybe I was reading more than was actually there, but his response sounded a little wistful.

"Who's Rathmann?" Dwight asked.

"A wannabe art critic at the party to-night," said Elliott. He speared an artichoke heart and said, "Tell me about Sigrid's grandmother. Is she as strong-minded and eccentric as she sounds?"

"Well, she's certainly strong-minded," I said cautiously, remembering her steely determination to keep her cancer from her daughters. "I don't know that I'd call her eccentric."

"No more than most ninety-year-old women who've always had the money and power to set the rules for others," said Dwight. "I doubt if all of 'em live in the South."

"Point taken," said Elliott. "I didn't mean to imply —"

"Neither did I," Dwight said with an amiable smile, and offered him another slice of tenderloin.

From there, the talk circled back to the murder, and we speculated freely about how and why the super had returned to the apartment when he'd already made certain that there were no leaks in the ceiling.

"He probably didn't trust us to call him if we'd seen any dampness," I said.

"Maybe he came in at the very moment someone was stealing those pillboxes or the Streichert piece," Elliott suggested.

"And the thief panicked and lashed out?" Dwight considered it, then nodded. "People can do stupid things when they feel cornered."

"Is it valuable?" I asked.

"Could be."

"What's a maquette anyhow?" Dwight asked.

"It's a scale model for a larger piece. A way to work out proportions before trying to cast a final version."

"Would someone who came in to use the bathroom know what it was?"

"Well, Rathmann certainly would, and there were at least three others at Luna's party tonight with a background in art. Maybe more. Her boyfriend is an artist who's starting to make a bit of a name for himself. And yes, that maquette's probably worth a few thousand. I still don't understand how Sigrid's grandmother wound up with something like that."

He glanced at his watch. "Almost two. Wonder what's keeping them?"

As if on cue, one of the detectives appeared in the kitchen doorway with his parka zipped and the hood up. "Major Bryant? We're finished here for now. Lieutenant Harald will probably be back tomorrow, but she said she'd call first and —"

Elliott swung around sharply. "She's already gone?"

"Yessir. Did she know you were waiting to see her?"

"I guess not," he said with a rueful shrug that had me feeling sorry for him.

We were nearly through a second round of ale and he emptied his glass, thanked us for his impromptu supper, then stood to go. "Sorry to have kept you unnecessarily."

"No problem," Dwight said easily.

We walked out into the deserted hall with him and rang for the elevator. The doors to the other two apartments were closed and there was a tucked-in-for-the-night feel. The portable coat racks were still there but the hangers were empty except for a gaudy Hawaiian shirt and a fake orchid lei.

"Looks like someone's gone off with my overcoat and scarf," Elliott said. "Unless Luna's got it." He checked his watch again. "A little late to ask her tonight, I guess."

The elevator door slid back and a beefy white-haired man with a droopy white mustache opened the cage door.

"You'll freeze out there without a warmer coat," I said.

"No. I'll hop in a cab and I'll be fine."

"I don't think so," said the night man, whose name, according to his brass tag, was

Jani. "The snow's over a foot deep and still coming down. The crosstown streets are pretty well blocked and not much is moving on Broadway. The ambulance barely made it to the door, and that was a good forty minutes ago."

"Ambulance?" asked Dwight.

"Phil Lundigren's wife flipped out when she heard about Phil and they had to call an ambulance for her."

Elliott turned back to us. "I don't suppose you have an extra coat I could borrow? Or a heavy sweater so I can foot it down to the subway?"

All four of us looked down at his shoes. Leather hiking shoes, not boots, and barely ankle high.

Dwight gave me an inquiring glance and I nodded.

"Looks like you'd better stay here tonight," he said.

"Here?" Elliott looked around the hallway in puzzlement.

"With us," I told him. "You can't go out in this weather dressed like that. Not when we have an extra bedroom."

"Oh, but I couldn't," he protested.

"It's pretty rough out there, sir," said the night man.

"Then I'll try the hotel down the block."

"Full, sir. You're not the only one stranded. I heard one of Luna's party guests say they got the last room."

Elliott turned back to us and stretched his hands out in surrender. "If you're sure you don't mind?"

"Of course we don't mind," I told him.

While Dwight put away the food and Elliott helpfully stacked the dishwasher, I pulled extra towels from the linen closet in the hall and made sure there were clean sheets on the bed in the guestroom.

We were all too tired for further socializing, and when I handed Elliott a robe that Rob had left in the owner's closet, I said, "Sleep as late as you can. I certainly plan to."

Yawning, Dwight said, "I went ahead and filled the coffeemaker. If you're up first, all you have to do is switch it on."

"Thanks again," Elliott said as we headed for our own room. "I've heard about Southern hospitality all my life, but I never expected to find it in the middle of Manhattan."

CHAPTER 7

It is generally supposed that the police of a city have but one duty to perform, namely to arrest law-breakers; but the New York police have other things than that on their schedule.

— *The New New York,* 1909

Sigrid Harald — Sunday morning

When Sigrid joined him in the kitchen of 42 1/2 Hawker Street on the edge of Greenwich Village, Roman Tramegra said, "Oh, good! I was about to tiptoe down the hall to see if you were awake yet. Have you seen the snowdrifts? A *perfect* winter morning for a hearty breakfast."

Her housemate flourished his whisk at her and, in a deep voice that was a mixture of cinema English and educated Midwest, said, "What will it be, my dear? Hash browns, quiche, omelets, or waffles?"

Now in his early fifties, Roman fell somewhere between friend and surrogate uncle. He was an overly adventurous chef and his culinary experiments were often inedible, but breakfast was usually safe.

"An omelet would be good. Just cheese, though."

"Only cheese? Not a few jalapeño peppers or chopped shallots and tomatoes?"

"Cheese," Sigrid said firmly, and when Roman brought out a hunk of something with an odd color, she emended it to, "Cheddar cheese."

Sighing, he returned his first choice to the refrigerator and exchanged it for the familiar orange wedge.

Sigrid poured herself a cup of coffee. "I don't suppose the paper came?"

"Actually, it did. At least there's a plastic bag wedged in the snowbank inside the gate." He broke two eggs into a bowl and gave them a brisk stir with the whisk. "I suppose you should get it before it's completely buried."

Sigrid smiled. Despite his bald dome and portly size, there were times that Roman reminded her of a large fluffy cat. He had a cat's aversion to strenuous exercise and to the cold and wet. Snow might be beautiful, but that did not mean he wanted to walk across their small enclosed courtyard in it.

"If you go out for it, do you think you could manage to walk backwards?"

"Excuse me?"

"It's for my book. I want to see if a killer could make it look as if he only came *in* after a snowfall. Not that he went *out.*"

"It wouldn't," she said flatly. "Sorry. It's not just the shoe tracks. Snow this deep will show which direction the legs were moving."

Sigrid had first met Roman through one of her mother's impulsive charitable acts. Due to an improbable set of circumstances, he had wound up camping in her tiny guestroom, and when her building went condo, he took it upon himself to find her a new apartment. Several frustrating fiascos later, he had brought her to this house built onto the side of a commercial building near the river on one of the shortest streets in Greenwich Village. The half-furnished rooms formed a sort of flipped L shape around a small courtyard with a high fence. The kitchen, utility room, and maid's quarters were on the short segment, with a master suite on the long segment, along with a living room, dining area, and guestroom. The eccentric space was much too big for one person, yet the rent he quoted was quite reasonable.

"What's the catch?" she had asked suspiciously.

"I have to live here, too," he confessed. "It belongs to my godmother. Some of the furniture has been in her family for four generations, and I seem to be the only person she'll rent the house to. I'll live in the maid's quarters and I *promise* I shan't get in your way. You'll hardly know I'm here."

That had not proved even remotely true, but Sigrid found that he was less intrusive than she had feared, and there were times that she was even grateful he was there. When Nauman's death sent her into a deep depression, Roman's constant presence and determined badgering had helped bring her out of it.

He had a magpie curiosity about everything that crossed his path and was entranced to learn she was a homicide detective, because he wanted to write mystery novels and thought she would be a handy resource. She could not convince him that most of her cases were open and shut and came with very little mystery attached. All the same, she could and did clarify points of police procedure for him, and she was quite touched when he dedicated his first book to her.

He had now written four books, and they were moderately successful. None had made the *New York Times* bestseller list, but they did sell well enough to pay his share of the rent, rent he now paid to her.

Buying this house was her only big indulgence after Nauman's death, and his robe still hung in her closet. It no longer held the scent of his mellow pipe tobacco or aftershave, but merely touching it once in a while comforted her in ways she would not try to analyze.

There was a snow shovel in the utility room, and by the time she had cleared a short path out to the newspaper and made sure the gate could be opened, Roman had sautéed peppers, onions, and tomatoes for his own omelet and was ready to lay the plain cheese one on her plate.

She shook the snowflakes from her coat, slipped off her boots, and joined him. However, instead of lingering over the paper and a third cup of coffee as was usual on Sunday mornings, she ate quickly and told Roman that she would be going in to work.

"But it's still snowing." He gestured first to the window and then to the tiny television screen that hung under one of the cabinets. The sound was off, but they saw a reporter standing in Central Park. Falling snow frosted her bare head. Behind her, skiers and sledders were happily frolicking in the deep drifts. "Most of the crosstown streets are blocked. People are skiing from their apartment buildings straight over to the parks. They're asking people not to drive. Cars are skidding into each other everywhere."

"Our street may not be plowed," she said as she put her plate in the sink, "but I'm sure West or Sixth will be passable. I'll have a car pick me up."

Roman looked at her with sudden eagerness. "You *never* go in on Sunday unless it's something interesting. And to brave the elements? Do tell!" He immediately began scanning the pages of the metro section. "Would it be in today's paper?"

"I doubt it. And it's not that interesting except that the murder weapon is probably a little bronze model my grandmother sent up for Mother." Knowing that he would not leave it alone until she defused his interest, she gave him a bare-bones synopsis of last night and then went down to her room to dress.

9:15 and Grandmother Lattimore had always been an early riser, so she dialed the 919 area code. After two rings, a soft

Southern voice answered, "Lattimore residence."

"May I speak to Mrs. Lattimore?"

"I'm sorry, ma'am," said the unfamiliar voice. "Mrs. Lattimore is sleeping. May I take a message?"

Surprised, Sigrid identified herself. "Grandmother's not sick, is she?"

"She said she was just a little tired, ma'am, but I'm sure she'll be awake soon."

"Tell her I'll call back this afternoon after church." Her grandmother might be past ninety, but she had an iron will and Sigrid doubted that a little tiredness would keep her from Sunday morning services.

Moments later, she was speaking to a desk sergeant at a nearby precinct house who promised that he would have a car meet her at the corner of the closest uptown street.

At the office, Sam Hentz gave a tight smile when he saw her and held out his hand to the others, who groaned and handed over their dollar bills.

Sigrid seldom bantered with them, but their chagrined looks amused her and she paused to push back the hood of her white parka and unwrap the fleecy turquoise scarf that had protected her face from the worst of the icy wind sweeping off the Hudson

112

when she made her way to West Street earlier.

"What?" she said. "You thought a little snow would keep me home?"

"Some of the drifts are three feet high in places," said Urbanska.

"So how did you get in?" Sigrid asked.

The younger woman grinned. "Snowshoes. My brother sent me an old pair of his as a joke last year when we got those four inches, and I mushed over to my regular subway stop."

"Very resourceful," Sigrid said dryly.

If Hentz occasionally reminded her of a Doberman pinscher, Dinah Urbanska was a golden retriever — just as friendly, just as eager to please, if no longer quite as clumsy as when she first joined the department and they had all learned to keep coffee cups, laptops, and stray chairs out of her path. The sounds of broken glass or a "Jesus Christ, Urbanska!" followed by a string of curses as detectives rescued a pile of now-muddled case files from the floor were less frequent these days, but there were times when a crash from the squad room would penetrate Sigrid's office and make her wonder yet again why Hentz, who normally kept himself slightly aloof from the others, had appointed himself her mentor. Under his tutelage, though, the klutzy young woman had become a good detective.

Sigrid hung her outerwear on a coat tree in her office, then came back into the squad room for a cup of coffee and the morning briefing.

Yesterday's rain and snow had caused a dip in the usual Saturday night violence. A brawl outside a popular club had sent two men to the emergency room, another had been stabbed at a poker game, and an old woman was badly clubbed because she would not give her son money, but Phil Lundigren was their only homicide. City-wide, his was the first of the year. Last year, less than five hundred cases had been documented and the homicide rate kept dropping. Murder by gunshot still led the statistics, with blunt instruments a distant third. If they could shut off the trafficking of illegal guns from other states, the number of murders could be cut by half. In the meantime, the city's controversial stop-and-frisk program did seem to be finding fewer and fewer guns.

Turning to their case, she learned that Hentz had already briefed them so that they were up to speed and ready to get the wheels moving.

"Any word from the ME yet?" Sigrid asked.

"Not yet," said Hentz.

"What about Mrs. Lundigren?"

"Still under sedation," Urbanska reported. "Yanitelli stopped by on his way in to work and got her prints."

She set her own coffee cup on the edge of her desk and flipped open her notebook. Hentz reached over and moved the cup away from her hands before she could forget it was there and send it flying.

"The doctor on duty's going to give her a mental evaluation this morning. He said we could probably question her after lunch, and if that goes okay they might release her this afternoon and let her go home."

Sigrid turned to Hentz. "She told us she had no relatives. What about him?"

"None that the elevator man knew about. Want me to get a search warrant for the apartment? See if there's anything there to point us toward his killer?"

She nodded.

With an urban detective's disdain for someone who drawled like a hick, Hentz asked, "What about the stuff that was stolen from Sheriff Mayberry and his wife?"

"Major Bryant and Judge Knott?" Sigrid remembered that Kate had once said that

115

her brother-in-law was former Army Intelligence, but why spoil it for Hentz? "It would appear that the only things taken from that apartment were an earring and a small bronze sculpture that my grandmother had sent up with them."

That statement hung in the air for an awkward moment. Only Urbanska was artless enough to look up from her notes and say, "Your grandmother, ma'am?"

"Judge Knott is distantly related to her." Her tone did not invite further exploration of that relationship.

"What's this sculpture thing look like?" asked one of the detectives.

"I've only seen pictures, but it seems to be several small male figures crammed into a roughly cylindrical shape about the size of a tall beer can." Her slender fingers sketched the size and shape.

"Solid bronze?" Hentz asked.

Sigrid nodded.

"That much metal would have real heft to it. We didn't find anything in the apartment that looked as if it had been used to clobber the victim. You think that could be our murder weapon?"

"Very possibly. I'm told that it could be valuable, so when you're questioning the people who were at the DiSimone party last

116

night, concentrate first on anyone who might have an art background."

While Sam Hentz went off to find a judge who would sign a search warrant for the Lundigren apartment, Sigrid handed out the day's assignments. In addition to last night's violence, there were ongoing investigations into a mugging and some burglaries, and an arrest was imminent in a rape case. Detectives Elaine Albee and Jim Lowry were tasked with interviewing Luna DiSimone, who flatly refused to try to come to the station when they called her that morning.

"She says the snow's too deep," Albee reported, wrinkling her pretty nose in scorn.

"Then you'll have to go to her," Sigrid said. "We need a complete list of everyone who was there last night, especially anyone with a knowledge of art."

It occurred to her that perhaps Deborah Knott or her husband could email them the pictures on their digital camera, so she went into her office and called Deborah's number. One ring and a male voice said, "Deborah Knott's phone."

"Elliott?"

"Sigrid?"

She glanced at her watch. "You're out early."

"I never left," he said and explained about his missing overcoat, his shoes, and the sold-out hotel. "The Bryants were kind enough to offer me a room, and I took it. It was after two before we got to bed, though, and I don't think they're awake yet, but if you want I can knock on their door and — oh, wait a minute! Hang on, here's Bryant now."

She heard Buntrock explaining, and a moment later Dwight Bryant said, "Lieutenant Harald?"

"Sorry to bother you, Major, but I saw that your wife has her laptop and I was hoping one of you could send me a picture of that maquette that my grandmother sent up?"

"Be glad to if Deb'rah brought along the little gizmo that reads the camera card."

Sigrid gave him the address, then asked to speak to Buntrock again.

"Elliott, I'm sorry about last night. I'm told that you expected me to come back up to the sixth floor. I didn't realize."

"No problem," he said easily. "Miscommunication on my part."

"We're on our way over there in a few minutes. Will you still be there?"

"If I haven't totally worn out my welcome here, sure." She heard an exchange of male voices, then Buntrock said, "Bryant says we'll keep the coffee hot."

Five minutes later, they were looking at a picture of the Al Streichert maquette, the scale easily discernible because of the hands that held it. The picture filled the screen.

"Holy shit!" said Lowry, and Albee giggled. "Talk about cocksuckers."

As their focus switched from the penises to the caricatured faces, their grins faded and Albee, who was Jewish, took an involuntary step backward as she worked out what it depicted. One of the black detectives said, "This is your grandmother's?"

"I haven't talked to her yet," Sigrid said. "I don't know why she had it."

He flashed her a cynical look. "She's Southern, isn't she?"

Sigrid's cool gray eyes met his warm brown ones. "Not all Southerners are racist, Johnson."

"If you say so, ma'am."

"I do say so."

Ray Johnson shrugged and turned back to the screen.

"Make some printouts," Sigrid told him as the others went back to work. "It's disgusting, but it may be valuable and it may also be our murder weapon."

Lowry broke the tension by handing her a

list of sixty-seven separate names that had been gathered at the murder scene. A touch typist, he had entered the names into the computer, with Albee and Urbanska double-checking to make sure none were left off. He finished sorting them alphabetically and printed out several copies to take over to the apartment building.

Sigrid pointed to two of the names. "Elliott Buntrock and Charles Rathmann are both tied into the art world and should be able to name any others. Buntrock's still at the building, but call Rathmann and invite him to come down and help us."

She took a copy for herself and told them to leave the handwritten sheets and a print-out on Detective Tildon's desk. Tillie shone at detail work like this and Sigrid planned to turn him loose on the list when he came in the next morning. She was quite sure he would soon have each name cross-referenced five or six different ways so that he could eliminate any guests who had been together all evening and could alibi others.

By the time Hentz got back with the search warrant, Lowry had signed out a car. Broadway was clear enough for them to make decent time, although the windshield wipers had to labor to push the falling snow aside. While it helped that today was Sunday, which meant fewer vehicles on the streets, the sidewalks were lined with piles of snow so high that with the thickening flakes it was hard to see the jaywalking sledders and skiers headed for the park before they stepped out into the street.

The detectives were two blocks from Luna DiSimone's apartment building when Sam Hentz's phone rang. He answered, then murmured, "ME's office."

He listened intently for a moment or two and his face registered total surprise. "*What? The hell you say!*"

He hung up the phone, shaking his head in disbelief. "Turns out that the Phil may be short for Phyllis. Lundigren was a woman."

CHAPTER 8

Possibly the dining room is the most useful room in the whole apartment, aside from the kitchen.

— *The New New York,* 1909

I awoke Sunday morning to silence. No honking horns, no sirens, no pulsing beeps from big trucks backing up. Even without lifting my head from the pillow, I could tell by the quality of light coming from the window that the world was white outside. The bedside clock read 10:40.

10:40? Even on my days off, I almost never slept past nine anymore. I rolled over to kiss Dwight good morning and found his side of the bed empty. Although the bedroom walls were thick and the door was solid, the smell of coffee and bacon somehow managed to reach my nose.

I was up and dressed in five minutes and when I walked out, Dwight and Elliott were at the dining table working on a breakfast of Danish pastry, crispy bacon, and scrambled eggs. I was fairly sure that neither eggs nor bacon had been in the refrigerator before we went to bed last night. Both men were dressed, but I saw that Dwight was in his stocking feet.

I paused in the archway on my way to the kitchen for the biggest coffee mug I could find and fixed my husband with a stern eye. "I'm guessing that those damp boots over there by the door mean you've already been to that market again?"

Dwight nodded sheepishly and Elliott finished ratting him out. "I thought I was the first one up, until he came walking in with a couple of Fairway shopping bags."

"Well, we couldn't offer you stale bagels, could we?"

They waited till I was back with my coffee to tell me that Sigrid and a team of detectives were on their way over.

Elliott passed me the bacon and pastries and said, "She wants me to tick off the names of anyone who might have recognized that Streichert maquette, so I'm afraid you're stuck with me a little longer."

"Not a problem," said Dwight. "The way it's still coming down out there, I doubt if we'll be going anywhere today."

I suppose I should have been disappointed to come five hundred miles just to get snowbound, but a day spent relaxing with Dwight and reading the Sunday *New York Times* from front page to last, and relaxing with Dwight, and . . . well, you get my whim, as my brother Haywood would say.

Without his jacket on, I got the full effect of Elliott's blue sweatshirt, which was emblazoned with a pair of silver Yamahas.

"You ride?" I asked.

He followed my eyes to his thin chest and looked down to remind himself what he was wearing. "Motorcycles? God, no! My sister sends these things. I ran over her foot with my tricycle when I was in nursery school, and she's never forgiven me. She still thinks I'm a terrible driver."

He asked what we'd planned for the week.

"We're just playing it by ear," Dwight said.

"And leaving ourselves open to serendipity and suggestions," I added. "You have one? A suggestion, I mean?"

"Well, if you like jazz and find yourself down in the Village some evening, there's an authentic little club I like. It's just a hole-in-the-wall, but Sam Hentz sits in on piano sometimes."

I drew a blank on the name, but Dwight

was surprised. "Detective Hentz plays jazz piano?"

"Put himself through college playing in bars and restaurants. He's not half bad either. I've gone down to hear him a few times."

He pulled out his phone, scrolled through till he found the address, and gave it to Dwight. "Take the One train down to Christopher Street, then walk one block north to Tenth. Smalls. You can't miss it."

"Actually, Dwight and I do have one item on our dance card."

Dwight raised an eyebrow. "We do?"

"Someone at the party last night gave me a pair of tickets to the matinee of *The Mikado* on Wednesday."

"You like Gilbert and Sullivan?" Elliott asked.

I nodded. Dwight made a *comme ci, comme ça* gesture with his hand.

"That's how Sigrid and I got to know each other," Elliott said. "She was investigating a death at the Breul House — and if you're interested in some of the worst excesses in nineteenth-century art collecting, you owe yourself a visit. Bad taste preserved in amber, although the house itself has good lines, architecturally speaking. Anyhow, she heard me whistling one of Gilbert and Sullivan's patter songs and I was hooked as soon as I realized she knew all the words."

"Really?" I took the last dab of scrambled eggs from the bowl. "She doesn't strike me as a person who would like anything so frivolous."

"I thought that, too, at first." He cut a raspberry Danish in half and slid it onto his plate. "On the other hand, Gilbert and Sullivan may be frivolous, but they aren't stupid." He licked raspberry jam from his finger. "Remind me to give her that magazine article we found."

"Right. I stuck it back in the box."

When I went out to the kitchen to start a second pot of coffee, I took out the pages and started to flatten the box so it would fit into the recycle bin easier. Upon disposing of the bubble wrap at the bottom, though, I discovered a small white envelope underneath, an envelope addressed to Anne Harald.

Sealed, unfortunately.

(*"Not that you would read someone else's letter if it were unsealed,"* my internal preacher said starchily. His pragmatic roommate gave a cynical snort. He has no illusions about my strength of character when my curiosity's in full gallop.)

Elliott regarded the envelope with equal

curiosity when I brought it and the magazine pages back to the dining room.

"Let's hope Sigrid won't wait till Anne gets back from New Zealand next month," he said.

I topped off his coffee cup and paused to look out the dining room window. Blown by the wind, snowflakes swirled down and around like confetti at a political convention.

"People were out on skis before," Dwight said. "Why don't we buy you some boots and maybe walk over to the park?"

"Will a shoe store be open on Sunday?"

"Some guy was selling cheap plastic boots on the sidewalk in front of the market. Right next to a woman selling mittens and scarves. How do you suppose they do it? How did he put his hands on a bunch of boots in the middle of a snowstorm?"

Elliott nodded in amused agreement. "Street vendors are a breed unto themselves. Two drops into a downpour and you'll see them hawking umbrellas on every corner. They —"

He was interrupted by a knock on the door.

I looked at Dwight. "I thought people had to be buzzed in first."

"They're cops," he reminded me.

Of course.

But when I answered the door, it wasn't Sigrid and her team. Luna DiSimone stood there looking perfectly adorable in a coral gym suit and a silk hibiscus behind her ear. She held a platter full of assorted canapés and hors d'oeuvres covered by a sheet of plastic wrap. Over her shoulder I saw that she'd left the door to her apartment standing wide open at the other end of the hall.

"I was hoping you could take some of this food off my hands," she said. "The party broke up so early, I've got tons of the stuff left. Oh, hi, Elliott. Do you know these people?" She laughed at her own question. "Well, of course you do or you wouldn't be here, would you? Have you seen the snow? Isn't it just *gorgeous?* Nicco keeps calling me to bitch about it, but I love snow, don't you?"

Without being invited in, yet never questioning her welcome, she walked past me and put the platter on the table. Dwight and Elliott had come to their feet, Elliott unfolding himself one storklike joint at a time as he leaned over to accept her kiss on the cheek.

"Don't let me interrupt your breakfast," she said with that gurgling lilt that made her commercials so easy on the ears.

128

"Please," I said, gesturing to one of the empty chairs. "We're pretty much finished. Can I get you a cup of coffee? I just made a fresh pot."

She circled the table to sit next to Elliott and smiled happily. "Coffee would be absolutely wonderful. Black, please, and no sugar."

I brought it to her and said, "I think you left the door of your apartment open."

She dismissed my warning with an airy wave. "That's okay. Everybody's honest on this floor."

Elliott cocked his head at her. "Luna, you do realize that someone was killed here last night?"

A shadow crossed her smooth face. "Poor Phil! It's so *awful.* I still can't believe it. He was so sweet when he brought up the coat racks for me last night. I absolutely had to *force* him to take a tip. Who on earth do you think could have done that? It must have been someone who pretended he was invited to my party. Sidney's going to be so mad at himself when he realizes what he's done."

"The elevator man? What'd he do?" Dwight asked.

"He brought the killer up, didn't he? Without asking if he was one of the people

I'd invited."

Elliott frowned. "He wasn't checking IDs when I came up, and I didn't see a list."

"I didn't give him one, but —"

"But he should have recognized the mark of Cain on the killer's forehead and refused to let him get on the elevator?"

"Okay, I guess that was silly," Luna admitted with another graceful wave of her hand. "But none of my friends are killers. Honest. I won't say they wouldn't stab you in the back if they thought it would get them a part in a TV series, but really kill? *Never!*"

"Any of your guests have sticky fingers?" Dwight asked casually.

Luna half turned in her chair and her eyes widened as if she were seeing him for the first time and rather liked what she saw. Her eyes moved deliberately down his muscular body and she reminded me of a golden retriever when it suddenly spots an unguarded bone.

"Sticky fingers, Dwight? It *is* Dwight, isn't it?"

He nodded. "Several of your guests were in here last night."

"And something's missing? What?" Her eyes swept the dining room and vestibule in undisguised interest. "I just realized that this is the first time I've been in Jordy's apartment. How do you two know him anyhow? I don't think he's ever been further south in America than the Village, so you must have met him here. And this place is so *him,* isn't it? Traditional landscapes, old pieces of wood furniture. Oh, look! Are those strips of stained glass original to these windowpanes?"

She didn't seem to expect any answers to her cascade of questions, and when she stood up and walked toward the living room, there was no way to stop her short of putting my foot out to trip her.

"Where did it happen? In here? Ewww! Is that Phil's blood on the floor? How could you stand to stay here last night, Deborah? Doesn't this gross you out? It would me. I'll give you my cleaning guy's number. You certainly can't ask Denise to come and clean up her own husband's blood, now can you?"

I suppose I should have taken offense, but her chatter and her questions were those of an artless child. Dwight, Elliott, and I exchanged raised eyebrows and the three of us trailed her into the living room in time to hear her shriek, "My cat! Oh my God! That's my Oaxacan cat! How did it get here?"

She snatched up that brightly painted

handcarved wooden cat from the side table. Graphite smudged her fingers, but she didn't seem to notice. Cradling it protectively in her hands, she looked at Dwight and me in bewilderment. "Did you take it?"

"Certainly not," I said indignantly. "Last night was the first time I noticed it." I appealed to Dwight. "Did you?"

He shook his head. "When did you last see it, Miss DiSimone?"

"Oh no!" she wailed, her long blonde tresses swirling around her face. "Please, Dwight. Don't go formal on me. I'm sorry. Of course you and Deborah didn't steal it. I know you didn't. I'm so confused by all this — Phil getting killed, my party messed up, police taking down our names like we're criminals — I'm not thinking straight." She set the cat on the nearest surface and clutched the sleeve of Elliott's Yamaha sweatshirt with both hands, leaving traces of fingerprint powder. "Elliott, tell them I didn't mean it like that!"

Shaking his head at her dramatic apologies, he said, "What can I tell you? She's an actress. She needs a scriptwriter to keep her on track."

He looked at his watch and frowned. "I wonder what's holding Sigrid up? Luna, dear, stop posturing and tell me that my overcoat and scarf wound up in your apartment last night."

"Was that your coat? I knew it belonged to somebody really tall and skinny. It was still on the rack last night when Nicco had to leave. He could barely get it buttoned and it was practically dragging the floor on him. He had to go to his studio to walk his dogs and then it was snowing too hard to get back, but I'm sure he'll bring it with him when he comes. What time is it? He swore he'd be here by eleven so we could have brunch with the *Tiempo* people, although they may cancel because of the snow. He'll be so pissed if they do because he was hoping they'd run an in-depth interview about his new paintings and —"

Elliott held up a hand to stop her chatter and herded her toward the front door. "It's well past eleven and he's probably sitting on your swing at this very minute, wondering where you are."

"Oh. Right."

I followed them to the door and reminded Elliott that he'd left his jacket on a chair in the dining room.

"I'll be right back if Marclay has my coat," he said.

I left the door on the latch and fetched a wet cloth from the kitchen to begin wiping surfaces that had been dusted for finger-prints, including the cat that Luna had forgotten ·to take. Dwight came down the hall from the second bathroom with a bath mat in his hand. "I'm going to put this over that bloodstain till we can get it cleaned," he said.

The chenille mat had interlocking circles of blue and green and didn't exactly go with anything in the room, but yes, I was glad to have the blood covered.

CHAPTER 9

The citizen of Gotham and his wife dodge the servant question at the start by taking an apartment instead of a whole house. . . . A maid looks after the sweeping and cleaning, messenger boys and the telephone do the errands, and the janitor fights off agents, gas men, and beggars. One does not have to think about light or fuel or ice or ashes.

— *The New New York,* 1909

Sigrid Harald — Sunday morning (continued)
Once the others had gotten past the obvious raunchy remarks and readjusted their theories in light of the ME's report, Sigrid said, "Not a word of this to anyone unless it appears to be common knowledge. Until we learn more about the whole situation, Lundigren is a 'he.' Understood?"

Her words were meant for the whole team, but it was Urbanska who flushed bright red, aware that her impulsive tongue had spoken out of turn more than once.

"Understood, ma'am."

The street in front of the apartment building had not been plowed when they arrived, but employees from the buildings along here seemed to be keeping the sidewalk shoveled and blown fairly clean as snow continued to fall. The pure white drifts turned New York's gritty streets into a New Year's greeting card, and even Sigrid, who seldom paid much attention to nature, found herself caught up in the beauty of bare tree limbs etched in white against the dark brick or stone of the buildings.

Hentz nosed the car in as close to the curb as possible. Last night's rain meant that ice had formed beneath the snow, but they managed to get to the sidewalk without falling, although Sigrid and Elaine Albee both grasped the nearest arms when their booted feet almost slipped out from under them. The front door was locked, and Sigrid was surprised by the elevator man, who opened the door for them in his neat brown uniform.

"Weren't you on duty last night?"

There were shadows under Sidney Jackson's almond-shaped eyes and his face seemed pale and tired beneath its faint golden skin. "The day man walked off the job this morning so I got called back in. I couldn't believe it when Mrs. Wall told me Phil got killed last night."

The elevator was small, but the six of them managed to squeeze in.

"Vlad — he's a porter and he got called in, too. He says Denise flipped out and they took her to Bellevue. She gonna be okay? How'd Phil die anyhow? Somebody cut him?"

"Why do you say that?" Hentz asked.

"I'm back and forth to the sixth floor all night and I didn't hear anybody say anything about a gunshot. Jani took over for me around eleven so I could get home before the snow got too deep, and he told Vlad the same thing. So what did happen?"

Ignoring his question, Sigrid asked, "Did you see Lundigren last night around ten?"

"No, but he would've used the back elevator or the back stairs."

"How well did you know him?"

"Good as anybody, I guess. Friendly enough, but he doesn't hang out with us. He's a hard worker an' he keeps at it. Building this old, something's always breaking down and the boiler needs watching like a baby — that's why they called Vlad in. He knows boilers. But Phil, he's right on top of things. He'll get on you bad if he thinks you're slacking off or not being a good representative for the building." He gestured over his shoulder to the open elevator car. "He makes us keep the cage polished and we can't let stuff pile up in the corners because Denise, she vacuums it out every day."

The detectives noted that nothing in Sidney Jackson's words gave any indication that he knew the victim's true sex.

"Mrs. Lundigren is on the payroll?" asked Lowry.

He shrugged. "She helps Phil out with stuff like that. She's okay as long as you don't talk to her. She wants you to act like you don't know she's there. She cleans for Mr. Lacour and Mrs. Wall, and that reminds me: Mrs. Wall said for me tell her when you get here."

"Who's she?" asked Hentz.

"Chair of the co-op board." A loud buzz interrupted him. "Gotta go."

"One minute," said Sigrid. "Lowry, you and Albee go talk to this Mrs. Wall. See if Lundigren had a personnel file. You know what to look for."

They nodded and stepped into the elevator. Sidney looked at the remaining three dubiously as he pulled the brass accordion gate closed. "What about you? You can't get to the stairs without a key."

Hentz jingled the key ring they'd taken off Lundigren's body. "We'll manage."

Followed by Dinah Urbanska, he and Sigrid walked across the Arts and Crafts ceramic tile floor and turned a corner into a short hall that led to two doors. One was for the fire stairs. After three tries, Hentz found the key that unlocked it. Inside the stairwell was the service elevator. While one could exit from the stairwell without a key, the door could not be left unlocked for access from the lobby side. The elevator here was larger and more modern than the one out in the lobby and it appeared to be self-service when they rang for it. The doors opened automatically without a key. Like the stairwell, the floor of the car was spotless and even gave off a strong smell of a pine-scented cleaner. The elevator walls were hung with quilted plastic pads, and there was the usual panel with a button for each floor.

Urbanska looked at Hentz and stated the obvious. "So once someone's on an upper floor, they can get down and out, but if you don't have a key, the only way to get up is on the front elevator that's manned twenty-four/seven?"

"So it would appear," he said.

They stepped back into the hall and Hentz unlocked the door to the Lundigren apartment. They were met by a white Persian cat that mewed loudly upon seeing them.

Urbanska immediately stooped and crooned reassurances, her hand stretched out to the animal. Cautiously, the cat sniffed her fingers, then rubbed against her knee and accepted her strokes. When Urbanska stood up, the cat walked to the archway that led deeper into the apartment, looked back at the young woman, and gave a soft cry.

"He's probably hungry," she said. "Okay if I look for his food?"

Sigrid, who had never owned a pet and was not particularly fond of cats, nodded.

Urbanska glanced around the little jewel box of a living room. "Pretty room," she said.

"Doesn't look as if it gets much use, though, does it?" asked Sigrid.

The small space was indeed pretty, but as impersonal as a doctor's waiting room. No family photos, no magazines or newspapers, nothing out of alignment. Behind the gauzy white curtains, a window overlooked a narrow alley that probably led to the street. Although sparkling clean on the inside, the window was dirty on the outside and was not only barred, but painted shut as well. Hentz noted that there was a ramp up from the basement and that someone had swept it clean within the past hour, for there was only a light dusting of snow.

"Seems to be letting up," he said as he dropped the curtain.

Beyond the formal living room lay the kitchen, bedroom, bath, and a den that had probably begun life as a dining room. Everything was neat and tidy, but the den was clearly where the Lundigrens had done their living. A large plush recliner faced the plasma screen, and the remote lay on a table beside the chair along with a copy of *TV Guide* and Al Gore's book on climate change.

All very masculine, thought Sigrid.

The couch was probably Denise Lundigren's usual seat. It was upholstered in a bright floral print and several ruffled cushions picked up those colors and formed a cozy nest at one end. A half dozen shelter magazines were neatly stacked on the shelf of the nearest end table. Here, too, were the photographs that had been missing in the living room, but all seemed to be of Denise. Denise as a pretty little girl in a ruffled dress and patent leather Mary Janes. Denise in a high school cap and gown. Denise in a polka-dot dress on the observation deck of the Empire State Building. Denise curled up on this very couch with that white cat in her arms.

But none of Phil. And none of anyone else.

Out in the kitchen, they watched Urbanska spoon a small tin of cat food into a delicate china saucer that sat on the floor beside a matching bowl of water. Here, white tiles, white cabinets, and white appliances were brightened by floral dishtowels and pot holders. The magnets on the refrigerator were enameled cats and flowers, and the magnetized shopping list — *soap, carrots, cat food, O.J.* — continued the motif. A tall narrow window at the end of the room had been frosted, then fitted with glass shelves that held a collection of shiny crystal animals, mostly cats but also porcupines, rabbits, and birds, each one cut and faceted to reflect light from every angle. The bottom shelf was reserved for small glass perfume bottles that looked to be hand-blown. The thin glass stoppers were fanciful swirls, and they, too, glittered under the lights that were concealed at the top of the window.

"She must wash those things every day," Urbanska marveled. She rinsed out the tin and put it in a waste can under the sink. "My aunt collects crystal figurines and they're always dusty."

The bedroom was clearly decorated by and for Denise. A floral perfume lingered on the air here. The white furniture featured curlicues and piecrust and was stenciled in thin gold lines. The king-size bed was outfitted with ruffled pillow shams and matching dust ruffle, floral comforter, and pale blue sheets. The comforter had been turned back but only one side of the bed was rumpled. A biography of Eleanor Roosevelt sat on the nightstand next to the unrumpled side.

"Looks like she went to bed alone while her husband —" Urbanska caught herself and looked at Sigrid in confusion.

"Husband's fine for now," Hentz told her. "Keep thinking of our victim as a man and you won't slip up when you're questioning the others."

Sigrid said nothing, but doubted if Urbanska could stop herself from turning red every time she was reminded of the victim's true sex.

Urbanska doggedly continued. "So she went to bed and he went up to check on the noise. Why would he go into a different apartment?"

"The night man said that he hadn't seen

Lundigren all evening, so he probably took the stairs or the service elevator," said Hentz. "Did we check to see whether 6-A's service door opens onto the main hall or a back hall?"

"I saw a service door in the kitchen," Sigrid said, "but I couldn't say where it went."

As they returned to the search, the white cat came in and wound himself around Urbanska's legs. She gave him an absent-minded stroke and he jumped up on the bed to begin washing himself.

A dainty dressing table held little bottles of creams and lotions, additional fragile perfume bottles, and a chrome makeup mirror that was framed in lights. Opening a side drawer, Sigrid found a tangle of costume jewelry and a blue velvet jeweler's box. Inside that was an elaborate crystal necklace and a handwritten gift card: *Happy anniversary, xoxo, Phil.*

One drawer of the tall dresser held masculine socks and underwear, the other four drawers were filled with lingerie and feminine sweaters.

Ditto the two closets. Denise's was stuffed to overflowing with the usual women's apparel. Phil's held three brown coveralls in plastic dry cleaners' bags, a brown suit, several shirts and ties, a sports jacket, and four pairs of slacks.

In the bathroom's medicine cabinet were over-the-counter painkillers, vitamins and calcium supplements, first aid remedies, Band-Aids, and three prescription bottles. One was an antidepressant in Denise's name. Another, also in her name, held mild sleeping pills. The third, in Phil's name, contained pills to control high blood pressure.

Once they had walked through the apartment, they spread out to search more intensively. On the floor at the back of Denise's closet, underneath three rows of shoeboxes, Urbanska found a cardboard box with dividers that had originally kept jars of mustard from bumping against each other. Each compartment was now stuffed with even more shiny knickknacks. She saw a crystal long-stemmed rose, a pretty cloisonné pillbox, a kitten of frosted gray glass, a porcelain shepherdess figurine, a pink glass perfume bottle, and a silver Santa Claus bell that tinkled when she picked it up.

"What's that?" Sigrid asked.

"Looks like her overflow collection. She probably switches them out with each other. That's what my aunt does, anyhow." Urbanska paused and almost to herself murmured, "My aunt doesn't have any children either."

At the end of another ten minutes, they had found nothing with writing on it except for that one card and the shopping list.

"Everybody has papers," Sigrid said. "Bills, bank statements, insurance policies. Where are theirs?"

The cat followed them back through the apartment.

"I guess he'll be okay," Urbanska said with a concerned look on her face. "I put out some dry food, too. And fresh water. The litter box was pretty clean, too."

"You looked?" asked Hentz, amused.

Before he took them up to the twelfth floor, Sidney Jackson used the house phone to tell Mrs. Wall that two detectives were there to see her, and she was waiting at the door when Elaine Albee and Jim Lowry stepped off the elevator. Mid-fifties and confident with it, she was small and slender and carried herself like someone who was used to being photographed at opening receptions and charity functions. Her straight silver hair curved to frame a pointed chin, and ragged bangs softened her strong forehead. She wore black stretch pants and a slouchy black sweater with the sleeves pushed up to show several silver bracelets. Despite the laugh lines and wrinkles, she had beautiful skin, and her only makeup was lipstick that had almost worn off. She might have started the morning with mascara and eye shadow, but her hazel eyes were red-rimmed now and they realized that she had been crying.

They introduced themselves and Mrs. Wall invited them into an apartment that was harmoniously furnished in earth tones and sturdy Arts and Crafts oak furniture. Craftsman touches were everywhere, from the rugs on the wooden floors to the brass lamps and slatted wood radiator covers. An earthenware teapot and a full cup of hot fragrant tea sat on a hammered brass tray atop the coffee table, and they declined her offer to bring more cups.

"Everybody in the building is just devastated by Phil's death," she said when they were seated. "All sorts of rumors are flying around. Please tell me what really happened."

"The only thing we know is that he was struck down in apartment 6-A sometime between nine-thirty and eleven," said Lowry.

Mrs. Wall sat there slowly shaking her elegant head and her eyes filled up again. "He was just the dearest man. There's no way we'll ever find someone half as good again. Why was he killed, Detectives? He never hurt anyone or anything. Not even spiders. Our middle child used to go all Annie Hall on us whenever she saw one, and if my husband or I were out, Phil would come right up and catch it in a plastic cup and put it out on the balcony."

"How long had he worked here?" Albee asked gently.

Struggling to keep her voice steady, Mrs. Wall said, "We moved in seventeen years ago and he was here at least two years before that."

"What about Mrs. Lundigren?"

It seemed to Elaine that Mrs. Wall's lips tightened when she said, "Denise? We've heard that an ambulance had to be called when they told her. Will she be all right?"

"I think they expect to let her come home later today."

The older woman shook her head. "Poor woman. Her condition is so . . ." She hesitated, searching for the right word. ". . . so fragile. I honestly don't know how she will manage without Phil."

"Do either of them have family?"

"I never heard him mention anyone. He listed Denise as next of kin when he applied for this job, and I do know he had a mother who died about eight years ago, because they went up for the funeral."

"Up?"

"To New Hampshire. That's where he was from originally. I don't know if that's where she'll want to go, but part of the super's salary is the free apartment and we'll be needing it for Phil's replacement."

"Is the building a co-op or condo?" Albee asked.

"Co-op," Mrs. Wall replied, which meant that the tenants were technically shareholders, not owners, who paid the building's monthly expenses based on the size of each apartment. Newcomers who wish to buy into a co-operative building have to be approved by the building's board, unlike a condo, where the conditions are less constrictive and tenants hold regular deeds to their own individual apartments.

Mrs. Wall's silver hair swung forward as she leaned over to retrieve a thick file folder. "I was looking at Phil's records this morning to notify the insurance company. One of his benefits was a policy the board took out on his life with Denise as the beneficiary."

"How much are we talking about?" asked Jim Lowry.

"A quarter-million. I know that's not much in today's economy, but it should allow her to start a new life. If she can. But here." She handed him the folder and her thin bracelets tinkled softly against each other. "I made copies of the job application he filled out when he first came, along with his references. I wasn't on the board then, of course, but it all seems very straight-forward and I see no reason you shouldn't have it."

Elaine Albee looked over his shoulder as Lowry opened the folder and read through the simple job application form. Their eyes immediately went to the box labeled *Sex* and saw that the *M* had been checked. *Marital Status* had the *M* checked, too. He turned the sheet over and they saw three references listed.

"Do you know if the board actually checked these references?" he asked.

"Probably not," she replied with a sad smile. "I'm told that the building had been without a reliable super for several months. I don't know who found Phil, but he came over in an emergency and handled it so promptly and without any dramatics that the board practically begged him to apply for the full-time position."

She took a sip of tea and cradled the cup in her hands. "Besides, anyone could see that Phil was competent and dependable and so honest that he could make George

Washington look like a pathological liar."

"So if we told you that he had taken a gold earring?"

Her fingers tightened around the cup and then she set it back on the tray very deliberately. "Phil steal? Never! He wouldn't pick up a penny in the lobby without trying to find out who had dropped it."

Albee sat back in her seat and decided it was time to go fishing. "Mrs. Wall, you say that everyone loved Phil, but is that really accurate? Isn't it true that there's at least one shareholder who didn't get along with him?"

Mrs. Wall sighed. "You mean the people in 7-A?"

"For starters," Lowry said, trying to sound as if there might be several others.

Resigned, the woman tucked a strand of hair behind her ear and said, "We should never have approved the Rices. We should have realized they were trouble when they were willing to pay ten percent above the asking price in a down market. And all those glowing references from their former neighbors? They lied through their teeth just to get those awful creatures out of their own building. The Rices started alienating people here even before they moved in."

She ticked off several incidents on her

fingers: the remodeling that went on too long because they tried to ignore building codes, the extra two dogs, the cavalier manner in which they repainted and recarpeted the common hall to suit their own questionable taste without asking anyone, their rudeness to the other owners, the tub they let overflow twice, and finally the illegal electrical wiring that could have burned the building down.

She topped her cup from the teapot and took another long swallow. "They tried to bribe Phil not to report it and they threatened to sue him for slander when he testified at their hearing before the board. We've begun the eviction process, but it takes time, and Phil was worried that they might try to do something to hurt the building before they're actually gone even though they would be hurting themselves if it lowers the value of their own apartment."

"Judge Knott and Major Bryant found him in 6-A when they got in Friday evening," said Lowry.

"Who?" She looked puzzled and then her face cleared. "Oh, yes. I forgot. Jordy Lacour did say a couple from North Carolina would be using his place this week. This is awful for them, too. Have they left?"

Albee shook her head. "No, ma'am. I

think they're planning to stay. Anyhow, Lundigren told them he was worried about a leak from the apartment overhead."

"The Rices! It would be just like them to think that if the Lacour apartment was empty, no one would notice a leak until it had done considerable damage." She set her teacup down so firmly that it rattled the spoon in her saucer. "Unconscionable!"

"What about the other employees in the building?" they asked.

"So far as I know, there are no serious animosities, but you'll have to ask them." Again, she reached into the file and pulled out another sheet of paper. "Here's a list of all the employees and the outside service people that we use."

"Could we see those personnel files?" Albee asked casually, but Mrs. Wall balked at that.

"I'm sorry, Detective. That would be an invasion of their privacy. The only reason I can give you Phil's in good conscience is because it may help you find who did this awful thing."

"What about a list of the building's occupants?" asked Lowry.

"Those you could get from the directory at the front door, so I drew up a current list for you," she said, handing him a third sheet.

"One further thing," said Lowry. "How would you describe Lundigren's marriage?"

Mrs. Wall hesitated, then pushed up one of the sleeves that had crept down over some of her silver bracelets and lifted the teacup to her lips.

The two detectives exchanged glances, both suddenly aware that Mrs. Wall had been using her tea as a stalling device throughout the interview.

"Was it a good marriage?" Lowry asked.

"You know about Denise's condition?"

"Her social anxiety disorder?"

The older woman nodded.

"It was hard on Phil, but he absolutely adored her and was very protective of her. We all understood and we did what we could to help. There's no way she could go out to work, you see. You may have heard that she cleans some of the apartments? I know Jordy uses her on a regular basis, and I started using her, too, when my last woman moved out to Long Island, so Denise is used to us, but if you were having unexpected guests and you wanted her to come clean the bathrooms and change the sheets because your own cleaning person couldn't come, you would have to make the arrangements through Phil, and he would bring her up and tell her what had to be done because she simply couldn't handle having to talk to unfamiliar people."

"So you would say it was a happy marriage?" Albee persisted.

"He was very devoted," said Mrs. Wall. "And very protective."

"And what about her?"

Again that hesitation. "She needed him."

True to Elliott Buntrock's prediction, Luna DiSimone's current boyfriend was lounging on her wicker swing when they walked into the apartment, and he gave her a sour look.

"Where the hell have you been? And why didn't you answer your phone? I've been trying to call you for the last hour."

Barrel-chested, with short legs, Nicco Marclay had once boasted a head of luxuriant red hair. Here in his twenty-seventh year, however, it had receded well past the crown and was now not much more than a fringe. He had taken to wearing flat golfing caps with narrow bills, and today's was a tattersall check in shades of brown and gold that clashed with his red flannel shirt and jeans.

His truculence faded as he realized who was with Luna. "Oh, hey there, Buntrock. I was hoping to talk to you last night, but then things got crazy."

Buntrock knew what "talk to you last night" meant. That was the opening feint of almost every artist on the make. It meant, "If you're looking for the next Picasso to write about for *The Loaded Brush,* I'm your boy." Indeed, it was his inclusion of Marclay in an article about emerging young artists two years ago that helped the man get into one of the better galleries.

"Wish you'd found me before you went off with my topcoat," he said mildly.

"Was that yours? Sorry. I did bring it back, though." He gestured to a stool at the bar that was now draped in a damp wool coat.

"What about my scarf?"

"Scarf? Didn't see a scarf."

"Check the bowl there by the door," Luna said. "Anything I found on the floor this morning, I stuck in there." She went over to the swing, lifted Marclay's cap, and planted a kiss on his bald head.

"Dammit, Luna!"

"Oh, lighten up, Nicco. And you haven't been calling me for an hour, because we talked thirty minutes ago. Did the *Tiempo* people call?"

"Yeah. They cancelled. Afraid of a little snow."

"Just as well," said Buntrock. To get to his scarf at the bottom of the large green glass punchbowl that Luna used as a catchall for keys and other odds and ends, he had to move a couple of phones, a tube of lipstick, a flamingo-shaped earring, and a pair of new-looking red rubber flip-flops. A lei of silk orchids had tangled itself around his scarf and it took him a moment to untangle it. "The police want to talk to us."

"Us? Why? The only time I ever met the dead guy was when he and his creepy wife were up here yesterday morning."

"Creepy wife?"

"Don't be mean, Nicco," Luna said. She sat down at the far end of the long swing, slipped off her shoes, leaned back against the pillows, and put her stockinged feet in the artist's lap.

"I'm not being mean. I'm being honest." He began to massage her feet absentmindedly. "But you've got to admit that it's creepy when somebody won't look at you and you have to tell her husband what you want her to do before she'll do it."

"She has a psychological hang-up," Luna told Buntrock. "I forget what it's called but it's like being pathologically shy. Anyhow, the last time the caterers came, they said they had to start with a clean kitchen and mine was a total mess, but my regular guy doesn't work on weekends, so when I asked

Antoine if he knew anybody, he told me that Phil's wife helps out sometimes, so I called Phil and they came up. He asked me what I wanted done and I told him, and then he took her out to the kitchen and asked us not to go in till he came back for her, that it made her nervous."

"Creepy," Marclay muttered. "But that's the only time I saw the man, so I don't have anything to tell the police."

"I think they want us to go through Luna's guest list and mark everybody who knows anything about art."

"Art?" asked Marclay. "Why?"

"Ours not to reason why," Buntrock said lightly. He finished untangling his scarf and dropped the lei back in the bowl. When he put the flip-flops back in, something clinked against the glass and he saw that a shiny button or something had embedded itself in the spongy sole.

"Guest list?" said Luna. "I don't have a guest list. I just went through the contact names on my phone and sent invitations to the people I like."

"Which is how that asshole Rathmann got invited," Nicco Marclay said truculently. Charles Rathmann occasionally reviewed for one of the throwaway weekly papers and he had not been kind to Marclay's last show.

"So how do you know police people like that Lieutenant Vaughn and that professor from John Jay?"

"The pilot I made for StarCrest Productions."

Marclay tweaked her big toe. "The one where you were supposed to play a Coney Island police officer?"

Luna nodded. "They were consultants on the shooting and we got to be friends."

Of course they had, thought Buntrock. Luna was as friendly as a six-month-old puppy and just as confident as any puppy that everyone wanted to be her friend, too. Buntrock had to admit that such artlessness was appealing.

Marclay gave the ball of her left foot a final rub, then began on her right. "Too bad it didn't get past the pilot. You could've made some serious bread."

Buntrock lifted a cynical eyebrow. Trust Marclay to keep his eye on the economic ball. He himself had met Luna through the owner of Marclay's gallery back when she was with another artist. Marclay had soon cut the other guy out. Out of the gallery and out of Luna's life. Luna DiSimone might not be an A-list actor — hell, she was probably barely B-list — but she was a connection to that world, and it never hurt to

159

have a sprinkling of showbiz glamour at your openings.

"You add any names to the guest list?" he asked.

Marclay shook his head. "It was her thing, not mine."

"But you did ask if I'd invited Elliott and Mischa and Orton," Luna said. She gave a contented sigh as Marclay kneaded the ball of her foot with his knuckles. "Ummmm, that feels so good."

CHAPTER 10

Many of [the drawing rooms] resemble
nothing so much as antique shops. . . .
Louis Seize cabinets back up against the
walls and hold Chinese porcelains, silver,
glass, miniatures.
— *The New New York,* 1909

The doorbell rang and I called, "It's open,
Elliott. Come on in."

"Sorry," Lieutenant Harald said, "it's not
Elliott."

Dressed in a white parka with the hood
pushed back, she entered through the
unlatched door, followed by Detective
Hentz, whom we had met the night before,
and a Detective Dinah Urbanska, a sturdy
young woman in a navy blue jacket with
golden brown hair and light brown eyes.

Lieutenant Harald seemed a little surprised to realize Elliott Buntrock wasn't
with us. "He left?" she asked.

"No, I'm still around," he called, striding down the hall. He wore a white silk scarf around his neck now and had a heavy black overcoat draped over his arm. "Luna and her boyfriend said they would try to construct a guest list for you."

"She doesn't have the original?" asked Hentz.

"In case you haven't realized it yet, Hentz, our Luna is a creature of impulse," said Buntrock. "She decides to give a party, and two minutes later she's scrolling through the numbers on her phone to text everyone she thinks might like to come to a beach party in January. Amazing how many of us are amused by her impulsiveness."

"I didn't find being accused of theft all that amusing," I said. "And after making such a fuss about that cat, she went off and left it here."

"Cat?" asked Detective Urbanska. She looked around as if expecting to see a real one emerge from behind a chair.

I lifted the brightly painted wooden cat from a nearby table. "This one. It was over there with those pillboxes. Luna said it was hers. Accused my husband and me of stealing it last night."

"Now, now," said Elliott. "She merely blurted out the first thing that came into her head to explain how it got here. She really doesn't think you stole it."

"No?" I was suddenly feeling cranky and tired of all these people and wished they would go away and leave Dwight and me alone. I was sorry that someone had died here. Phil Lundigren had seemed like a nice enough person and he probably didn't deserve to be killed. All the same, it wasn't as if he were someone we'd had any kind of a relationship with.

"Anyhow," Buntrock said, "it's just a cheap Mexican souvenir. Probably didn't cost her ten bucks."

"Let it go, shug," Dwight said quietly. "Any of those guys who helped themselves to our facilities last night could have set it on that table."

Sigrid held out her hand and I gave her the cat. No more than two inches tall and approximately four inches long from tail tip to nose, it was carved to look as if it were about to pounce. "It was over here, right?"

She carried it to the table halfway down the living room wall and set it down next to the two pillboxes. By lamplight the rich deep enamel had made them glow like jewels. By daylight, they were merely shiny and pretty.

"I can't swear to it," I said, "but I think

163

there were at least five or six more of those little boxes there before the cat appeared."

"Are they valuable?"

"I have no idea. I guess it depends on their age and who made them." I lifted one and saw some indecipherable characters engraved on the bottom. "Anybody here read Chinese?"

"Is it important?" Elliott asked her.

Sigrid shrugged. "If they're valuable and if someone wished to steal two or three, putting an equally colorful object in the middle of them might distract a casual eye from noting the loss." She restored the figurine to its original position, and even though it really didn't go with the exquisite little boxes, I realized it could indeed serve as a decoy.

Intrigued, Elliott Buntrock began to lift the boxes and hold them up high so he could study the markings on their bottoms. For some reason, he reminded me of a long-ago springtime on the farm when two of my brothers decided to raise chickens for a 4-H project.

"You ever sex biddies?" I asked.

His lips twitched. "What?"

"Baby chicks. You look at their bottoms to see whether they're male or female so that you don't wind up with too many roosters."

164

"I grew up on the East Side," he said dryly. "Not many baby chicks there. But this one's got a hallmark on its little bottom. Probably gold, if I'm not mistaken. Could be worth a tidy sum." He carried it over to the French doors to study it in better light.

"I don't suppose you found a pillbox in the victim's pocket?" Dwight asked as we moved back to the vestibule.

"Or my other earring?" I asked.

Sigrid shook her head. "Sorry."

While we had been distracted by the Mexican cat and the pillboxes, Detective Hentz had stepped into the hall to answer his phone, and now he said to Sigrid, "Lowry and Albee are on their way down, Lieutenant."

"Good." She turned to Dwight. "I'm sure I don't have to tell you, Major, that if anything about last night occurs to either of you —"

"No," Dwight said. "You don't. And we do have your number."

"Oh wait!" I cried. "When I pulled all the bubble wrap out of the box that Mrs. Lattimore sent, we found an envelope."

I darted into the dining room and retrieved the envelope we'd left on the table beside the magazine pages. When Elliott realized what was happening, he hastily set the box back on the table and joined us.

To my disappointment, Sigrid merely turned the envelope in her hand, then put it and the magazine article in the pocket of her white parka.

"Come on, Sigrid," Elliott complained. "Aren't you going to tell us what she said?"

"It's not addressed to me," she said coolly. "Shall we go see how Miss DiSimone's getting on with her guest list?"

Okay, I had wanted them to clear out and leave Dwight and me alone, but it was frustrating not to know what was in Mrs. Lattimore's letter.

Elliott slipped on his jacket and gathered up his overcoat. "Thanks again for sheltering me from the storm. If you're free one night, perhaps you'll let me treat you to dinner?"

"That would be great," I said before Dwight could say no.

We exchanged phone numbers, and when everyone was gone, Dwight shook his head in amusement. "You don't fool me, honey. You're hoping he'll find out what Mrs. Lattimore wrote."

"Aren't you at all curious, too?"

"Maybe, but I'm more patient. Besides —" He took a business card from his pocket and flourished it. "Detective Hentz gave me his card. He's playing at that jazz club down in the Village tomorrow night. I thought perhaps we could buy him a drink."

CHAPTER 11

There is the reach for happiness — the attempt to gain it by and through possessions.

— *The New New York,* 1909

Sigrid Harald — Sunday (continued)

Last night, apartment 6-C had seemed as packed with festive beachcombers as a Hamptons jitney on an August weekend. Today, through the open front door, it looked more like Coney Island on the Tuesday after Labor Day. Plastic wineglasses and half-empty drink cups littered the surfaces. Bits of food had been ground into the planks of the floor and the colored toothpicks that had held tasty morsels were scattered everywhere. Several black plastic trash bags were heaped in the middle of the oversized living room. One was stuffed and already tied shut. Luna was still adding to the other three: wine and liquor bottles in one, aluminum cans in another, while a fourth bag almost overflowed with food-smeared plastic plates, napkins, and other party detritus.

With dainty fingers and an expression of distaste on her pretty face, Luna DiSimone lifted a napkin filled with olive pits by the edges and dropped it into that trash bag.

"Miss DiSimone?" Sigrid said as they paused in the doorway.

"Yes?" She brushed a tress of long blonde hair back from her face and her frown turned instantly to sunshine. "Are you the police Elliott said wanted to talk to us?"

"I'm Lieutenant Harald and these are Detectives Hentz and Urbanska," she said, "and yes, we did want to speak to you. And to Mr. Marclay, too?"

Sigrid cast an inquiring eye in the direction of the stocky man wearing a flat cap and received a sour nod. She had given the guest list sheets a quick scan on the drive over. Nicco Marclay's name had appeared so often throughout the evening, she was fairly certain he could not have left the party during the relevant time.

"Excuse the mess and come on in," said Luna DiSimone. "I had a party last night and the caterers stiffed me on the cleanup part."

"Didn't I see you here last night?" Marclay asked.

"Yes," Sigrid said, surprised that he would have noticed her amid so many.

"Charlie Rathmann said something that ticked you off and — hey, wait a minute! Lieutenant Harald? You're *Sigrid* Harald, aren't you? You and Oscar Nauman?"

Sigrid gave a tight nod.

"Well, I'll be damned! You really are a police detective. I thought that was some gallery hype to make you seem more mysterious. Why the interest in which art people were here last night?"

"That isn't something I can talk about right now," she said.

Elliott Buntrock hesitated in the open doorway. From the neutral look Sigrid gave him, he realized that he was not supposed to mention the missing maquette. He entered without speaking and sat down on a green Adirondack chair. If he was going to have to mark names on a list, the chair's broad flat armrest would act as a desktop.

Sam Hentz explained what they wanted from the two men while Urbanska huddled with Luna DiSimone to go through the contact list on her phone and text the pertinent names over to their computer back at the station.

"You won't tell anyone where you got their info, will you?" the actress asked. "Some of these numbers have *never* been public."

"We'll destroy them as soon as the case is closed," Sigrid promised. "And we may not have to contact all of them."

Leaving the others to labor over the lists, she and Hentz walked out into the hall to meet Lowry and Albee as they stepped off the elevator.

"Learn anything?" Sam Hentz asked.

"Mrs. Wall gave us Lundigren's personnel file," said Lowry. "Mrs. Lundigren was with him and he was passing as male when he was hired nineteen years ago. Before that, he worked as a janitor over on Amsterdam and West Ninety-First. He listed his mother in New Hampshire as next of kin, but she's dead now."

"Was she aware that he had any issues with anyone?"

"Other than a nutty wife? No, ma'am. According to Mrs. Wall, everyone loved him."

Hentz groaned. "And how many times have we heard that?"

Lowry grinned, then reported that the building employed seven men in addition to the usual service providers. Referring to the list Mrs. Wall had provided, he ticked them off on his fingers: "Lundigren was the super, of course, then two porters and four guys that handle the door and elevator twenty-four/seven. It's like a little UN here — Jamaica, Croatia, Hungary, you name it, they got it."

Typical New York, thought Sigrid. "Hentz and I will go over to the hospital and talk to Mrs. Lundigren. While those three finish IDing any guests with an art background, you and Albee can start questioning the employees."

She gestured to the third apartment on this floor. "That door was open to the party last night, so talk to them first. Ask if they expanded DiSimone's guest list to any art people. I gather that she doesn't have a firm handle on who she invited, much less who actually came."

When Sigrid reentered Luna DiSimone's apartment, she found Urbanska questioning the actress about the dynamics of the building and how well the Lundigrens got along with the owners and the other employees.

"I honestly can't say. He was darling to me, but I've only lived here about two years. It took me forever to convince my mom that this wasn't the back side of the moon. She really didn't want me to move so far away from her."

"Where's home?" asked Urbanska, who still had moments of homesickness for South Jersey.

"Over in the East Sixties."

Suppressing a smile, Sigrid saw that Elliott had finished annotating his list and told him that she and Hentz were headed downtown.

"Can we drop you?"

"Sure," he said, reaching for his overcoat.

When they got outside, the snow had finally stopped falling for the moment. The windshield and back window of the car were covered in white, but it brushed away easily. Traffic was still light and Hentz executed a U-turn that headed them in the right direction. On the way, Sigrid read aloud the names that Elliott had checked off and he elucidated each.

"Mischa Costenbader? He runs the gallery that exhibits Nicco Marclay. I saw him when I first arrived, but he can't stand Rathmann, so he didn't come over once Rathmann collared me. Would he take a Streichert maquette if he could get away with it? In a heartbeat. Orton owns a gallery in NoHo that's two cuts above Costenbader's. Marclay may be trying to get taken on there. I've never heard much negative about him except from artists that he won't give a show to. Rathmann you met, of course. Wishes he were a bigger name as an art critic, but who doesn't? I got to the party at nine-thirty and he was already there buzzing around Orton and me till you arrived. Kenneth Burtch? He's starting to make it as a fashionable portrait painter. He's done the mayor and one of the Kennedy women and a Rockefeller, too, if I'm not mistaken. You've got him on the guest list, but I didn't see him. I did see Cameron Broughton, though. He's one of those professional Southerners whose accent gets stronger the longer he's out of the South. I'm not sure how he makes his living, but he talks knowledgeably about antiques and the decorative arts. He might not know what a Streichert maquette was, but he'd probably recognize that it wasn't something off eBay."

"And would he stick it in his pocket if no one was watching?" Sigrid asked.

Buntrock cocked his head and looked out the window to orient himself by the passing street signs. "Sorry. I don't know him well enough to say. You can let me off at the next corner, Hentz."

"You got it," Hentz said as he stopped for a red light.

Buntrock fastened the top button of his coat and began winding his scarf around his neck in preparation for facing the bitter winds that whipped through the unplowed cross streets. "When's your next gig at Smalls?"

"Tomorrow night, as a matter of fact." He pulled in as close to the curb as possible. "Here okay?"

"Fine. Thanks for the lift. See you at the Arnheim reception next week, Sigrid?"

"I haven't decided," she said.

"I'll call you," he told her, opening the door. Two strides of his long legs and he was over the snowbank and onto the sidewalk. Without looking back, he gave a high wave of his hand as he walked away.

Hentz forgot to flick his turn signal when he pulled back into traffic, and an annoyed limo driver gave him a horn blast and the finger as he swerved around their car.

At the hospital, they inquired at the desk for directions to Denise Lundigren's room. Once on the proper floor, Sigrid asked for her doctor and was told that he expected them. "He'll be finished with rounds in about ten minutes," a nurse said, "but I'll let him know you're here."

By now it was well after twelve, so Sigrid excused herself and walked down to the end of a quiet hall to call her grandmother.

The same soft voice as before answered the phone. "I'm so sorry, Miss Harald. Mrs. Lattimore said for me to apologize when you called. She said to tell you that she was invited to Sunday dinner with another friend out in the country and that she'll try to call you tomorrow, unless you want to leave a message . . . ?"

"If you would, tell her it's about the package she sent my mother and — Oh, never mind. I'll talk to her tomorrow," Sigrid said and hung up feeling unsatisfied and slightly uneasy.

For better or worse, that maquette was involved in Phil Lundigren's murder, so niceties be damned. She pulled Mrs. Lattimore's letter from her purse and worked her fingernails up under the flap until it pulled loose.

My dear Anne,

I've spent these past few months sorting through the house, ridding myself of decades of mindless stuff. I've labeled the items I've heard one of you girls admire or that I think you or one of your own children might like. As for this disgusting object, I had completely forgotten that it was locked in an old suitcase up in the attic until my Smithsonian magazine arrived before Christmas. How I acquired it is not important. What is important is that it be returned to the sculptor's family — perhaps to the granddaughter who gave the interview? — and that the return be managed discreetly without my name coming into it. Surely you or Sigrid must know someone in the art world who can be trusted to do this? The first time I saw it, I realized that it was a piece of racist vulgarity. Nevertheless it is probably a valuable piece of racist vulgarity and not mine to destroy or keep.

Mother

Puzzling as it might be not to learn how her grandmother wound up with something she found disgusting at first sight, Sigrid knew it would be pointless to ask if she had decided not to tell. Maybe when Anne came home? Her mother and grandmother spoke the same language, a language that could charm confessional secrets from a priest, and one that Sigrid had never mastered. Yes, let her mother deal with it, she decided.

Down by the nurses' station, a short fat white-haired man had approached Hentz, who immediately signaled to her.

When she joined them, he held out his

pudgy hand. It was like shaking hands with marshmallows. "Dr. Penny, Lieutenant. I believe you wanted to speak to me about Mrs. Lundigren?"

"Is there someplace we can talk privately?" Sigrid asked.

He led them to a small room down the hall that held a couch and two armchairs. Although Sigrid and Hentz remained standing, he took the farther chair and said, "I'm sure you realize that Mrs. Lundigren is not one of my regular patients, so I don't have her whole history. Even if I did, I could not discuss the particulars of her case."

"We understand that, Doctor. We only want your professional opinion. Is she stable enough to answer questions?"

"As long as you don't get too close physically or try to force her to make eye contact." He glanced at his watch. "I think I've established a bit of trust, and if you can make it brief, I'll stay in the room if you like."

He rose, but Sigrid lifted a hand to keep him from leaving. "Something you need to know, Doctor. Mrs. Lundigren's husband was murdered last night."

Again the doctor looked at his watch and gave an impatient scowl. "I'm perfectly aware of that, Lieutenant. Her grief and panic are precisely what we are dealing with here."

Sigrid stopped him with a cool, level-eyed look. "Are you also aware, Doctor, that her husband was a woman, not a man?"

"What?"

"He — *she* — had evidently been passing as a man for years," Hentz said bluntly. "According to the ME, she had not been surgically altered and everything was intact."

Dr. Penny sank back into the chair. His belt disappeared into his belly and his chubby thighs strained the seams of his pants. "Well now, that *does* put a different spin on the ball. One hesitates to leap to conclusions based on insufficient data, yet one immediately has to wonder if her social anxiety disorder has been exacerbated by a closeted lesbianism. Not once in our talks did she refer to her partner as anything but 'he.' Surely she knows?"

"There was only one bed in their apartment, Doc," said Hentz, "and they've lived there together for at least nineteen years."

"I see." He heaved himself to his feet. "Very well. But please try not to upset her more than she already is."

"Will she be released today?" Sigrid asked.

"Before your revelation, I would have said

yes. Now it will depend on how this session goes."

They followed him halfway down the hall. He lightly rapped on a door and pushed it open. "Denise? It's Dr. Penny again. These are police officers and they have some questions for you."

Denise Lundigren sat in a chair by the far wall on the other side of the single bed. Her hair was neatly combed this morning, but her pretty heart-shaped face was scrubbed clean of the heavy makeup she had worn the night before, although a faint trace of eyeliner remained. Despite the dark shadows beneath her frightened eyes and the inevitable wrinkles, she actually looked younger and seemed more vulnerable than when they last saw her. Her hospital-issued gown and robe had been washed so many times that the floral pattern had faded to pale pink, and she hunched into the robe, pulling the front sides protectively across her thin chest.

Sigrid remained near the door. Hentz had been able to calm her initial fears last night until they told her of Phil Lundigren's death, and she was quite willing to let him try to connect again.

He sat down on the near end of the bed and began talking to the pillow in a soothing voice. "We're very sorry for your loss, Mrs. Lundigren, and we hate to have to bother you again, but you do want to help us catch whoever did this to Phil, don't you?"

Hesitantly, the woman nodded.

"We're not going to be able to unless you can tell us about last night. Did Phil seem the same as usual? Was he upset about anything?"

"Yes," she whispered as tears filled her eyes. "He was upset."

"What about, Denise?"

She shook her head.

"Upset with someone in the building?"

She didn't reply, just clutched the faded robe tighter, but now she was watching Hentz's face.

Without looking at her, he smoothed the pillow that lay between them and kept his voice low and matter-of-fact. "Was it one of his coworkers or one of the tenants?"

No response.

"Was it you?" Sigrid asked.

Startled, the older woman half swiveled in her chair and turned her face to the wall.

"Sorry," Sigrid said.

"All couples have their squabbles, Denise," Hentz said quietly. "Did you and Phil fight last night?"

She kept her face averted.

"What did you fight about, Denise?"

There was another long moment of silence, then the woman sighed and said, "I — I sometimes take things. I can't help myself. Little things. Mostly animal things."

"Was that what you fought about? You had taken something?"

"I try not to, but sometimes I just can't help it and he gets mad if I don't remember where I got something. Like the cat."

"The cat?"

Relaxing a little, she released her white-knuckled grasp on the robe. "It was so cute. Purple and pink and little yellow whiskers! But Phil got mad and said I was going to get him fired and he had to put it back. He knew I'd cleaned 6-A the day before, so he thought it was Mr. Lacour's. I was pretty sure it was Luna DiSimone's, though, but he made me so mad, I wasn't going to tell him it was hers."

"You like cats, don't you?"

Sudden concern crossed her face. "Puff-Daddy! Is he all right?"

"Don't worry," Hentz said. "Your cat's been fed and has fresh water, but he's probably missing you."

Dr. Penny nodded approval. "You need to be there for your cat, Denise."

"Yes," she said, her voice slightly stronger than before.

"Did you want to keep the wooden cat?" Hentz asked.

She shrugged. "It was sweet but it wasn't crystal, so I didn't care if he took it back. But he said some mean things. He knows I can't help it."

"So you and Phil fought about the cat?"

"And the watch."

"You took a watch, too?"

"I don't think so. I don't always remember when I take things, but he kept yelling at me and said he was going to lose his job if he didn't give it back to Mrs. Wall. It's like when he thought I took a necklace from 4-B and he went through all my things looking for it."

"So he took the cat up to 6-A?"

"Yes. He called up and nobody answered so he said he'd go while they were out."

"What time was that, Denise?"

"About ten o'clock? I was trying to watch my program on HGTV and he kept going on and on about the cat and Mrs. Wall's watch. Right after he left, that nice young colored couple chose the very same house I would have picked."

"And that was the last time you saw him?"

She nodded. "I thought he was coming

right back, but he didn't, so I watched my channel for another hour and went to bed a little after eleven."

Her eyes darted to Hentz's face. "What happened to him?"

They told her as concisely as possible. "We think he may have interrupted a robber or it might be that someone followed him into 6-A. Was there anyone in the building that he didn't get along with, Denise? The other employees?"

"If he had problems with them, he never mentioned it. He didn't like Antoine."

"Why not?"

"He thought Antoine was sneaky."

"Why?"

She shrugged.

"What about the tenants?"

"They thought he was Mr. Wonderful." Her tone turned bitter. "They felt sorry for him because of me. Like he could have had his pick of perfect wives." She flashed an angry glance at Hentz. "You don't have to keep pussyfooting around."

"What do you mean?"

"I've watched enough crime shows. I know what happens when someone gets killed. The autopsy. You want to ask about Phil and me, don't you?"

"That he was a woman?"

"He wasn't!" she said, beginning to cry. "And don't you go thinking dirty things about us. Don't! You want to make out that I'm a lesbo and he was a dyke, but we weren't. I like men and he *was* a man in every way except for his equipment. From the time he was a little kid, he knew he was a boy trapped inside a girl's body. That's how we could love each other — why we got married. He took care of me."

Her sobs grew louder and she turned to Dr. Penny helplessly. "What's going to happen? How can I live without Phil? Who's going to look after Puff-Daddy and me?"

CHAPTER 12

And [society] seems to be very happy, for it wears a beatific smile and sheds an extra beam of pleasure when its members bend to speak to each other.
— *The New New York,* 1909

There was no getting around the reality of murder. A man had been killed in this apartment, and yes, it was awful to think about, but Dwight and I have both seen our share of violent deaths and we know that life does move on whether or not we dwell on it. Besides, we had been together less than eighteen months and we were still new to married love. Which is to say that despite the way the day had begun, once everyone cleared out, Dwight and I reverted to honeymoon mode, and it was even more delicious than I had thought it would be.

For starters, we took our coffee and the *New York Times* back to bed, and while he leafed through the sports section, I slipped into the bathroom and changed from sweater and slacks to my new see-through confection of black ruffles and lace.

I know, I know. Silly and a total cliché, right? All the same . . . I mean, sometimes a man (Dwight) likes to see his woman (me) in something besides an oversized Carolina sweatshirt, okay?

He was too absorbed in what the Hurricanes were doing to pay any attention when I slipped under the covers beside him, so I quietly picked up the magazine section and tried to concentrate on world affairs.

As an academic exercise, Dwight had seemed to enjoy his brief busman's holiday, looking over the shoulder of those New York detectives and mentally comparing their procedures to those he used back in Colleton County. Now, as if hearing my thoughts, he said, "It does feel weird, though."

"What does?"

"To be on the outside looking in on this investigation." He lowered the sports section and his eyes widened the instant they touched my new negligee.

I pretended not to notice. "Given your druthers, you'd be out there right this minute, questioning everyone in the building," I teased. "Right?"

"Wrong." He dumped the sports section on the floor in favor of a new sport, and pulled me toward him.

More newspapers slid off the bed and I flung aside a sheaf of colorful advertising inserts that tried to insert themselves between Dwight's chest and mine.

He pushed back my hair so he could nuzzle my neck. "You know that thing Mrs. Lattimore sent up?"

"Yes?" I tried to tug at the waistband of his shorts, but he had begun to lower the skinny straps of my gown and my arms were briefly imprisoned. "What about it?" I asked as innocently as possible, considering that my negligee had now become a crumpled ball of soft black silk that he tossed to the floor.

"I've been thinking. If we put your leg *here*" — he positioned my leg across his bare shoulder — "and my head here, and then your hand *here* while I —"

The rest of his words were lost as an electric spasm shot through my body. I gasped, and after that, all coherent thoughts and words disappeared beneath an avalanche of physical sensations that culminated in a firestorm of explosions.

"Dear Lord in the morning!" I said when I could talk again.

"Well, it is Sunday," he murmured smugly.

Once everything quit pinging like an overheated motor cooling down, I spooned my back against the curve of his muscular body and we fell asleep with his hand cupped around my breast.

I awoke an hour or so later to find his lips touching mine and his hands gentle on my skin, but moving with increasing urgency. This time, our lovemaking was slower and more conventional, but it was very sweet and every bit as satisfying. We showered together afterwards, soaping each other down carefully. For the first time since our first shared shower over a year ago, I only got a halfhearted salute.

"Sorry, shug," he said. "The spirit's willing, but the flesh is gonna need a little time to regroup."

After that big breakfast, I wasn't particularly hungry, but that didn't stop me from joining Dwight when he got into Luna DiSimone's party goodies. Afterwards, we called Cal, who was on his way out the door to a birthday party with Mary Pat and did not seem to be missing either one of us bad enough to make him want to be late to the party.

I talked briefly with Kate, who commiserated about the weather. She was shocked to hear about Phil Lundigren and asked me if I would take some flowers or a potted plant down to his wife.

"She has an anxiety disorder that makes it hard for her to connect with strangers, so don't try to make her your best friend, Deborah. Just tell her that the flowers are from me — she probably still thinks of me as Kate Honeycutt from 6-A — and that I'm thinking about her, okay?"

"Good as done," I told her.

As he took the last cold shrimp from the platter, Dwight said, "What do you want to do this afternoon?"

"Well, we're not far from the Planetarium and the Museum of Natural History."

He frowned. "You really want to look at stars or dinosaur bones?"

"Not really," I admitted. I'm all for culture and I know New York's museums are world-class, but we have a great natural history museum in Raleigh and a fine planetarium over in Chapel Hill.

Dwight seemed to feel the same. "Why don't we take the camera and walk over to Central Park? See what city folks do in the snow."

We piled on a couple of layers of warm

clothes and were soon heading out the door, this time making sure that it was really locked. I felt a bit vindicated when Dwight had to pull on it firmly to make the latch fully engage.

The man on the elevator was the same one as from Friday evening. Sidney. He was a mixture of regret for the death of a fellow worker and sympathy for our messed-up vacation. Mostly though, he was avid for details.

"What happened?"

"Looks like he interrupted a robbery," Dwight said, "and someone smashed him in the head."

"Robbery? Was anything taken?"

"We think part of Mr. Lacour's collection of gold and enamel pillboxes," I said.

"And your earrings," Dwight reminded me.

"One of them anyhow," I said. "And a little bronze sculpture."

"You didn't happen to notice people going in and out of our place last night, did you?" asked Dwight.

Sidney shook his head. "But then I was busy with people coming and going and the hall seemed to be packed full every time I came up. Someone on the fifth floor was threatening to call the fire marshal on

Luna." His wry smile turned mournful. "Poor Phil, though. You could've knocked me over with a feather when they told me. I guess you heard that his wife flipped out when they told her and had to be taken to a psycho ward?"

We hadn't, and he told us about Mrs. Lundigren's mental problems in more detail than Kate had. Kate had told me that the West Side was very liberal and socially tolerant of human failings, but to tolerate a klepto?

"I probably ought not to be talking about it, but I heard that you're a police officer yourself?"

Dwight nodded. "So what happened to the regular morning guy?"

"Antoine? Who knows? They say he started work as usual and then just left."

"So that's why the elevator never came this morning," Dwight said. "Even the service elevator wasn't running. There was someone on duty when I got back. Didn't seem like a happy camper, though."

"That would be Vlad," said Sidney. "One of the board members called him to come in because of the boiler. The front sidewalk needed shoveling, too. We're all having to take up the slack. The night man's still asleep downstairs, but he's getting too old to pull a double shift."

"He spent the night here?" I asked.

"Yeah. Antoine, too. See, Phil always said if we were gonna get snowed in, we better get snowed in here and not at home, so he and Jani bunked here. Jani took over around eleven last night so I could get home before it got too deep. My place is only a block from the stop, so I knew I could get back before four today."

"Why would the day man just up and quit?" I asked. "Was it because of Phil?"

Sidney shook his head and tried to smother a yawn. "He and Phil didn't get along all that good. Not that he wished Phil bad luck or anything, but I don't think he's gonna cry at Phil's funeral. No, it's probably that he's finally had it with teenage boys who think it's funny to hijack the elevator and leave it on another floor. Vlad was still ticked off about it when I got here." Beneath that impeccable gray mustache, his lips curved in wry humor. "But then with Vlad, everything's a big drama."

CHAPTER 13

Carts work at the snow for days and weeks trying to get it away to the docks and so into the river.

— *The New New York,* 1909

Sigrid Harald — Sunday (continued)

By the time Sigrid and Sam Hentz backed out of the hospital room, Denise Lundigren was in full-blown hysterics. Leaving Dr. Penny to calm her, they headed back for the car, and both gave involuntary sighs of relief as they got in and slammed the doors. It was one of those rare moments of solidarity and Hentz didn't push it.

Instead, he put the car in gear and said, "Think there's any chance she followed him upstairs and killed him?"

"The spouse is always a possibility." Sigrid leaned forward to adjust the heat controls with chilled fingers. "Remember what she said when we told her Lundigren was dead?"

Hentz nodded. "She asked if he was really dead and not just hurt."

"Which could suggest that she had hit him herself without realizing the force of her blow."

"And the door was secured with two chains," Hentz said thoughtfully. He eased down on the brakes so that a man pulling two laughing, well-bundled children on a sled could cross against the light. "Like she didn't expect him back."

"Unless he habitually came and went through the service door," Sigrid said, trying not to let herself be diverted by that sled and the bittersweet memory it evoked of sliding down a snowy Connecticut hillside into a tangle of blackberry vines with Nauman, another sharp reminder of all that she had lost when he died. "Their living room looks more like a furniture showroom than a place used by someone in coveralls."

"Between the crystal knickknacks and flowers and ruffles, the whole apartment felt girly to me. Wonder if he ever wore a dress and sipped tea?"

"Would you?" she asked dryly.

"Point taken," he said. "She did make it sound as if he really was a man trapped in a woman's body. Must have been hell on him growing up."

Up ahead of them, a sanitation truck fitted with a snowplow on the front trundled along, throwing up a three-foot high windrow that completely blocked a car illegally parked in front of a delicatessen. They saw the car's owner come hurrying out, gesticulating wildly.

Too late.

He shook his fist at the driver, who passed on, oblivious.

"Hope that poor bastard has a shovel in his trunk," Hentz said.

Although both of them were too young to remember the blizzard of 1969, when the city came to a virtual halt for three days, no succeeding mayor of New York ever forgot the political fallout, and surely this mayor was too savvy to let the streets stay closed for long. New Yorkers might enjoy a Sunday snow, but come Monday morning there would be a price to pay at the next election if too many streets remained blocked for more than two or three days. Private snow removal companies were already out at the major corners, and traffic had to swerve around a yellow backhoe that was loading snow into a big dump truck.

"Do you suppose the board knew about Mrs. Lundigren's klepto tendencies?" Hentz asked as he waited for the light.

Sigrid looked up from her notes. "I was wondering that myself. Lowry and Albee reported that this Mrs. Wall made a point of saying how honest Lundigren was. I think we should go back and ask her about the wife. From what I've read, kleptomaniacs steal for the thrill of stealing, not for any material gain. Most times, they'll just throw the object away. If Lundigren always took back whatever she stole, then maybe the board was willing to treat it as a quirk, something they could put up with in order to keep a valuable employee."

"Are you going to tell her about Lundigren?"

"Only if it's pertinent."

"Wonder where they got married? Were same-sex marriages allowed anywhere?"

"He was probably already passing by then, but it's an interesting legal point," she said. "The state recognizes common-law marriages between heterosexuals, but what's the standing for same-sex couples? Did he leave much of an estate? Is there a will?"

"I don't know about a will, but the Wall woman told Lowry that she'll benefit from a quarter-million insurance policy. That could be two hundred and fifty thousand reasons to kill."

"Maybe, but why do it in 6-A?"

Hentz flicked her a sardonic look. "Don't you mean 'why now'?"

There was a time when Sigrid would have frozen him with an icy narrowing of her gray eyes, but now she acknowledged his jab with a wry quirk of her lips. Sooner or later in any puzzling case, her team of detectives had learned to expect that pointed question, especially if they could show opportunity and motive for more than one of the victim's circle of friends, family, or fellow workers. "Why now?" she would ask. "Why not last week? Why not next Wednesday? What's different? What pushed the killer's buttons *now?*"

Her phone vibrated and it was Detective Albee checking in. She reported that the occupant of 6-B was a friend of DiSimone's. "They met on *Sesame Street* and she's the one who told DiSimone about the building when that apartment came up for sale two years ago. She wasn't able to add any names to the list, and when we showed her our master list, she didn't know who had art connections except for this Cameron Broughton. He styled her bedroom and helped her pick out some prints to frame."

"What about the other building employees?"

"The eight-to-four elevator man — Antoine Clarke — seems to have quit, but we've talked to the evening man who's covering for him and to one of the porters. The night man's around, but we haven't found him yet. Urbanska's gone back to the office to start collating the lists."

After bringing Albee up to speed on what they'd learned from Denise Lundigren, Sigrid said, "When you're talking to the staff, ask about any friction between Lundigren and Clarke. And tell Mrs. Wall that Hentz and I want to speak to her. We should be there in ten minutes."

Eight minutes later, Sigrid and Hentz were on their way up to the twelfth floor.

"So what's with Antoine?" Hentz asked him once the brass accordion cage was closed and the first-floor door slid shut.

"Ahh, him!" Sidney gave an annoyed twitch of his narrow shoulders. "You'd think he was never a kid himself."

"Kid?" asked Sigrid.

"Probably Corey Wall, although the Petersen kid in 11-B's done it a time or two as well."

"You mean someone took this elevator up when Antoine wasn't looking? And that's why he quit?"

"Who knows? Usually it's the night man who loses it, but Corey did get me once when I was delivering a package to 1-B and I stepped inside to set it down in the kitchen. Two minutes flat and it was gone. Used to happen to poor Jani at least once a month. He's pushing sixty-five and when he gets comfortable in one of the lobby chairs, he's out. The buzzer's loud enough to wake the dead, so that's no problem. If someone comes in at two in the morning and Jani's asleep in the lobby, adults will just wake him up. The boys, though? They don't do it as much as they used to, but they're kids and they think it's funny to hop in and take it up themselves, and then they just leave it on whichever floor and we have to go run it down."

"And Antoine takes it personally?"

"First time it happened to him, last summer, he bitched about it for three days. Not to Corey's parents or any of the owners, of course. Or to Phil either, for that matter. It's like Phil kept telling us: this is a good job. Good pay, good benefits, and anybody can learn it in an hour. I'll cover for Antoine today, but if he's not back here tomorrow at eight, they'll have a new guy in a brown uniform before noon. Just between you and me, though, I don't know that the kids take it as much as he claims. I think Antoine sneaks out for a cigarette and doesn't always hear the buzzer. Easy to say he's hunting for the elevator when he's the one that stopped it."

"I'm surprised they don't install a self-service elevator," said Hentz, who lived in an East Side high-rise.

"Never gonna happen," Sidney said, running his hand across the shiny brass fittings, almost like an affectionate owner petting a favorite dog. "People love this thing. It's been here since the place was built and it'll probably still be here when they take it down."

Mrs. Wall invited them into her living room and Hentz looked around appreciatively as they loosened their coats and stuffed their gloves into pockets.

"Roycroft?" he asked, touching the hammered copper tray on the coffee table.

Mrs. Wall seemed surprised and Hentz said, "My aunt's big on the Arts and Crafts movement. She has a Craftsman house on a lake upstate."

Sigrid kept her face carefully immobile. She was the only one in the department who had connected Lizzie Stopplemeyer, the aunt listed as Hentz's next of kin in his personnel file, with the Mrs. Irving Stopplemeyer, whose late husband's face was as familiar to strudel lovers as Colonel Sanders's was to chicken lovers. She waited until the amenities were done before describing Denise Lundigren's present mental state.

Mrs. Wall seemed to grow uncomfortable when they asked about thefts in the building. "Phil Lundigren was the most honest person I ever met. As I told those other detectives who were here earlier, if he found a penny in the hallway, he would go door to door looking for the owner. Denise's kleptomania distressed him no end, but he always brought anything back as soon as he realized she had taken it. She doesn't leave the building very often and never alone, so it was easy for him to keep track of anything new in the apartment. It's so sad and it's not even that she *wants* the things she takes. I can't tell you how often Phil or one of the porters finds a missing item on the service steps. Phil said that taking things gives her an adrenaline rush. It's not the object, it's the act of stealing itself." She opened the drawer of a nearby end table and showed them four or five little glass animals. "I've started putting these out on Thursdays when Denise cleans for me. So far, it's working."

She sighed and her straight silver hair gleamed against the rich brown of the wall behind her. The silver bracelets on her slender arm tinkled as she pushed back her artfully ragged bangs. "So, so sad," she repeated.

"She said something about a watch and a necklace," Sigrid said.

"Denise didn't take my watch," Mrs. Wall said quickly. "I misplaced it and Denise had cleaned here the day before, so I did ask Phil to look for it. As he pointed out, though, she's never taken jewelry and I did find it later."

Her eyes slid away from Sigrid's thoughtful gaze and she busied herself with the manila employee files that still lay on the coffee table.

Hentz picked up on her body language, too. "Was it a valuable watch, ma'am?"

"Yes," she said reluctantly.

"May we see it?"

"Why? I told you. I carelessly misplaced it and then I found it again. I felt so bad accusing Denise. I was going to apologize to Phil today."

"Nevertheless, if we could just see it?" Sigrid persisted, feeling more strongly than ever that there was something about the watch that was making Mrs. Wall uncomfortable. "It will help us understand what objects appeal to Mrs. Lundigren's weakness."

"Oh, very well. It's in my bedroom."

The woman stood and her bracelets jingled down her wrists as she reached into her pocket for something.

Sigrid and Hentz shared a puzzled look. As soon as Mrs. Wall turned the corner, Hentz quietly crossed the room and paused just beyond the doorway to listen intently. A few seconds later he returned to his chair, and Sigrid said, "She keeps her bedroom door locked?"

He nodded in confirmation. "Everything else in this place may be Craftsman brass and copper, but that sounded like a Yale lock to me. A steel lock with a deadbolt."

Mrs. Wall returned shortly and handed them a black velvet box. Inside was a cocktail watch disguised as a bracelet. The flat links of white gold were set with a blinding array of pavé diamonds, the thin square dial was outlined in emerald-cut diamonds, and the knob of the winding stem was a small rose-cut diamond.

"It was my mother's," she said. "My father had it designed for her."

"Not exactly a Swarovski crystal cat," said Hentz.

Mrs. Wall smiled. "No."

"But it certainly sparkles like one of those figurines," said Sigrid.

"Which is why I first thought Denise had taken it, but Phil swore to me that jewelry was something she never took."

"Who had the missing necklace she mentioned?"

"It's never been recovered, but we're fairly certain that it was taken by someone else. 4-B had men in to measure for wallpaper. He probably snagged it in passing when no one was looking. By coincidence, Denise had cleaned up after a party there that very morning, so when the owner finally missed the necklace she had left on her dresser, she automatically assumed Denise had taken it. But then Phil remembered that Denise was only hired to clean the kitchen and dining room. She would have had no reason to go into the bedroom. Especially with other people in the apartment. She couldn't bear to interact with strangers." Mrs. Wall shook her head ruefully. "Besides, she took a glass ring holder from the windowsill over the kitchen sink that morning, and so far as I know, she's never stolen more than one item at a time."

Sigrid closed the velvet jeweler's box and handed the watch back to Mrs. Wall. "You must have been relieved to find where you left this."

"Yes," the older woman said, slipping it into her pocket. "I should very much hate to lose it. My husband thinks I ought to keep it in our bank vault, but I love wearing it to parties."

"I don't suppose you were at Luna DiSimone's party last night?" Sigrid asked.

"You suppose correctly, Lieutenant. I did have to listen to several complaints, though."

"Did you relay those complaints to Lundigren?"

"Heavens, no! We try" — her eyes glistened with sudden tears — "*tried* not to bother him after hours."

She gave a deep sigh. "I've called an emergency meeting of the board for this evening, but I don't know how our management company will ever find someone as good to replace him."

Hentz said, "Mrs. Lundigren said there may have been some animosity between Antoine and her husband. Would you know why?"

"Absolutely not. Whatever happened in the basement stayed in the basement as far as Phil was concerned. Unless it was a firing offense, he wouldn't speak of it."

"Have there been many firing offenses?" Sigrid asked.

"We had to let someone go about two years ago," said Mrs. Wall. "That's when we hired Antoine Clarke." She pulled one of the manila files from the pile and quickly scanned the contents. "There's nothing to indicate a conflict between them."

Catching sight of a small photograph clipped to the top sheet of paper, Hentz said, "Is that Antoine's picture?"

Mrs. Wall immediately closed the folder with a clash of silver bangles.

"What about the man who was fired two years ago?" Hentz persisted. "Could he be harboring a grudge?"

"It was not pleasant," Mrs. Wall conceded. "He made inappropriate comments to some of the young women in the building and even tried to touch them. I don't have the inactive files at hand, but if you'll give me an email address, I'll send you his name and last known contact information."

"Is your son around?" Hentz asked.

Startled and suddenly apprehensive, she said, "My son? Why?"

"Corey Wall *is* your son, isn't he?"

"Yes," she said cautiously.

"His name shows up on two of the lists as

being at that party."

Some of the tenseness went out of her face and she gave a rueful smile. "He probably crashed it."

"May we speak to him? Is he here?"

"I'm sorry, Detective. He went sledding with some friends this morning. One minute they want to be treated like adults, the next minute they're five-year-olds playing in the snow. Is it important?"

"That's okay," Hentz said easily. "It's just routine. We'll catch up with him later."

"I'm sure he doesn't know anything that could help you." She stood as if to indicate that this meeting was over.

The others stood, too, but as she rose, Sigrid said, "Were you aware that the day man walked off the job this morning because someone took the elevator when his back was turned?"

Her brow furrowed. "I knew that Sidney was covering for Antoine, but I didn't know why Antoine wasn't here."

"Is taking the elevator when it's unattended something your son does very often?"

"They told you that? None of the men have ever complained to us about Corey's behavior. Besides, we try to compensate with very generous Christmas bonuses." She flushed under Sigrid's steady gaze. "He's only seventeen, Lieutenant. Adolescent humor is sometimes hard for adults to understand."

CHAPTER 14

The number of restaurants, cafés, lunch counters — places where food is cooked and served — is something amazing to strangers. Some of the side streets are lined and dotted with eating establishments.

— The New New York, 1909

Sigrid Harald — Sunday (continued)
As they left the Wall apartment, Sigrid's phone vibrated in her pocket and she glanced at the screen. Elaine Albee.

Once they were out in the hall with the door closed, she answered the phone and heard Albee say, "Lieutenant? We're down here in the basement. Does Hentz still have Lundigren's keys? I think we've found where he kept his papers."

A few minutes later, she and Hentz stepped off the elevator into a basement that smelled of musty cement overlaid with a faint aroma of motor oil and a stronger one of hot pastrami. Off to the left lay the boiler room, and beyond that, a hall that terminated at a steel door to an areaway outside. A high window in the door had bars embedded in the glass for security. The hall was lined with garbage bins that had wheels and tight-fitting lids so that no odors escaped. Although gray and utilitarian and crowded with the equipment needed to keep a building like this running, the basement felt clean and there was a sense of orderliness and purpose.

Straight ahead was a short hall that seemed to open into a locker room where the men could change from their street clothes into the brown wool uniforms provided by the board. Many articles of indoor and outdoor clothing hung from hooks along the wall. Through the arched opening, they saw two large men who sat with their backs to the door while they ate sandwiches at a Formica-topped table. Judging by the sounds from deeper in the room, they were also watching some sort of loud sports program on television. The announcer spoke excitedly in a language that was neither English, Spanish, nor French, the only languages Sigrid could confidently identify.

She glanced at her watch. Almost three. No wonder their fragrant sandwiches were making her hungry.

Battered chairs and occasional tables stood around, castoffs abandoned from above and rescued by the staff. A miscellany of pictures hung on the walls — everything from kitsch framed in ornate gold leaf to a cover of a *National Geographic* magazine signed by a well-known photographer and framed in bamboo.

"Down here," Lowry called from somewhere off to the right.

They followed his voice through the dimly lit passage to a double bank of ceiling-high wire cages that measured about four feet wide by six feet deep. Each bore the number of an apartment and served as a storage locker for off-season clothes, luggage, or anything else an owner could not find room for upstairs. Most were neatly arranged; others looked as if the doors had been opened and stuff thrown in with a snow shovel.

Lowry pointed to a unit at the far end where Albee waited. "This one's assigned to the Lundigren apartment," she told them.

Somebody — Lundigren? — had built shelves to the ceiling to accommodate several cardboard boxes and two rows of books, but had left an alcove large enough to hold a rump-sprung swivel chair, a two-drawer file cabinet with wheels, and a small steel desk that was missing one of its original legs. A fairly new-looking laptop sat on the desk.

Hentz handed the super's set of keys to Albee, and after four tries she found one that turned in the lock. They rolled the files out into the passageway, and after they found its key, Hentz and Sigrid each took a drawer while Albee tackled the laptop and Lowry went through the desk.

Sigrid hit paydirt immediately. "His birth certificate," she said and handed it to Hentz.

There it was: Phyllis Jane Lundigren, female, born fifty-three years ago in Littleton, New Hampshire. In the same folder was a marriage certificate dated twenty-four years earlier for Phillip James Lundigren, age twenty-nine, and Anna Denise Katsiantonis, age twenty-seven.

"Cute," said Lowry. "Don't change the body, just change the name."

Another folder was devoted to Mrs. Lundigren. It held her birth certificate and her medical records, including a stay in a New York psychiatric facility for treatment following a pseudocyesis when Denise was thirty.

Puzzled, Hentz said, "What's pseudocyesis?"

"Hysterical pregnancy," Sigrid told him. "Where a woman thinks she's pregnant and develops all the symptoms, including morning sickness and actual birth pains."

"Jeez!" said Lowry. "Talk about a screwed-up couple."

Lundigren's medical files showed no hospital stays, only annual physicals. On all the forms, the sex box was checked *M,* which would indicate a live-and-let-live doctor.

"Here're their wills," said Hentz. "Looks like they were pretty careful about the wording. No mention of husband or wife. He leaves everything to Anna Denise Katsiantonis Lundigren, and hers leaves everything to Phillip James Lundigren, both of this address."

"Hey, Detectives!" someone called from back near the elevator.

"Yeah?" Lowry called back.

"You guys order pizza?"

"Yeah," said Lowry. "Be right there."

"I ordered an extra-large," Lowry told them. "Figured maybe you hadn't eaten lunch either."

The promise of pizza was welcome news.

"You didn't happen to order coffee, too?"

Sigrid asked.

He grinned. "Sure did."

Before he could reach for his wallet, she pulled out hers. "Let me get this, Lowry."

His refusal was only pro forma. He took the bills she handed him and headed down the long passageway to the outer basement door. Minutes later, the appetizing fragrance of oregano and mozzarella reached them. They dragged chairs over to a rickety card table and were soon pulling apart the slices.

"Postal Pizza?" Sigrid asked. The red-white-and-blue box was printed to look like priority mail.

"Neither snow nor rain stays the swift completion of their deliveries," Albee said with a laugh. "We got the number from the porter down there. This place delivers twenty-four/seven. The night man says he orders from them all the time, and when you get a look at his figure, you'll know he's telling the truth."

"What's he doing in so early today?" Hentz asked as he tried to keep sauce from dripping onto the folders he had brought from the files.

"He never left," said Lowry, handing him a napkin. "The snow was so deep this morning when his shift ended, he just sacked out here. Same as Antoine Clarke. Both of them heard the weather report last night and were here by nine before it got too deep. There's a set of bunk beds down there."

"And a fridge, a TV, and a microwave," said Albee, "plus a shower. All the comforts of home."

Hentz listened as he leafed through the papers in the folder he had brought to the table. All were stamped by the management company that had hired the men. "Copies of the personnel files," he said. "I guess he was their on-site eyes and ears."

A copy of Lundigren's own original job application was there, too, and they saw a younger version of the victim. In the grainy black-and-white photograph, his eyes appeared open and candid beneath those very bushy eyebrows.

Jim Lowry shook his head. "Even knowing he's a woman, he doesn't look like a woman. He must have taken hormones in the early years."

Sigrid took the personnel file. The forms for later hires had color copies of their photographs and she lingered on that of Antoine Clarke. He had honey brown skin, brown eyes, and a clipped Afro. A trendy half-inch-wide beard outlined his square chin from ear to ear with a small pointed goatee in front. According to his application form, he was five foot seven, weighed 135, and was twenty-seven years old. Born in Jamaica, he became a naturalized citizen at age eleven when his parents were granted citizenship. An address in Queens had been crossed out and a new one up on West 146th Street penciled in. To the question of previous arrests, he had copped to a shoplifting charge eight years ago and a D&D two years after that.

None of the other employees listed arrests. Either they were less forthcoming or had each led spotless lives.

"Have someone run these names for us," Sigrid said. "See if they're as clean as they claim."

She declined when offered one of the extra pizza slices. "So all three elevator men were here in the building last night? Too bad we didn't get a chance to sit down with this Antoine Clarke before he quit. What about the porters? Any of them here overnight or during the party?"

"No, ma'am," said Lowry. "They worked their usual eight to five on Saturday. Sidney got here about twenty minutes before we did."

"Who else have you interviewed?" Sigrid asked as she retrieved a wayward olive that had rolled off her slice of pizza.

"Vlad Ruzicka, the porter working today, and Sidney, who normally has the four-to-midnight shift. Jani Horvath — he's the night man — just got back from the deli, so we were giving them a chance to finish eating first." He licked a dab of sauce from his fingers.

"Learn anything useful from either of them?"

"Not really. Lundigren ran a tight ship, but he doesn't seem to have been a micro-manager. He let them know what was expected, then left them to it. Wasn't looking over their shoulders all the time, and they respected that. Didn't socialize much, though. They said he spent a lot of time back here reading. Most of the books on the shelves over there are biography or current history. The others never knew if he was here or not unless they saw him or heard him or came and looked, and I get the impression that it kept them on their toes. They knew that management and the board would support Lundigren if he thought there was cause to fire one of them."

"They tell you if Lundigren was having trouble with Antoine?"

"I think Vlad might know something, but Sidney said we'd have to ask Antoine, so

Vlad clammed up, too."

"Anything interesting on that computer?" Hentz asked Albee, who had made a quick scroll through Lundigren's files.

"Nothing yet. I get the impression that he wasn't all that comfortable with computers. Nothing's password protected. There are some records for the building, and there are emails going back two or three years, but none of them look personal. Mostly it was business-related or tenants asking him to come change a lightbulb or do something about a leaky faucet."

She wiped her lips and took a sip of coffee. "Mrs. Wall mentioned that their antiquated security system's been on the fritz for the last few weeks, which is why we have no videotapes of who came and went last night. He seems to have been researching new systems and had narrowed it down to two companies. The rest of his Internet history is mostly reading the *New York Times* and anything about Lindsay Lohan."

While they ate, Hentz brought the other two up to speed on their own interview with Mrs. Wall. "That watch she 'misplaced' had to be worth at least fifteen thousand," he said.

"Easily," Sigrid agreed, looking up from a color copy of Jani Horvath's photograph.

"Run her son's name through the system, Albee. Corey Wall. See if he's the reason his mother keeps a lock on her bedroom door."

Elaine Albee wiped cheese from her fingertips and made a note of the name. "Corey Wall? He the kid that hijacked the elevator this morning?"

"Sidney thinks so," said Hentz, adding his crumpled napkin to the debris on the table. "And he seems to have crashed the party last night. Sounds like a kid with a healthy sense of entitlement. If he steals from his own parents, maybe he stuck his nose inside 6-A, too."

Sigrid took a final swallow of what had been surprisingly good coffee and pointed to the phone number on Antoine Clarke's file. "Invite Clarke to come speak to us tomorrow. And while you're at it, run a check on him, too. In the meantime, Lowry, you and Albee can go talk to the people in 7-A."

She repeated what Mrs. Wall had told them about the Rices and their anger that Lundigren had reported them for various violations of the co-op rules. "They tried to bribe him not to and then threatened to sue him for slander when he did. The board has begun the eviction process and the Rices probably blame Lundigren for their troubles."

Lowry nodded. "The Bryants did say that Lundigren was in their apartment looking for water damage from 7-A, right?"

Albee saw where he was going with that. "You think he could have brought one of the Rices in through the service door to prove negligence and it got out of hand?"

"Except that there wasn't any new damage," Sigrid reminded them. "Not last night, anyhow. But ask them."

They put their dirty napkins and coffee cups on top of the uneaten pizza crusts and Jim Lowry carried the box to a wheeled bin lined with a large plastic bag. On his way back past the locker room, he stepped inside where two bulky men sat watching television. The porter, Vlad Ruzicka, wore the building's brown coveralls, but the other man was in his own street clothes, thick black corduroy pants and a green wool sweater.

The television was so loud that Lowry had to shout. "Horvath? Jani Horvath?"

The man nodded, stood up heavily, and joined Lowry out in the passageway. "Lieutenant Harald wants to talk to you about last night," Lowry said.

"Wait a minute," said Horvath. His thick white hair covered his ears and he fiddled with the hearing aid in his left ear. There was a high-pitched squeal that faded as he adjusted the volume. "My pal there keeps the TV so loud, I have to turn this thing down or it'll blast my ear off."

His walrus mustache was as thick and white as his hair. It flared across his top lip and drooped longer on each side of his mouth. Could use a trim, thought Lowry. "I think you've got mustard in your mustache."

Horvath pulled a grease-stained rag from his pocket and vigorously rubbed it across his upper lip till all the mustard was gone. "Now what'd you say before?"

"Down there," Lowry said, pointing to the other end of the basement as Elaine Albee rang for the service elevator. "Lieutenant Harald."

"Going my way, sailor?" Albee said from the doorway of the service elevator. She batted her eyes flirtatiously and Lowry laughed as he joined her. There was a time when he had tried to get past the banter, wanting a personal relationship; but she had dialed it back, refusing to get involved with someone on the job. These days they were each seeing someone else and their partnership was strictly professional. Except that sometimes Elaine would look over at his farmboy face when they were winding up the paperwork on an intense case or relaxing with colleagues at the cop bar down from the station and she would find herself wondering if it had been such a wise decision.

As the door of the elevator closed and she pressed the button for the seventh floor, she was swept with such a sudden urge to turn and kiss him that it took all her willpower to keep her voice steady and her hands in her pockets, to look as if she actually gave a flying flip about how they should play the Rices when all she wanted to do was stop the elevator, stop time, and say to hell with being sensible.

When Jani Horvath reached the card table, Sigrid had his file open and invited him to sit. He parked his wide bottom on one of the metal folding chairs across from her while Hentz leaned against the wall.

They had met the night before, so without ceremony Sigrid verified his name and address, then said, "I see that you've been working here fourteen years?"

He smoothed the ends of his mustache and nodded. "Fifteen this June. I worked as the day man, but when they fired the night guy and hired Antoine to take his place, I asked to switch. Not as much walking back and forth to let people in, no packages to haul in and out of the elevator. Not as many tips either, of course. My wife's gone, so the night shift's fine. The new kid said it was okay by him. He likes the tips. Likes the nightlife, too, see? So it works out for everybody."

"Last night you said you hadn't seen Lundigren come up to the sixth floor."

"No. He would've used the back elevator, though."

"So when did you last see him?"

"I got here about eight. Stopped off to pick up a beer and a cheeseburger for my supper. I like to have something to eat about four in the morning. Phil came in while I was putting them in the fridge and he loaned me a Sharpie so I could write the date on it, 'cause Denise checks by every few days and tosses anything that's been in there a week. Keeps the fridge nice. Is she gonna be okay?"

"Her doctor hoped she could come home today," Sigrid said. "You like her?"

"Sure. She's okay once she gets used to you, and she always keeps the place good. Clean sheets on the bunks, washes the dishes if we forget. She was real kind when my wife left me last year. Sewed a button on my jacket for me." He stretched out his meaty hands. "I don't do too good with needles, see? Got a little arthritis in my fingers."

"Was there anything different about Lundigren when you saw him last night?" Sigrid asked.

"Different?"

"Did he seem upset about anything?"

"Nope. He told us to keep an eye on the people in 7-A. The board's gonna evict them and he was afraid they might do something to hurt the building before they get out. They're not really our kind of owners. I don't know why the board let them buy in. The rest of the shareholders act like regular people. The Rices act like we're dirt. We're not worth saying good morning to unless they want us to do something for them. Anyhow, I told Phil okay and he said he'd see me this morning. I went on in back to sack out and I guess he went to his apartment upstairs. Wish I'd had a chance to really tell him goodbye. He was a good man to work with."

"About the new man. Antoine Clarke?"

"Yeah?"

"We've heard that he and Phil Lundigren didn't get along too well."

Horvath propped his elbow on the table and began twisting one droopy end of his mustache between his thumb and index finger. "I wouldn't know about that."

"Sure you would," said Hentz. "You're here the longest after Lundigren. You had to've heard if they didn't hit it off."

More twisting of his mustache until that end was nothing but a tight string, at which point he sighed and capitulated. "I don't know what really set them off, but it started with the kids, especially the Wall boy."

"Corey Wall?"

"Yeah. See, Antoine wanted to haul him up short the first time Corey stole the elevator on him. Wanted Phil to take it to the board. But Phil's been here since before Corey was born. Used to let him stand on the polisher and hold on to the handle when he was little. Taught him how to ride his first bicycle right up there in the lobby. He really loved that kid. But Corey was fifteen when Antoine came and he didn't like it when Antoine tried to make him quit horsing around in the lobby. Antoine's not that much more than a kid himself, you know? Phil says they're jealous of each other. Antoine's already a man, see, but Corey's gonna go off to college, have a good job, make a lot of money, and Antoine's gonna be running an elevator the rest of his life."

"Did you see Antoine last night?"

Horvath shook his head. "Not to talk to. I

had to take a leak around nine-thirty and he was watching TV. Said the snow was starting to come down heavy. Next time I woke up, it was around eleven and he was climbing into the top bunk, so I told Sidney to go on home early. Right after that's when all hell broke loose and you people wouldn't let me take anybody down for a while. Antoine was still sleeping when I came down to eat my cheeseburger, see, so he didn't know about Phil till I told him this morning when he took over for me and I came back here and sacked out again."

Sigrid and Hentz exchanged glances. This definitely put Antoine Clarke in the building and awake when Lundigren was killed.

"Thanks, Mr. Horvath," she said. "We'll probably be talking to you again before this is over. Would you tell Mr. Ruzicka we'd like to speak to him?"

"Okay." He stood to return to the locker room. "I got nobody to go home to, so if you need me, I'll be bunking here again this evening. They're saying we could have more snow."

As he walked away, Albee and Lowry returned.

Hentz glanced at his watch. "That was quick."

"The Rices lawyered up," Lowry said.

"Said that given all the animosity in this building, they weren't speaking to us without one present and theirs won't be back till late tonight. They'll come down to the station tomorrow morning."

Vlad Ruzicka was a big expansive man. Fifty-two now, according to the job application he'd filed seven years ago. His face was broad and flat with merry blue eyes and an infectious laugh.

When Sigrid introduced herself, he bounded over and shook her hand enthusiastically. "Lieutenant!" he exclaimed. "All day I'm hearing about the beautiful lady cop with eyes that can see into a man's soul, and now here you are!"

"Have a seat, Mr. Ruzicka," she said, reclaiming her hand.

"Call me Vlad. Everybody here calls me Vlad."

He described at great length how shocked he'd been when Mrs. Wall called him this morning, how unbelievable it was, how hard it was going to be without Phil around to guide them, and what about poor Denise? The longer he talked, the sadder his face became, until his blue eyes filled to overflowing.

She interrupted to ask when he last saw

Lundigren, and in a quavering voice he said, "Friday, near quitting time. He comes down to see the sign-up sheet for the coat racks. He says Luna DiSimone's having a party on Saturday, so he puts her name on the sheet and tells me to have a good weekend and he'll see me Monday. And now he's gone."

"Tell us about Antoine and Lundigren," Sigrid said before his eyes could fill up again.

The tears vanished as quickly as they had come and with exaggerated caution he pretended to look first over one shoulder and then the other. "Sidney. He's not here, is he? Not listening? And you won't tell him what I say?"

"Your secrets are safe with us," Hentz said dryly.

"It's not a secret. Everybody knows that those two are like a cat and a dog with their tails tied together. Phil, he wants us to do everything by the rule book. Me? I don't care. Sidney don't care. You know the rules, you follow them, everybody's happy, true? But Antoine, he doesn't want to follow the rules if the owners don't. Or the owners' kids."

"Boys like Corey Wall?"

Vlad clapped his big callused hands together in delight. "You got it! Corey Wall. He's a little bastard right now, but his people are good people and he'll be good people, too, when he finishes growing up. But Antoine gets mad every time Corey or his friend talk back to him or steal the elevator. Last time it happens, Antoine wants to ring the bell on 12-B and hit Corey with a glove."

Bemused, Sigrid said, "With a glove?"

"Like those old movies where one guy hits another guy in the face with a glove." He pantomimed the act with a backward flip of his hand. "Then next thing you see, it's swords or pistols and somebody dies."

"He wanted to challenge Corey to a duel?"

"No, no. Not really. I mean that's how *Antoine* feels. Like Corey's insulting him, and he wants to insult back. But Phil says he can't and keep his job, so today it's like take this job and shove it. He just quit. But Mrs. Wall swears it couldn't be Corey who took the elevator. Not today. She says the only time he left the place today was to go sledding in the park. Besides, we don't even know what floor the elevator was on. When I got here this morning, it's right there in the lobby."

Vlad Ruzicka could tell them nothing new about the Rices, although he would have

230

happily walked them through the board meeting where it was decided to begin the eviction process. "Well, no, I wasn't there, but Phil tells us about it. The Rices say they're going to sue him and the board and the whole co-op."

They thanked him for his help, but he was reluctant to take the hint that they were finished with him for the time being.

"I just hope you find whoever it is that sneaked in and did that to Phil."

Hentz frowned. "Sneaked in?"

"Yeah. See, everybody thinks this place is like a bank vault. No way, Jose. I'm here six years but the locks on the service doors have never been changed. And people aren't always careful with their keys, are they?"

CHAPTER 15

Inevitably comes the snow; and that in a city is always regarded as something of a misfortune. Up in Central Park and along Riverside Drive it looks very beautiful.
— *The New New York,* 1909

The street in front of the apartment building had not been plowed when Dwight and I got outside, although it was clear that some trucks or other vehicles had driven through, because the snow had been flattened down to ice in the middle. The sidewalk out front was fairly clear but elsewhere there was barely enough room for two people to pass. We walked single file around the corner to Broadway, where the boot vendor had spread his wares on a plastic shower curtain atop a pile of snow. His boots had flat heels and were made of clear plastic with elastic loops and some buttons near the top so that they could be put on over shoes and slacks and then tightened around the calf. They reminded me of my Aunt Zell's gardening boots except that hers were made of heavy vulcanized rubber. I rather doubted these flimsy things would get through more than one or two wearings, but at least they would keep the snow and ice out for now.

We walked down Broadway to 72nd, then two blocks over to enter the park near Strawberry Fields and the memorial to John Lennon. With the temperature hovering right around freezing, there were lots of puddles and slushy patches, but Dwight swung me over the rougher spots.

The park was magical. All the lampposts and every twig of every branch were rimmed in soft white. The benches carried thick cushions of snow, but someone had cleared the "Imagine" mosaic and a bouquet of fresh flowers made a bright spot of color against the black-and-white tiles.

A mother and child passed us on skis, and we followed a family carrying inflated pool tubes to a slope where dozens of children were sliding in high glee. I never saw so many different contrivances: tubes, sleds, and molded plastic sliders of every description. Maybe two years out of seven, Colleton County will get enough snow to go sledding. When that happens, we rummage through the sheds and barns for old patched inner tubes and flat-bottom trays or make-shift sheets of heavy plastic.

As we stood at the top of the rise to watch the activity, a nearby couple picked up on our accents and said, "Guess you guys don't get much of this, do you?"

"We were just saying we never knew anyone with a real sled," I told her as two red-cheeked preadolescents trudged up the hill with their tubes and announced that they were ready for some of the hot chocolate from the Thermos their mother was holding.

The dad conferred with his sons, then said, "Want to take a turn?"

We didn't have to be asked twice. Seconds later we were spinning downhill laughing like kids when our tubes collided.

"You could go again if you like," said the boys, who were now dunking cookies into their steaming cups of hot chocolate.

After two more runs, we were pretty winded and they were ready to reclaim their tubes. We thanked them profusely and moved on.

Crossing a humpbacked little stone bridge, we paused to look down at the water. Although there was ice on each side of the stream, enough of a channel remained that a mother wood duck and some half-grown ducklings were able to swim past. The mother duck wheeled and paddled back to look up at us with a hopeful gleam in her black eyes. She quacked and I patted my pockets. Empty. But Dwight found a little packet of crackers from God knows when. The cellophane was wrinkled and the crackers were already reduced to crumbs. He emptied them into the water, setting off a greedy fight.

"We're probably not supposed to feed them," I said, and Dwight laughed.

"If they aren't used to being fed, then why'd that mama ask for a handout?"

We passed a group of teenagers putting the finishing touches on a tableau that represented Goldilocks and the three bears. A little further on, a snow Eve offered a snow Adam a real, bright red apple. No fig leaves in sight.

After two hours of trudging through the snow and taking pictures of incredibly beautiful vistas, we had circled back around to the 79th Street entrance, past the Museum of Natural History. By now we were cold and hungry and we found a sandwich shop where we could sit by the window and watch the passing parade with hot coffee and franks nestled in buns loaded with sauerkraut. Snow had begun to fall again from the lead-gray sky.

"How come we never have sauerkraut on our hot dogs at home?" Dwight wondered, wolfing his down.

"Because we never have it on hand?" I asked. "Or because we automatically reach for coleslaw and chili?"

"Maybe. This sure is the taste of New York, though. You gonna eat the rest of yours?"

I handed it over, and while he finished it off, I turned on my phone and checked for messages. Nothing of importance.

Four-thirty and heading for dark now. Daylight had faded, streetlights were coming on, and fresh snow was falling so thickly that I had to hold on to Dwight's jacket as we mushed back to the apartment building. Central Park's beauty had allowed us to forget about the murder for a couple of hours, but now Dwight was wondering if Sigrid and her people had learned how and why Phil Lundigren had died in our apartment.

"Maybe they'll extend you some professional courtesy," I said. "She owes it to us to at least tell how Mrs. Lattimore acquired that bronze thing."

He swung me over a puddle of dirty water at the next intersection. "You reckon professional courtesy's in her vocabulary? She doesn't strike me as the talkative type."

"That's okay. I'll bet there's a pretty active grapevine in the building. And we can always bribe the elevator man with a midnight snack."

When we got to our corner, Dwight said, "Do you want to go out tonight or eat in?"

With the snow coming down so steadily, that was a no-brainer. "Why don't I stop in this liquor store for some bourbon while you go see what your market has to offer?" I said.

He grinned and kissed me on the forehead. "I knew there was a reason I married you."

North Carolina still has a monopoly on selling distilled spirits, which means no private liquor stores. This can be a real annoyance if you want a decent blackberry cordial for your champagne or some esoteric brand of whiskey and it's not on the ABC list. Competition keeps whiskey slightly cheaper in New York and I've never noticed more drunks here than back home. Of course, I do get a lot of alcoholics in my courtroom, so maybe I'm getting cynical about blue laws.

I paid for the bourbon and carefully crossed the street, avoiding a wave of dirty slush splashed from a passing bus.

When I walked down the street to Kate's apartment building, a man roughly the same height and shape as Phil Lundigren was cleaning the sidewalk out front with a snow blower. Dressed in the building's brown coveralls, brown work gloves, and a brown knit stocking cap on his head, he finished with the blower and began to scatter salt on the few stubborn patches of ice that remained. He gave me a friendly smile when I pulled out Dwight's keys, and he held the outer door open for me.

Before I could insert the key in the inner lobby door of the building, Sidney hurried over to let me in. On the ride up to the sixth floor I discreetly tried to pump him for information about the investigation. Other than saying that the police had left only minutes earlier, he had heard nothing new. Nothing that he was willing to share, anyhow.

Back in the apartment, I put my boots and my coat in the guest bathroom's shower stall to drip dry and changed into a long skirt and a pair of sexy high heels. Shoe stores are for me what grocery stores are for Dwight, and we've both been guilty of sneaking our purchases into the house when the other wasn't looking.

While I waited for him to come back, my eyes fell on Luna DiSimone's little wooden cat and it occurred to me that maybe she had heard something.

Out in the kitchen, I transferred the party food that she had brought over onto a plate from the cabinet, washed and dried her platter, then left the door on the latch for Dwight, who should be getting back soon burdened with shopping bags.

When I rang Luna's bell, she came to the door still dressed in the coral gym suit she'd had on earlier. It didn't look quite as fresh as before, though. The hibiscus was gone from behind her ear and her hair was pulled back in an unbecoming ponytail that only accentuated her long chin. Nor was her apartment as invitingly funky and festive as last night. After hiking through snow for two hours, I found that bare wood floors and summery patio furniture had lost their appeal.

But she was still as friendly as if we'd been best friends forever. "Deborah! How lovely!" she caroled in that distinctively attractive voice as she threw the door open wide and took both the platter and the cat from me. "You're just in time to help us put my house back together."

As she spoke, two men came through a far door struggling with a large rolled-up carpet. One was the Nicco Marclay I'd heard about this morning. I recognized him from the party because he wore a flat cloth golfing cap similar to the one he'd had on then. Probably going bald and hating it.

The other was Cameron Broughton, and he rolled his eyes behind those pale blue lenses when Luna introduced us again. "Deborah's from North Carolina, too, Nicco, and she and her husband are probably the only two in the state with absolutely no connection with Cam. Another myth shattered."

Luna had stashed her rugs in the back service hall and now the guys were helping her put everything back. She told me she had wool and velvet slipcovers to go over the summer furniture, including the swing and the Adirondack chairs. Linen cloths would cover all the glass-topped tables and gas logs would go back in the fireplace as soon as someone packed up all the white candles and driftwood candlesticks that were in the fireplace now. She gave me a hopeful look reminiscent of that mother duck in the park, but I smiled sweetly and said I really wished I could stay and help, "But I only came over to return your plate and your Mexican cat."

"Love the shoes," she said. "Blahniks?"

I didn't deny it. If she couldn't tell four-hundred-dollar Blahniks from forty-five-dollar no-names, why should I enlighten her?

"Did Lieutenant Harald have any idea how the cat got over there?" I asked.

"I don't think she cares. She was more interested in knowing who came to my party that might know about art. Like Cam and Nicco."

I looked at Broughton. "You're an artist, too?"

He shook his head and turned his back on us to help Luna's boyfriend straighten the rug.

"Oh, but you *are* an artist," Luna insisted. "Cam designed this room for me, Deborah, and found all the right pieces. Wait till you see it with all its winter clothes on."

"Which isn't going to happen tonight," said Nicco Marclay. "I'm ready for a drink."

As I apologized for the interruption and made to go, she gestured to a large green glass bowl on a nearby table. "You didn't lose a phone last night, did you? Or a tube

241

of lipstick?"

I glanced into the bowl at the lost phones, keyrings, pill bottle, and lipsticks and did a double take. "That's my earring!" I grabbed the red rubber flip-flop that had my missing gold earring embedded in the sole and said, "Whose flip-flop is this?"

For a moment I thought Cameron Broughton was going to claim it. He gave me a startled look, then bolted through the back door. The elevator dinged from down the hall behind me and I turned to see Dwight emerge. Snow covered the brim of his hat and he was loaded down like a Sherpa guide.

"Catch you later," I told Luna as I whirled away. "Thanks again for the food and the great party."

A moment later, I was pushing open the door of 6-A for Dwight. I threw the flip-flop on the vestibule sideboard and helped him take some of the bags into the kitchen. He stowed some ale in the refrigerator and stooped to pick up a lemon that had rolled off the counter.

"Nice shoes," he said as he straightened up. "New?"

I waggled one foot at him and lifted a carton of outrageously expensive buffalo cheese. "They were right next to the fresh mozzarella," I said.

CHAPTER 16

The department is broken up into many divisions, with just as many different functions as there are divisions. . . . For example, there [is]the Detective Bureau, with its interesting machinery for the detection of crime and criminals.
— *The New New York,* 1909

Sigrid Harald — Monday morning
Upon succeeding to Captain McKinnon's position, Captain Jane Fortesque had instituted formal weekly briefings. After that first uncomfortable session in which she patted Sigrid's hand and sniped at the lieutenant's celebrity status, Sigrid was careful to get there early enough to choose her own chair rather than being stuck with whichever was left over. Today she greeted the other early arrivals and took a seat halfway down the long conference table. She was well aware of the psychological inferences that could

be drawn if she sat at the far end, but she had no desire to put herself within patting distance of Fortesque if she could help it. She had not resented the woman's promotion from another house, and had Fortesque continued Mac's hands-off style, the new order would not have bothered Sigrid.

Gruff and demanding, Mac had been of the trust 'em or bust 'em school of leadership. Even though he was now married to her mother, he had never patted her hand and he had not cared what his subordinates did on their own time as long as it did not reflect badly on the force.

Not only was Fortesque a micromanager, she also believed in team spirit. Some NYPD cynics held that the only way a woman could advance to a position of true power within the system was on her knees while trying not to get her tongue caught in the zipper. This was not a charge that had ever been leveled at Captain Fortesque. The luck of being in the right place at the right time and seizing the initiative had earned her a spot on a narcotics squad in Harlem where she had, without question, done solid work.

It was known that she was not shy about taking a generous share of the professional credit when she turned in her reports and that she had a talent for dropping innocent-sounding double-edged remarks about colleagues when in the presence of power, but she deflected serious criticism by becoming a tireless cheerleader for the personal milestones of those she worked with and for. She noted birthdays and anniversaries with cupcakes or a box of doughnuts and was a relentlessly hearty worker. Even those who resented her found it hard to voice that resentment when their mouths were full of Krispy Kremes.

("They probably recommended her for promotion just to keep from choking on the sugar," Hentz said when he realized that Sigrid was gritting her teeth.)

Pictures on the captain's wall showed versions of a tall, rawboned woman in varied attire through the years. There she was in her official police uniform at her swearing-in ceremony, and here she was wearing shirts with lettering across the chest and holding enormous bowling and softball trophies, several of which now stood on the shelves in her office. By the time of the latest picture, wherein the police commissioner shook Fortesque's hand in congratulation while Mac looked on, the captain wore an artfully draped suit meant to disguise the extra pounds she was packing.

She occasionally spoke wistfully of the softball and bowling teams she had played on and of the camaraderie such activities fostered. So far, she had not insisted that similar teams be formed here, but Sigrid lived in dread.

Nevertheless, even though she could no longer run baselines or bowl strikes, their new captain seemed determined to encourage off-duty personal relationships among her squad leaders. Sigrid had been forced to attend more than one after-work session at the cop bar near their station so that the captain could offer a toast to someone's birthday or to celebrate the confirmation, bar mitzvah, or graduation of a colleague's child. Worse, Sigrid had been horrified to find herself the recipient of a fulsome toast on her own birthday the previous February and had already planned to be on vacation when her next one rolled around.

"That woman needs a hobby," she had muttered to an amused Sam Hentz.

"Or a husband," he had murmured back.

"Muffins on me!" Captain Fortesque said, setting two fragrant boxes and a stack of napkins on the conference table in front of one of the squad heads. "Lieutenant Hess became the grandmother of twins Thursday night. A girl and a boy. Amanda and Jackson, right, Lieutenant?"

"Annabelle and Jack, right," Lieutenant Hess said, beaming proudly as she pulled the first muffin from the box. "Almost seven pounds each."

As the others murmured congratulations, Hess passed the boxes and napkins on down the table.

"I've decided that bran muffins are healthier than our sugary doughnuts," Fortesque said as the boxes made their way past Sigrid, who took a muffin and set it on the napkin before her. "Most of us could stand to cut back on the calories." She patted her ample middle. "Not you, of course, Lieutenant Harald. In fact, you really ought to eat two. And start adding cream to your coffee."

Sigrid forced herself to smile and broke off a piece of the muffin. This was not the first time the captain had implied that she was too skinny. It would be futile to point out to the woman that one of these "healthy" muffins — rich and buttery and thickly studded with walnuts and raisins — probably packed more calories than two or three doughnuts. Instead, having skipped breakfast this morning, she took a second bite and opened her notes.

Saturday night's homicide put her at the top of the agenda, but did not keep her there. No sooner had she finished reporting the bare facts of Phil Lundigren's death and what lines her squad were pursuing than Fortesque gave her a beneficent smile, said, "I'm sure you and your squad will do your usual superb job, Lieutenant," then turned to Narcotics with happy anticipation.

During yesterday's snowfall, a Nissan sedan with a Florida license plate had crept cautiously up Eighth Avenue. Instead of going with the flow when the green light changed to yellow, the Nissan slammed on its brakes and a cab skidded into its rear end. It was the usual snow-related fender bender with no real damage to either car.

Except that it sprung the lock on the Nissan trunk.

A passing patrol car stopped to assess the situation, whereupon the driver of the Nissan and his passenger tried to flee. One thing led to another, as it so often does. After picking the driver up from the icy pavement where he had slipped and fallen, the officers asked for and received permission to look into the trunk even though it was standing wide open and they could see several clear plastic bags full of fresh green vegetable matter, which as they now knew had been harvested the night before over in a Bensonhurst basement and was then on its way to a packager and distribution point in Morningside Heights.

"Eleven arrests so far and more to come," Narcotics crowed. "The feds are very happy with us right now."

Captain Fortesque was moved to tell how aspects of this incident paralleled her own rise through the ranks. "If those two on the beat had driven on past without stopping, that stuff would soon be out on the streets. Good police work makes good opportunities."

And stupid criminals make good police work easy, Sigrid thought as she tried to match the respectful interest she saw on the faces of her colleagues. She wondered if any of them were also thinking, *Who's dumb enough to let a Floridian drive a valuable load of weed in a snowstorm?*

When they were dismissed and Sigrid returned to her own squad room, she was pleased to see progress.

IAFIS had turned up a second shoplifting charge against Antoine Clarke only two years ago, and Vlad Ruzicka had been charged with an assault in what looked like a fistfight with someone in his neighborhood over a leaf-blowing incident last year. He had been fined and put on unsupervised probation. The others seemed to be as law-abiding as they claimed.

Detective Tildon was already engrossed with cross-matching the guest lists. "I've eliminated eight names that left before nine o'clock and four that didn't get there till after ten," he said, a satisfied smile on his round face. "Another bunch claim not to have left 6-C from the time they arrived till after the body was discovered, and they can cite friends to back them up."

Although a husband and father first, Tillie loved the details and minutiae of police work, especially if they could be reduced to a list or a simple diagram. As a schoolboy, his orderly soul had found joy in diagramming compound-complex sentences or in working out complicated quadratic equations. Merging the many partial lists that the officers had collected from Luna DiSimone's guests was a real treat for him.

Yanitelli had made rough IDs for several of the fingerprints. "I've matched prints from the toilet seat with the first guy who said he went in. His and Mrs. Lundigren's were the only prints in that front bathroom. Nothing but smudges in the master bath. Our Brit, the guy with the blue Mohawk?

251

He left one clear thumbprint on the lower outer corner of the medicine cabinet mirror and a corresponding index print on the inside corner, so he probably had a look-see at the contents. Maybe after prescription drugs?"

"Or an antacid," Hentz said pessimistically as he took off his tailored charcoal jacket and hung it on the back of his chair. "He did imply that he was there longer than normal because he wasn't feeling well. What about the French doors?"

"Nothing usable from them, but we found Lundigren's on that wooden cat. They overlapped his wife's prints."

"That tallies with what the wife told us," Sigrid said. "She admits taking the cat from DiSimone's apartment and that she let Lundigren believe it came from 6-A. According to her, he went up that night not to check on the noisy party, but to return that cat." She glanced over at Tillie. "Does anyone mention seeing the super go into 6-A?"

"Not that I can see."

"Lieutenant?" Elaine Albee had her hand over the mouthpiece of her desk phone. "Mrs. Wall on two."

Sigrid picked up the nearest phone. "Mrs. Wall? Lieutenant Harald here."

"I'm sorry to bother you, Lieutenant. I

have emailed you the name of the elevator man that we let go — the one that Antoine Clarke replaced — but I thought perhaps I should speak to you personally."

"Yes?"

"You're aware that Antoine left his post yesterday morning without any notice?"

"Yes, we were told that." Sigrid held up her hand for silence and pressed the phone's speaker button so that the others could hear.

"The thing is, his girlfriend's called twice this morning," said Mrs. Wall. "She says Antoine never came home yesterday and he's not answering his mobile. She's worried that something's happened to him."

"Give me her name and number," Sigrid said, "and we'll check into it. In the meantime, we still want to speak to your son Corey."

"I'm sorry, Lieutenant, but he's not due home from school until three."

By the time she hung up, the others had begun to connect the dots.

"Antoine Clarke's done a runner on us?" asked Yanitelli.

"He was in the building Saturday evening," said Lowry.

"And we know that he has at least two Class A misdemeanors," Albee chimed in.

Hentz leaned back in his chair and clasped

his hands behind his head. Stainless steel links gleamed in the French cuffs of his crisp white shirt. "If he's worked there two years, he's probably had opportunity to acquire a few passkeys."

Tillie walked over to their whiteboard and began constructing one of his detailed timetables. At the top, he wrote, *Time of Death — 9:50–11 p.m. Saturday night.*

To one side he wrote, *Employees in the Building,* and in alphabetical order listed Antoine Clarke, Jani Horvath, Sidney Jackson, and Denise Lundigren as being there at the relevant time.

"Jackson worked the elevator until eleven," Sigrid said, "and everyone says people streamed in and out all evening."

Hentz went back to his notes. "Horvath said he slept till he relieved Jackson a little before eleven, which is when Jackson said he went home. You think Jackson would have had enough time to sneak back up and kill Lundigren before you and Judge Knott entered the apartment?"

"Maybe," Sigrid said slowly, "but Denise Lundigren says her husband called right before he left her to see if the Bryants were there. Tillie, contact the ones who admitted being in the apartment and ask if they heard the telephone ring around ten o'clock. It wouldn't take him an hour to return the cat and no one seems to have seen him after he left his own apartment. Did a canvass of the building turn up anything?"

"There are forty-five apartments," Elaine Albee said, reading from a list compiled on Saturday night. "The uniforms say they knocked on every door. No responses from twenty-one, and eight of those twenty-one still didn't answer the door when we tried them yesterday. At least half of those were out of town, according to their neighbors. The Rices in 7-A will be in with their lawyer today. The owner in 3-C told one of the officers that Lundigren fixed a leaky faucet in her kitchen around five-thirty. No one else admits to seeing or speaking to him after that."

"The wife says they watched television that evening and they had words about her taking things from various apartments," Sigrid said. "So he leaves with the cat about ten."

Tillie added that to the neat timetable he was compiling.

"Let's say he lets himself in through the back door and surprises Antoine in the act of stealing those little gold-and-enamel boxes and the judge's earrings. Antoine hands the earrings back, then picks up that chunky bronze piece and smashes Lundigren on the head. Lundigren goes down, Antoine tries to stash the body on the balcony but doesn't quite get the door shut."

"Did he take that bronze with him or did someone else?" Lowry wondered aloud.

"Both are possibilities."

"Horvath told us that Antoine was awake at nine-thirty but just going to bed at eleven when he got up to relieve Jackson early," Hentz said, keeping his eye on the main ball. "So Clarke was around and awake all evening. And Vlad the Regaler did tell us that there was some animosity between Antoine and Lundigren, if that's not another of his embellishments."

"Either way, we definitely need to find Antoine Clarke," Sigrid said. "This doesn't look like a premeditated murder to me, so maybe we'll get a quick confession."

Dinah Urbanska tossed her empty coffee cup toward the nearest wastebasket. It missed and splashed its last few drops on Tillie's shoe. Flushing, Urbanska apologized and said, "Um, Lieutenant? I was wondering. Nothing much has been said about it, but do you think Lundigren's death had anything to do with the fact that she — I mean, that *he's* a woman?"

"What?" Tillie stared at her in surprise and

Sigrid realized that he had not been with them when the ME relayed that information.

"Sorry, Tillie. When Cohen had the super's body on the table yesterday, he discovered that Lundigren had all the physical attributes of a female," she said, and told him of Mrs. Lundigren's insistence that it was a heterosexual marriage. "And to answer your question, Urbanska, if anyone at his apartment building suspected otherwise, we haven't heard a whisper. As far as I'm concerned, there's no reason to make things more uncomfortable for Mrs. Lundigren unless it becomes an obvious factor in this death."

She referred again to her notes. "Speaking of Mrs. Lundigren?"

"I spoke to Dr. Penny," Hentz said. "He's going to send her home today with something to help her cope with her anxiety."

Jim Lowry looked up from his computer screen. "Here's the information Mrs. Wall sent us about the elevator man that Lundigren recommended for firing. Want me to follow up on it?"

Sigrid shook her head. "Let it ride for now. I'd prefer that you run the names of those guests with a known art background. See if any of them have priors. And, Tillie, let's have a list of all the guests who can't be alibied. We'll finish up here, then go back after lunch and see if we can speak to the occupants of those eight apartments that weren't home yesterday."

A uniformed officer appeared in the doorway. "Lieutenant? There's a Mr. and Mrs. Rice here with their attorney. I put 'em in interview room A."

"Thank you, Sergeant. Hentz?"

The Rice attorney was urbane in a charcoal pinstripe suit. He introduced his clients, assured Sigrid and Hentz that they were more than happy to cooperate in this terrible tragedy, then took a seat beside them.

In appearance, husband and wife were almost polar opposites. She was small and dark and impeccably dressed in a designer suit and thigh-high leather boots. He was big and blond and could have stepped out of a Lands' End catalog — turtleneck beige sweater, brown corduroy pants, and hiking shoes.

In temperament, however, they were mirror images — indignant to be here, irate at having to answer questions, indifferent to the death of a super they felt had thwarted their rights, and clearly irritated that this session necessitated their attorney, whose hourly fee would probably mean one less designer suit for Mrs. Rice.

"I believe your interest in my clients relates to the death of the building's super-intendent?" asked the attorney.

"That's correct," Sigrid said. "It seems that there was personal animosity toward him."

Both Rices started to argue and justify, but the attorney raised a restraining hand.

"Whether or not what you say is true, am I correct in thinking you wish to know if they have an alibi for the pertinent time of the man's death?"

Mrs. Rice sneered and Mr. Rice huffed at the word "alibi."

"Correct," Sigrid said. "Can they prove where they were between nine-thirty and, say, eleven?"

"Certainly." He drew a sheet of paper from his briefcase. "Here are the names and addresses of four people who dined with my clients from eight till ten-forty over on the East Side, as well as the doorman who let them in and out and who knows them by sight. I have included a photocopy of the receipt from their taxi. You will see that it is time-stamped eleven-oh-eight."

"Excellent," Sigrid said. She passed the

paper on to Hentz. "Thank you for coming."

"That's it?" asked Mr. Rice. "That's all you wanted to ask?"

Mrs. Rice was similarly stunned. "We dragged our attorney here with us and this is all? Well, why didn't those detectives tell us that? We could have saved a lot of time and money."

"I believe they tried," Sigrid said coldly. "You refused to listen and told them you had nothing to say."

"But we thought it had to do with our lawsuit."

"No."

"Damn!" said Mr. Rice, his beefy blond face turning an unhealthy red as he glared at their attorney.

Mrs. Rice picked up her expensive leather purse and stood to go. "Living on the Upper West Side is like living among Bolsheviks. The sooner we move back to the East Side, the better."

When alone in her office, Sigrid dialed her grandmother's number. Once more the soft-voiced woman answered. Sigrid identified herself and the woman immediately said, "I'm so sorry, Miss Harald. You just keep missing her. She asked me to apologize for not calling you back and to say she's visiting a sick friend. I did tell her you had concerns about the package she sent your mother. She forgot that Mrs. McKinnon was away and she wants you to open it and do with it whatever you think is best."

"When do you expect her back, Ms. . . . I'm sorry, but I don't know your name. Have we met?"

"I'm Chloe Adams, Miss Harald. I met you when —" She broke off, then continued smoothly, "when you visited Miss Jane back when you were in high school and I was helping out here. That was years ago and I'm sure you won't remember. Now, I'll be sure and tell her you called."

"Wait!" Sigrid said sharply, but she was too late. Chloe Adams, whoever she was, had hung up.

Chloe Adams. *Chloe Adams?* The name almost connected with a long-ago memory that she could not pin down. Troubled, she looked in her address book and dialed another 919 number.

After five rings, Kate Bryant's cheerful voice said, "You have almost reached the Bryants. Please leave a message."

Frustrated, Sigrid hung up.

After a lifetime of dealing with her mother's Southern speech patterns, she had learned that what a polite Southerner says is not always what a polite Southerner means. She mentally replayed her brief conversations with Ms. Adams until she finally pinpointed what it was about the woman's words that had her puzzled.

"Your grandmother told me to say . . ."

"Miss Jane said for me to tell you . . ."

"She asked me to say she's visiting a sick friend."

Not a straightforward "she's visiting a sick friend," but "she asked me to *say* she was." The subterfuge of a truthful woman who would not lie herself but would relay the lie? Why was Grandmother avoiding her calls? Was it that maquette? Was there something illegal about how she acquired that thing that made her unwilling to talk to a granddaughter who was also a police officer?

Once more Sigrid scrolled through her address book, and when the connection went through she said, "Judge Knott? Deborah? I'm sorry to keep interrupting your vacation, but could I come by this afternoon? Shall we say around three?"

CHAPTER 17

Snow mingles with the dust, is churned dirty by hoofs and wheels, and, if it melts, soon makes a slush underfoot.

— *The New New York,* 1909

"Three o'clock will be fine," I said and tucked my phone back into the pocket of my parka.

"Who was that?" Dwight asked, picking up the glove I'd dropped on the chilled sidewalk when I answered the phone.

"Sigrid Harald. She wanted to know if I'd be in around three."

"Why?"

"You think she stayed on the phone long enough for me to ask? God must've given that woman forty extra words to last a lifetime and I bet she still has thirty-six of them left. We'll just have to be there at three if we want to know why."

"Not me. I'm meeting Josh Cho, remember?"

"Oh, right."

"You sure you don't want to come, too?"

I was tempted. I've never sat in on one of Dwight's seminars and I've been told that he's a good speaker, but that would mean I'd have to call Sigrid back and sound wishy-washy and indecisive. Besides, I knew he wanted time with his old friend, and more importantly — okay, *most* importantly — there was a shoe store near the apartment that had an enticing pair of red patent leather heels in the window, shoes that would go perfectly with a red-and-black dress I had found at a summer's end sale last September. All I needed was a little free time without Dwight, and thanks to Josh Cho, this was it. Carpe diem, y'all. While Dwight went to John Jay College of Criminal Justice and spoke to his friend's students about rural police work, I could pick up a great souvenir of New York.

Hey, shoes beat a plastic Statue of Liberty, don't they?

We had been out since ten this morning, which was when the snow stopped and a dispirited sun almost made it through the gray sky.

A heavy snowfall is take-your-breath-away

poetry in white when left undisturbed. But plowed and shoveled into waist-high walls along every curb, dusted with soot, desecrated by dogs, and churned into gray mush by Monday morning's heavy wheels?

Sorry. Poetry it's not.

Despite the usual bitching from its inconvenienced citizens in the outer boroughs, the city was coping rather efficiently, all things considered. Most of the main arteries were cleared, and between the sun and the scattered rock salt, the sidewalks were getting easier to navigate except at the corners where water had pooled or the sewer openings were blocked. We took a bus down to Rockefeller Center, where we leaned on the rail to watch the ice skaters till we were thoroughly chilled, then poked in and out of the shops along the Channel Gardens before crossing Fifth Avenue to warm ourselves in the stately quiet of St. Patrick's Cathedral.

By then we were both in need of a restroom. If St. Patrick's has any, they aren't apparent, but there was a hotel nearby. Travel tip: hotel restrooms are spotlessly clean as a rule and some are luxurious marble and mirrored fantasies. Unless you look like a street bum, the staff won't pay you any attention.

Warmed and, um, shall we say . . . *rested?* . . . we wandered back toward Eighth Avenue and stopped for lunch at a nondescript café just off Broadway where we ordered steaming bowls of mushroom and barley soup before catching an uptown bus.

As Dwight got off at Columbus Circle to walk over to John Jay, he reminded me to turn my phone back on.

He knows I hate feeling like I'm tethered to the world and I had switched it off after Sigrid's call. In that short time, I had missed three texts from Emma, one of my many nieces. Nothing of substance, just lots of exclamation points exhorting me to call before her lunch period was over. Like I even knew when that would be. A final text told me to check my email. If I knew Emma, it was probably some extra-funny joke going around the Internet. Jokes could wait when shoes beckoned.

I had not intended to buy new boots, too, but those flimsy plastic ones had already popped an elastic loop, and when the salesman showed me a pair of sleek calf-high boots lined in natural lambswool, I succumbed to temptation.

"Boots are practical," I told myself. "A

necessity in all this ice and snow."

"Boots, yes," said my internal preacher, *"but what's Dwight going to say about those pricey red high heels?"*

"Bet Dwight won't say a word if she wears them with that new negligee," said the pragmatist.

"Besides, I can truthfully say they were on sale," I said. Never mind that the sale price was almost twice what I would have paid for an off-brand at home.

The preacher rolled his eyes, but kept quiet as I pulled out my credit card. The very nice salesman wrapped my old shoes without sneering, put them in a bag with the new red ones, and volunteered to dispose of those plastic horrors. "Now don't forget to wipe your boots with a clean damp cloth when you get home," he said. "Wet the cloth with a little diluted white vinegar. Rock salt is hell on leather."

Who says New Yorkers aren't friendly?

Walking back to the apartment wasn't too bad even though the temperature had begun to drop. The wind had picked up and felt as if it were blowing straight off the North Pole. I pulled my hat further down over my ears and wrapped my scarf around my face so that only my eyes were unprotected. By nightfall, these filthy puddles of water would be crusted in ice again.

The man on the elevator was the same as had taken us down earlier today. No brass name tag on his brown uniform. It occurred to me that he had the same slender build as the one who had quit yesterday. Could it be that men were hired for their ability to fit into existing uniforms? After all, how hard could it be to operate one of these things?

"Are you filling in for Antoine?" I asked.

"Permanently, I hope," he said with an easy smile.

He lacked a chinstrap beard, otherwise he could have been the other man's brother — same light brown skin, same clipped Afro. No facial hair and no Jamaican accent, though. He spoke pure New York without even a hint of the South. No slight softening and slurring of the words, which so many Northern-born blacks pick up from their expatriated elders or from summers with grandparents and cousins who still live below the Mason-Dixon Line.

I longed to ask him how many generations removed from the South he was, but I was afraid he'd take it wrong, so I told him my name and he said that he was Jim Williams. "Actually, all my friends call me James, but if you run an elevator, you get tired of people saying, 'Home, James,' so Jim's what I'll have them put on my badge if I get this job."

"Do you know Antoine?"

"No, I heard about him at the pizza shop down the street. How he walked off the job, so I went right over to the managing agent and applied. I don't know if they'll take him back if he wants to stay, but it's my chance to get in here."

"Good luck," I said and let myself into the apartment just as my phone rang. It was Dwight. "Elliott Buntrock called. Wants to know if we'd like to meet him down in the Village for dinner. Okay with you?"

"Sure," I said. "You finished with your class already?"

"Not yet. This is a ten-minute break at the halfway point. Josh and I will probably stop in somewhere for a beer when the class ends, but I should be back by five. Buntrock said eight o'clock, so that'll give us plenty of time."

By the time I finished wiping down my boots and disposing of the evidence of my shopping trip, it was almost three.

My phone rang. Emma again. School must be out.

"Didn't you get my message?" she wailed.

"I've been busy," I said. "What's up?"

"It's Lee. He's in really, *really* big trouble. Everybody thinks he did it, but Aunt Deborah, you *know* he wouldn't!"

"Wouldn't what?"

"Wouldn't post a dirty picture of Ashley Osgood. I mean, it's not her, of course, but it was on his Facebook page and it came from his phone, but he didn't do it." My niece's distressed words streamed through the phone like rushing water that drowned any coherence. "And now Ashley's all upset and Dad's furious and Mother'll probably make him take his page down and —"

"Whoa, slow down, Emma. I'm not understanding you."

"Don't you have your laptop up there?"

"Yes, but —"

"I've sent it all to you. Didn't you even look at it?"

"Sorry, I —"

"Just look at it, okay? You're good at figuring out stuff. There has to be a way to prove that Lee didn't do this."

I promised that I would look and then call her back as soon as I could.

Lee and Emma are eighteen and sixteen, the children of my brother Zach and his wife, Barbara. Zach's next to me in age, the second of what the family calls the "little twins," to differentiate them from Haywood and Herman, the "big twins." He and Adam are number ten and eleven in an unbroken string of brothers. Unbroken till they got to me, that is. I'm told Adam really resented my birth, and sometimes I think he still believes that the only reason he got born in the first place is because Daddy didn't want to quit till he got a daughter.

Zach's an assistant high school principal and has always been pretty tolerant of me, but his wife, Barbara, and I were never particularly close, although that's beginning to change a little. She heads up our Colleton County library system and she keeps her two children on a fairly short leash. She recently admitted that she had always envied the way the kids in the family seem to confide in me. My brothers and other sisters-in-law put it down to my unwillingness to finish growing up and settle into a conventional adult life. Until I decided to run for judge, I was still doing some of the same things they were — drinking too much, driving too fast, smoking the occasional weed — so the kids rightly figured I would understand when they found themselves on the verge of getting busted.

Sitting cross-legged on the bed in my stocking feet, it took me a few minutes to power up my laptop and find Emma's message. She had forwarded me the picture that had appeared on Lee's Facebook page around noon today. I immediately clicked on his page, but the picture was gone, so I went back to Emma's download.

At first glance, I thought it was exactly what people were supposed to think, and I was appalled. Especially since it was captioned, "Hey, y'all, Ashley let me take her picture last night. Who knew girls shaved their thangs?"

Then I took a second look and realized that it was a close-up of somebody's closed armpit that I was seeing.

Once I interpreted all the text-speak abbreviations and disjointed phrases, Emma's frantic message was that this picture had been posted on Lee's password-protected Facebook page.

But he's never told anyone the password. The picture's on his phone even though he says it's been in his locker all day and he's the only one who knows the combination. Ashley's freaking. She went home early and now her mom wants Lee's hide. Dad wants to believe him, but you know how he can't show favoritism and all the evidence is that Lee did it. Please,

Aunt D. Can't you or Uncle Dwight think how somebody could get his phone out of his locked locker and then could post something like this on his FB page????

Teenage boys are notorious for pulling stupid stunts without thinking or caring about the consequences, which is why many a young man's last words before he winds up in a coffin or a hospital bed are, "Hey, y'all! Watch this!"

Rural South or urban North. Makes no difference. Look at the boys in this building who think it's funny to take off with an unattended elevator.

If this had been one of my other nephews — A.K. or Reese, say — I wouldn't have thought twice before bringing my gavel down on a guilty verdict, but this was Lee, a conscientious by-the-book kid who's never even had a speeding ticket.

Running through various scenarios that might somehow exonerate Lee, I had totally forgotten about Sigrid Harald until the doorbell rang. As I passed through the vestibule, I saw something else I'd forgotten. I hadn't given that red flip-flop a second thought since tossing it onto the chest. I grabbed it up so that I wouldn't forget again and opened the door with it in my hand.

Sigrid's turquoise scarf was loosely looped around the neck of a black wool sweater. I invited her in and hung her white parka on the back of a chair in the dining room. I gestured her toward the living room, spotted the bath mat, started to change direction for the dining room, then realized that she probably wouldn't be bothered by what was under the mat. I also realized that all this dithering was making me look like an idiot. And it probably didn't help that I was standing there shoeless, with hat hair, no lipstick, and a red flip-flop in my hand.

"Sorry," I said. "One of my nephews is in trouble and I got distracted. Sort of a locked-room mystery. Can I get you coffee? Or a glass of wine?"

"Coffee, if it's already made."

"All I have to do is turn it on," I said. "My husband mainlines caffeine, so as soon as one pot's empty, he usually goes ahead and gets another ready to go."

She did not smile and it struck me that she might feel equally ill at ease. Instead of going on into the living room, though, she followed me out to the kitchen and said, "Locked room?"

I switched on the coffeemaker and we sat

on the kitchen stools while I gave her a brief recap of Lee's situation. It might have been my imagination, but she seemed grateful for an interlude before she got to the point of her visit.

When I had told her all I knew about the hot water Lee was in, she said, "And the picture was definitely sent from his cell phone?"

"That's what they say."

"Combination locks on the lockers?"

"Yes, and the kids are required to leave their phones there during class periods."

"Then he probably told someone the combination at some time."

"He swears he didn't."

"What about access to the master list?"

"No way. My mother-in-law keeps them in a locked file in her office."

"Your mother-in-law?"

"She's the school principal."

"And your brother is her assistant?" She lifted an eyebrow at that.

I shrugged. "What can I tell you? It's the country."

The coffee was done and I filled two mugs. She started to move the red flip-flop out of the way.

"Oh," I said. "I keep forgetting. Take a look at the bottom."

She turned it over. "Your missing earring?"

"Yeah, I've been meaning to call you. I took Luna's cat back to her yesterday and this was in a catchall bowl by the door along with other stuff that people left in her place Saturday night."

She took it by the spongy bottom, avoiding the smooth thong that might still hold a usable fingerprint even though both of us had touched it. Luna, too, probably. "Whose is it?"

I shrugged. "I can't say for sure, but I'll be surprised if it's not Cameron Broughton's."

I described how I'd found it and how I was pretty sure that he had started to claim it and then changed his mind as it registered that my earring was embedded in the sole. "The most logical place he could have stepped on it is inside this apartment."

Her wide gray eyes seemed to turn inward to consider the possibilities and I said, "Have you run his prints through IAFIS yet?"

She gave me a sharp look and I shrugged. "I'm not saying he's your killer, but there's something familiar about him. He says he's from the Wilmington area — North Carolina's Wilmington, not Delaware's — and I held court there a few summers back. I'm district court, so whatever it was had to be relatively minor and nonviolent. There's something familiar about those pale blue glasses he wears that makes me wonder if he came up before me while he was back visiting or something. I could ask the clerk of the court, if that wouldn't be interfering."

"Would it matter?" she asked with the first half smile I'd seen on her face.

"You sound like my husband. He's always saying I stick my nose in where it doesn't belong."

The coffee finished making and I poured us each a cup. "As long as I'm being nosy, did Mrs. Lattimore tell you where she got that bronze thing?"

She shook her head, laid the red flip-flop on the counter, and took a cautious sip of the hot coffee. "That's what I came to ask you about."

"Wish I could help," I said, "but she didn't give me a clue. Just handed me the wrapped box and asked me to bring it to your mother."

Sigrid set her cup back on the counter and looked me straight in the eye. "Do you know a Chloe Adams?"

"Chloe Adams? Sure." Almost immediately, I realized the significance of what she was asking, and that realization caused me to set my cup down so quickly that coffee slopped onto the counter. Grateful to escape her penetrating gaze, I reached for the paper towels to wipe up the mess. "She's a cousin of my daddy's housekeeper. I've known her most of my life. Nice woman."

Before I could go on chattering like a demented parrot, Sigrid's phone rang. "Harald here." She listened intently, then said, "When? . . . Is she sure? . . . Okay. I'll be right up."

"What's happened?" I asked.

She ignored my question and reached for the flip-flop. "Do you have a plastic bag I can put this in?"

Annoyed, I opened a drawer and handed her a box. "I want a receipt for my earring."

"Later," she said brusquely, already heading for the door. She grabbed her coat in passing and was gone before I could object.

CHAPTER 18

And yet there are other dark features of the city that are not to be slipped by unmentioned if one would make a fair survey and a candid commentary.
— *The New New York,* 1909

Sigrid Harald — Monday afternoon
Sam Hentz was waiting outside the open door to the Wall apartment when Sigrid reached the twelfth floor. The new man on the elevator seemed inclined to stay and see what was going on until Sigrid turned and said "Thank you" so pointedly that he closed the cage and left.

Having been on the receiving end of the lieutenant's chilly dismissal more than once, Hentz was torn between amusement and irritation.

An anxious Mrs. Wall joined them at the door. Her silver hair looked as if she had combed worried fingers through it, and her

279

face was as pale as the light gray turtleneck and slacks she wore. "Did he tell you?"

"That your son Corey is missing? Yes," Sigrid said. "When did you last see him?"

"Yesterday morning. He said he was going sledding in the park. When he didn't come home, I tried calling him, but he wouldn't answer. We — we'd had words and he was angry with me. Fine, I thought. I'd just back off and give him time to get over it. I thought he'd crashed with some friends and gone to school from there. He often does that without telling me, but when he didn't come home today, I started calling around. No one's seen him. He didn't meet them yesterday morning and he wasn't in school today."

"You've tried calling him again?"

"Of course I have." Her anger at being asked something so obvious did not mask her mounting fear. "Here."

She pressed a speed dial button on her phone and thrust it into Sigrid's hand. Almost immediately, a mechanical voice said, "The person you have called is unavailable. Please try your call again later."

"I've heard that the police don't consider someone truly missing until they've been gone forty-eight hours, but please. Corey's been gone more than thirty hours."

"You said your son was angry when you last spoke," Sigrid said. "Are you quite sure that his friends are telling you the truth? Is it possible that they're lying as a favor to him?"

Mrs. Wall hesitated and Hentz said, "What did you fight about, ma'am?"

She tried to shrug him off. "What don't teenagers and their parents fight about? Curfews, schoolwork —"

"Stealing your jewelry?" Sigrid asked quietly.

What little color had been in Mrs. Wall's face drained away and the vibrant woman they had interviewed yesterday now looked old and defeated. "How did you know?" she whispered.

"Drugs or alcohol?" Hentz asked.

She gave a long unhappy sigh. "Corey doesn't do either of those. He gambles. Last year he lost nearly six thousand dollars playing poker online. We put a block on his computer so that he can't do that anymore, but he's found live games here on the West Side. He's hocked almost everything of value in this house. His computer, his camera, his television, even the silver that's been in our family for four generations. If he realized the pottery was valuable, that would be gone, too."

Tears glistened in her eyes. "He's not a bad kid, but my father was an alcoholic and my brother's addicted to cocaine. Our therapist says addictions can be genetic. His sisters don't seem to have any, but maybe because he's a boy? And the youngest?"

She pushed back the hair from her face and looked at the detectives helplessly. "My husband's in Chicago. A business trip. I haven't told him yet because he wants us to kick Corey out. Tough love, he calls it, but Corey can't help himself. He needs that adrenaline rush and, really, if you think about it, if you're going to be addicted to anything, gambling's better than drugs or alcohol, isn't it? Not as destructive?"

"Do you think his disappearance is connected with his gambling?" Sigrid asked.

"I don't know. I just don't know. He swears he hasn't played since Thanksgiving, but he's lied before. He doesn't have any money, though. We've cut his allowance to fifteen dollars a week. We cover everything else ourselves — clothes, fare cards. We even prepay his school lunches. Can't you do something? An Amber Alert?"

"How old is Corey?" Hentz asked.

"Seventeen."

"I'm sorry," Sigrid said, "but Amber Alerts are primarily intended for younger

282

abducted children unless there's a clear indication of kidnapping, and you don't really believe Corey was kidnapped, do you?"

"No, but —"

"We can and will ask our patrol units to be on the lookout for him," Sigrid said.

They took the boy's description and that when last seen he was wearing jeans, boots, a Columbia University sweatshirt, and a Yankees hoodie.

"What about the sled?" asked Sigrid. "Are you convinced that's where he intended to go? Did he take it with him?"

"He keeps it stored in the basement," Mrs. Wall said. "I just assumed he went and got it and left from there."

"Show us," Sigrid said.

By then it was a few minutes past four, and when the elevator came, it was operated by the night man, Sidney Jackson, whose dark eyes were solicitous as he looked into Mrs. Wall's anxious face. "You feeling all right, Mrs. Wall?"

"I'm fine, Sidney, thank you. We need to go down to the basement."

Tactfully, the man did not ask further questions, and he ignored a buzz from the fourth floor in order to take them directly there.

Unaware that the detectives had already examined the basement, Mrs. Wall explained that every apartment had its own storage space. "But we have a common area with racks for bicycles and bulky equipment off to one side."

They walked down the shadowy passageway to the storage area where the detectives had examined Phil Lundigren's files over pizza yesterday. Mrs. Wall flipped a light switch in a side passage to illuminate an open storage room with many large hooks upon which to hang bicycles. Steel rings were bolted to the wall so that things could be secured with locked chains.

"That's his sled," she said in disappointment. "So he did lie. He didn't go sledding after all."

She pointed to a battered old Flexible Flyer that hung from a hook next to a bike that was missing its front wheel. The stenciled name — Fred Wall — had almost worn off. "It was my husband's. Corey sold the expensive Hammerhead we gave him for Christmas two years ago."

"What time did he leave your apartment yesterday morning?" Sigrid asked.

"Before nine. That was the crack of dawn

for him, but one of his friends called and woke him up. They were going to meet for breakfast at a diner on Broadway and then go on to the park. Or so he said. His friends say he never came and they went on without him."

"Nine o'clock," Hentz murmured. "That's around the time that Antoine quit, wasn't it?"

"Was it?" She looked up at him with a troubled frown. "Yes, I suppose it was, because someone on the eighth floor called me about nine-thirty to complain that the elevator wasn't working. I had already arranged for one of the porters — Vlad Ruzicka — to come in at ten to check on the boiler, so when I heard Antoine had quit, I called Sidney and he volunteered to come in early and work a double shift." She turned impatiently and switched off the light. "Oh why are we even talking about porters and elevator men? They don't have anything to do with Corey missing."

"No?" said Sigrid. "Some people think Antoine quit because Corey took the elevator when his back was turned."

"Don't be silly." Mrs. Wall looked from one detective to the other. "I know it's wrong for my son to annoy the men like that, but this is a desirable job for someone with little education and no marketable skills. Good benefits and lots of tips as well. Even though our management agent hasn't advertised it yet, we've already had three applicants for Phil's job and a substitute for Antoine as well. No, Lieutenant Harald. Antoine didn't quit because of Corey." Her tone became defensive. "Besides, the elevator is never supposed to be left untended. If Antoine had done his job properly there would have been no opportunity for Corey to take it."

Hentz said, "Sometimes people snap and say 'take this job and shove it,' Mrs. Wall. If Corey did play that trick on Antoine yesterday morning, maybe it was one time too many."

The older woman suddenly froze. "Are you saying that Corey — ? That Antoine — ? That Antoine could have hurt him? Oh my God! Antoine killed Phil, didn't he?"

Sigrid and Hentz escorted a panicky Mrs. Wall back upstairs. She gave them the names and addresses of the boys he was supposed to meet with Saturday morning. "Drew Narsetti's his closest friend. He lives around the corner on West End Avenue and he's called twice to ask if I've heard anything from Corey."

She gave them a recent snapshot that showed a boy with a marked resemblance to her: small frame, pointed chin, hazel eyes. They said they would put out a BOLO for him and promised to keep her informed.

"What do you think?" Hentz asked Sigrid when they were back out in the hall.

"Probably what you're thinking," she said slowly. "Corey was at the party Saturday night and Antoine was in the building during the relevant times. Now Corey and Antoine are both missing. I've never cared much for coincidences. Have you?"

They met in the lobby with Detectives Albee and Urbanska, who had finished their canvass of the eight apartments that had not responded earlier. Hentz and Urbanska pushed some of the lobby chairs over to a couch in a secluded corner so that the four of them could sit and spread their notes on the low table while they shared their findings.

"No help from any of them," Elaine Albee reported. "Two of them are still out of town." She gestured toward the elevator. "According to Sidney Jackson, neither apartment was occupied this weekend. 2-A is something in the movie business and goes out to California for weeks at a time. The people in 11-C own a condo in Florida and always spend January and February down there."

"I talked to the Peterson kid from 11-B," Urbanska said. "He spent the weekend skiing with some cousins in Vermont. He also says Antoine's lying if he says he stole the elevator anytime lately. He swears he only took it once. Over a year ago. His parents heard about it and took away his cell phone for a week, so that was his only time."

As the others talked, Albee leaned back in her chair and looked through the two glass doors to the dirty snow heaped along the sidewalk. She found herself thinking about sunshine, blue water, and palm trees. Then Jim Lowry came up from the basement to join them and the afternoon felt suddenly warmer. She patted the broad armrest of her chair to offer him a perching place.

Surprised, Lowry took it. She had held him at arm's length for so long, he had almost given up. Now he reported that he had separately interviewed the two porters on duty and he, too, had spoken with Sidney Jackson again. "To hear them tell it, they're just one big happy family here. They don't think Lundigren liked Antoine much, but they don't know why. Both porters agree that Antoine doesn't like Sidney because he only laughs when the Wall boy steals the elevator. They say Antoine doesn't like to be laughed at and he's always bitching about privileged kids. On the other hand, Vlad Ruzicka says he saw Antoine give Corey some money Friday afternoon."

Sigrid frowned. "Not the other way around?"

"Maybe Corey sold him something his mother hasn't missed yet," Hentz suggested.

He proceeded to bring the other three up to date on their interview with Mrs. Wall, her admission that Corey had a gambling addiction, that he got the money to gamble by selling things he stole from the Wall apartment, and that he was supposed to have gone sledding Saturday morning, yet never made it.

"And his sled is still in the basement," Sigrid said.

She turned to Hentz. "Try calling that Narsetti boy. If he lives just around the corner, perhaps he'll come down and talk to us."

All through this session, people had passed in and out through the lobby. Various delivery people came and went, including FedEx, Postal Pizza, and a dry cleaners. Now one of the building's older residents approached from outside, pulling a loaded shopping basket behind her. Urbanska jumped up to hold the inner door open and was rewarded with a sweet smile. Close on her heels came a tall and gangly teenage boy who followed the woman toward the elevator with a cell phone in one hand and a latte in the other. As he passed them, his phone rang and he answered immediately just as Hentz said, "Drew Narsetti? This is Detective Hentz of the NYPD. Mrs. Wall —"

"Hey, cool!" the boy said, turning back to them. "I never had that happen before. I'm Drew. Are you the detectives Mrs. Wall said were trying to find Corey? She asked me if I'd come talk to you, but I really don't know where he is."

He sat down on the couch next to Hentz, unzipped his jacket, and took the lid off his coffee. The warm aroma of caffeine and hot milk filled the air and the detectives looked at it longingly, but none of them wanted to risk the lieutenant's displeasure.

"Where did you get that?" Sigrid asked.

"There's a coffee shop on the corner. Want me to get you one?"

"I'll go," said Urbanska as the others quickly dug in their pockets. She took their money and their orders, then hurried out.

Drew Narsetti seemed like a nice all-American, Mom-and-apple-pie kid —

shaggy brown hair that was squeaky clean and a long thin face that seemed to have escaped most of the ravages of acne. He told them that he and Corey had been friends since their sandbox days when their mothers used to push their strollers over to the park. "He's five days older than me and we're in the same class."

"When did you last speak to him?" Sigrid asked.

"To actually talk to? Yesterday morning. I was his wake-up call. He didn't think he'd hear the alarm. But we were texting back and forth till like midnight. He was at a beach party here in the building and he freaked when he heard their super got killed."

"Did he send you pictures?"

The boy gave a reluctant nod.

Hentz held out his hand for the boy's phone. "May I take a look?"

Drew took a long swallow of his latte to hide the embarrassment that suddenly reddened his face. "Well . . . see . . . I mean, like he didn't know somebody was going to get killed."

With a wry smile, Sigrid said, "And there were girls in bikinis?"

He gave a sheepish nod. "One of 'em was smokin' hot."

"We may already have those," Hentz said, keeping his tone matter-of-fact. "We asked everyone who had taken pictures to send us copies. It helps us document who was on the sixth floor Saturday night."

Drew hesitated then, with a what-the-hell shrug, said, "Let me pull up just the ones he sent, okay?"

"Fine. And I'll forward them to our computer, if that's all right with you?"

The boy nodded.

"Let's talk about yesterday morning," Sigrid said. "Did Corey sound as if anything was bothering him?"

"No, everything was cool. I called him at like a quarter to nine and told him where we were meeting to grab a bite before heading over to the park. He was a little down about the super. He really liked the guy and couldn't understand how he'd get killed right there with a party going on down the hall. He said his mom was really bummed about it, too. She's the head of their co-op board. But he said he'd see us at the diner. We waited till almost nine-thirty, but he never showed. I called and texted, but he didn't answer. Just blew us off."

"Has he blown you off before?"

"Not like this. He usually lets me know if he's changed his mind."

"No problems at school?"

"He's flunking trig, but not like what you mean."

"What about at home?"

Again the hesitation, and he seemed grateful when Sidney held the lobby door open for a florist with a cellophane-wrapped plant and for Urbanska, who carried a cardboard tray loaded with paper cups of coffee thick with foam. If the teenager had hoped that the coffee would bring a change of subject, he was disappointed.

Even as she uncapped her latte, Sigrid said, "Is he gambling again, Drew?"

He gave her a startled look. "You know about that?"

"His mother told us. She also told us about the stealing."

"So is he?" Hentz asked. "Gambling again?"

It was almost painful to watch the conflict between loyalty and truthfulness in the boy's face. After a long silence, he said, "Yeah."

"Where's he getting the money?"

That got them a defensive negative shrug.

"He doesn't have anything left to hock and he's not stealing from his parents, so who is he stealing from, Drew?"

"He's not stealing from anybody."

293

Sigrid looked up from her coffee as she registered the faint stress the boy had put on the unexpected word. "*He's* not stealing? Then who is?"

Drew stood up so quickly that his gangly limbs almost knocked over his cup. "Look, I don't want to talk about this anymore. You need to find Corey and ask him all this stuff. Anyhow, don't I have a right to an attorney?"

"Sit down, please, Drew," Sigrid said with a calm level look.

Albee watched, fascinated. There was nothing menacing in the lieutenant's manner, but Elaine had never seen her lose a staring contest. Although the teenager clearly wanted to leave, his shoulders drooped in defeat and he did as she asked.

"The day man here. Antoine. Corey gets money from him."

"Why?"

Silence.

Elaine Albee leaned forward sympathetically and in her most coaxing voice said, "We know you don't want to rat your friend out, Drew, but if we're going to find him, we need all the facts. He may be into something over his head."

Again they saw the conflicting emotions.

"You won't tell anybody I told you? Not

Corey or anybody?"

Albee glanced at Sigrid, who said, "We can't promise that until we know what it is, but we'll do whatever we can to keep your name out of it."

He slumped down in the chair. "He has something on Antoine."

"He's blackmailing Antoine?"

Drew nodded.

"How? What's Antoine done?"

"Corey says Antoine's been stealing from some of the apartments. See, the super's wife is like a klepto or something, so everyone thinks it's her. I don't know how Corey found out about it, but he did and Antoine pays him to keep quiet about it."

"He's still stealing?"

"I guess. I don't know."

"How long has this been going on?"

"The stealing or the blackmail?"

"Both."

"I don't know. Like, a couple of months maybe? Not for much. Just enough to get him into a poker game once in a while."

"Where's the game?"

"Now that I really don't know. Honest. It's some office building down in the Fifties. He's never said and I don't ask. I think he's pretty good. He says he wins enough pots that with what he gets from Antoine he can keep playing once a week. He's like try-ing to taper off, you know? Like when you quit smoking or drinking? He used to want to play almost every night. Now he's down to only Tuesday or Thursday night. It's crazy. I mean, we all like to play cards once in a while, but just penny-ante stuff. I can understand coke or meth. That messes with your body. Changes your chemistry." He looked at them in bewilderment. "But gambling? How can it mess with your head that much?"

And of course, they had no answer to the boy's plaintive question. After a few more questions of their own, they thanked him and let him go.

Sigrid looked at her watch. Nearly five o'clock. "Let's talk to the porters again. See if they know more about Corey and An-toine. Are they still here?"

"Vlad Ruzicka is, I know," Lowry said. "He was on his way out to shovel the sidewalk when I came up. Tomorrow's their pickup day and he had to make a place to set the bags."

"Let's see what else he knows," Sigrid said as she took a final swallow of her coffee. "Might as well add our cups to his trash." She picked up her parka, which had been lying on the back of her chair, and realized that she had forgotten to tell them about the flip-flop that Deborah had found. She took it from her pocket to show them and Hentz immediately recognized that the earring stuck in the sole was a mate to the one they had found in Lundigren's hand.

"I doubt there are any usable prints on it," she said, handing the bag to Urbanska. "Judge Knott and I both handled it before we realized what it was, and I suppose Luna DiSimone did, too."

"I'll have it checked," Urbanska promised.

Hentz still had Lundigren's keys and he led the way across the lobby, unlocked the door to the stairwell, and held it for the others while Lowry rang for the self-service elevator.

Dinah Urbanska paused and looked up at him. "What do you think, Sam? Is our killer the person who wore that flip-flop or is it Antoine Clarke? And has Clarke killed the Wall boy?"

"Let's hope not," he said grimly.

When the elevator doors opened, they found themselves face-to-face with the excitable Vlad Ruzicka. The big ruddy man was white-faced and spluttering. "Thank God! I was just coming to find you. Oh my God, I can't believe it! It's horrible!"

"Calm down," said Lowry. "What's happened?"

Ruzicka immediately grabbed Lowry's arm and dragged him through the outer door where two large wheeled garbage bins sat ready to roll up to the curb for tomorrow's pickup. At the top of the ramp, on the sidewalk, the lid of a third bin was raised. "So heavy. Like a ton of lead. I said maybe somebody tossed another set of encyclopedias or some bricks or something, so I opened it up and oh my God!"

Lowry leaned over the open bin and gingerly turned back the top of a black plastic bag.

A young man stared back at him with open lifeless eyes.

"Oh shit," he said when he realized who it was.

Bracing herself, Sigrid stepped forward to look into the bin. Instead of the white teenage boy she expected, she saw the narrow chinstrap beard that outlined Antoine Clarke's dead face.

CHAPTER 19

... but while they occupy a series of little cells in the fifteenth story of a sky-scraper, reached by an express elevator, warmed by steam, and lighted by electricity, what is the use of trying to keep a cow or striving to grow lilac bushes?
— *The New New York,* 1909

Thinking to kill two birds with one rock, I started down the hall to Luna's apartment, remembered the door, and went back to give it a second pull. As I suspected, the latch had not fully engaged and I had to give it a hard yank before I heard a satisfactory click.

"Oh, hi, Deborah!" Luna said when she answered her door. "Did you come to see what my place looks like in its winter clothes?"

She pulled me in and I was astonished by the transformation. Gone was every trace of

Saturday night's summer ambiance. The oversized room actually had a warm and cozy feel now. Nothing remained to show that white wicker and rattan made up the bones of her furniture. The chairs and couches and even the swing were covered in thick plush slipcovers of rich jewel tones that glowed in the soft indirect lighting. It was still a good party space, but large Persian rugs defined various interlinked furniture groupings, and real-looking gas logs burned in the fireplace. A whole menagerie of colorful Mexican animals pranced across the mantelpiece. Huge abstract canvases added more warmth to the walls, and the windows were now draped in dark purple velvet over the white sheers that had made the room so breezy during the party.

"This is absolutely amazing," I said, thoroughly impressed.

Luna beamed. "I told you that Cam was a genius. He designed the slipcovers and found someone to make them. And he arranged everything so that the room doesn't overwhelm the furniture."

"Have you known him very long?"

"Just since last year. Phyllis knew him first."

"Phyllis?"

"Phyllis Parrish. She's the one who was

with me when we rode up in the elevator together Friday night. She lives next door. Plays the French maid on *East Jarrett*."

She saw my blank look. "One of the daytime soaps. It's only a bit part but it pays the mortgage, and she gets to do summer stock in New England. We've known each other since our *Sesame Street* days, and when I saw how Cam decorated her place, I wanted him to do mine, too."

"Does he have a shop?"

"Well, he does, but it's only by appointment when a client's ready to look at quirky accessories like my Oaxacan animals or —" She shrugged and grinned.

I gave her my best girl-to-girl smile. "Or things a little more bawdy?"

She giggled. "You know it! When he first staged my animals, I had to redo them before I could let my mother come over and see how the apartment looked. My cat was getting it on with the horny-looking horned toad. You should see his huge collection of little hand-blown glass figures that people bring him from Venice. There's one set that's like a symphony orchestra with all the players in tuxes and every single musician is doing something dirty, including the conductor who's using his willy as a baton."

As soon as she said that, memory snapped

into place. Of course! Cameron Broughton had been one of four men who pleaded guilty to a D&D when I held court in Wilmington a couple of years back. No wonder Broughton had tried to avoid me.

I couldn't wait to tell Sigrid. He might not be a killer, but he could well be the thief that had taken her grandmother's bronze thing.

"Are the paintings by your friend Nicco?"

She nodded. "And see how Cam picked up the fabric colors from the pictures? It almost makes me want to throw another party. How long are you and Dwight going to be here?"

"Just till the weekend," I said regretfully.

"I was hoping I could get Lieutenant Harald to come if you were going to be here. She never does the party scene, but they say she came to mine because of you. Nicco was so pissed that he didn't recognize her at first when she came back to question us yesterday. I mean, he'd heard she was a police officer, but you don't expect the owner of Oscar Nauman's pictures to show up at a murder, do you?"

"I guess not, but speaking of murder, Luna —"

"Oh, poor, poor Phil! Does she know why he was killed?"

"I'm afraid that's not something she would tell me."

"But Dwight's a police officer, too, isn't he?"

"Yes, but this isn't his jurisdiction. What I actually came for was to ask if you could recommend a nearby florist? I want to take his widow some flowers."

"I should do that, too!" she exclaimed. "Or do you think I should wait for the memorial service?"

She gave me the name and number of a shop three blocks away on Amsterdam Avenue. Back in the apartment and after talking to a pleasant clerk, I settled on a potted gardenia that he swore was covered in buds that were just coming into bloom. It was going to cost three times what a five-gallon bush from a Colleton County nursery would cost, but we were five hundred miles away from Colleton County and Mrs. Lundigren didn't have a garden anyhow. When I told him it was for a recent death, he said he would add a white satin bow instead of the usual red one and that it would be there within the hour.

While I waited, I called Emma and learned that nothing had changed on their end since we'd talked. "I can sort of understand why everyone's upset, but really, Emma, it's only a bare armpit, not a girl's full frontal."

"I know that. You know that. Even Ashley knows that. But it's the caption that was so awful. And that it was on Lee's Facebook page. Mother doesn't know about it yet, but when she does, it's really going to hit the fan."

"So run me through it," I said. "The school says you can't carry a phone to class, right? Not even if it's turned off?"

"Not even if it's turned off," she said. "If you bring it into the building, you have to leave it in your locker or it will be confiscated for the rest of the day and you have to go to the office to get it back. The only time you can use it is during your lunch break."

"But you can legally use it during lunch?"

"Right. That's how I could call you. I have the last lunch period. Lee has the first and he says he did use his phone, but then he put it back in his locker."

"And he's sure he locked it?"

"Ask him yourself."

I heard murmurings, then Lee came on the line. "Hey, Aunt Deborah. I'm sorry Emma's bothering you on your honeymoon."

"Don't be silly, honey. I just wish I could help."

"I swear to you I didn't post that picture."

"I believe you, but who did? Who doesn't like you and has the computer skills to hack into your Facebook account?"

I could almost hear his frustrated shrug. "I don't think it's somebody who hates me. I think it's probably someone who thought it'd be a big funny joke."

"Did Ashley have a boyfriend before you?"

"Well, duh, Aunt Deborah."

"Sorry. So did she break up with someone who might be mad that she's seeing you?"

"They broke up before Christmas and he's seeing somebody else, too."

"Back to your locker then. You're positive you locked it?"

"*And* twirled the dial so no one could just pull up on it. Some kids think it's cool to leave their lockers unlocked so they can get in and out quicker, but then other kids will switch the open locks around, and next thing you know five kids are in the office trying to sort out the serial numbers so they can get their own locks back and get into their lockers."

Ah, yes. Another example of adolescent humor.

"Where do you keep the combination?"

"I don't. One of the perks of being the assistant principal's kid is that I get to hold on to the same lock I got when I was a freshman."

"Okay, forget about the lock for a minute, who knows your Facebook password?"

"Nobody. Well . . . Mother knows it. That's the only way Emma and I are allowed to have a page. I suppose she'd give it to Dad if he wanted it, but nobody else."

I'm as clueless about electronic technology as anybody can be these days and still log on to the Internet, figure out how to tape a program for later viewing, or make a wireless phone call. I do not tweet, twitter, or Facebook though, and I can barely send a text message. "Walk me through the process, Lee. Once someone has your phone, how can they send a picture to your Facebook?"

"You do know that phones can connect to the Internet, right?"

"So I've heard. Mine doesn't."

"I know." His tone was dry. I'm not a total Luddite, but all the kids know that I think phones are for making and receiving calls. Anything else? That's what a laptop's for.

"It's easy," Lee assured me. "You just take a picture, crop it, save it, then log on to your Facebook page. Once you're there, you can click the photo icon, locate the picture on your phone, click CHOOSE, and send it."

There was a brief silence, then Lee said,

"Oh crap! You know something? I checked my page at lunchtime and I might not have logged off."

"What does that mean?"

"It means if someone got my phone, they wouldn't have to know my password. My Facebook page accepts anything from my phone till I actually log off."

I could hear Emma's excited, "That's *it*, Lee! You idiot! Of course that's how they did it!"

"But how did they get into my locker?" he howled.

"Who has the lockers next to yours?" I asked.

"I'm on the end, so there're only three. The bottom locker is a freshman girl. I don't know her name. On the left, the top one is Jamie Benton, and the bottom one's Mark McLamb. They're both juniors."

"Jamie Benton? Jenny and Max Benton's son?"

Murmured consultation between brother and sister.

"Emma says yes. Why?"

"No reason." I wasn't sure how general the knowledge was that the Bentons were divorcing and that they were locked in a custody battle over the boy. "He and the other boy — Mark? Are they good friends?"

"I guess. They horse around at their lockers, but there's no way they could get into mine."

"Two minutes ago you were saying there was no way anyone could post on your Facebook page. If you left your page unprotected you could've left your locker unlocked."

"No way," he said stubbornly.

"Do those boys have the same lunch period as you?"

More off-phone chatter, then Lee said, "A.K. says they have second lunch with his group."

If A.K. was standing right there, it's a safe bet all his teenage cousins were, too. Between them, they could cover a lot of ground.

"Get the others to see what those two were doing during lunch. And ask that freshman girl if she saw anybody fooling around with your locker today."

"Thanks, Aunt Deborah. I will. Everybody says tell you hey."

I heard a chorus of heys in the background. Before I could make any further suggestions, he broke the connection. He's a gentle boy, but maybe his sister and his cousins would teach him something about the art of intimidation.

■ ■ ■ ■

Had Phil Lundigren's death happened back in Colleton County, I would now be taking his widow a plate of homemade sausage biscuits, a casserole, or a cake I had baked myself. Food is the universal offering for a house of mourning when all the relatives pour in and need to be fed. Doing something tangible for the bereaved allows friends and neighbors to feel a little less helpless in the face of death. Hell, I've even carried a casserole to a presumably grieving widow, only to later learn that she was the one who had planned her husband's murder.

I had no idea if Mrs. Lundigren had an alibi for Saturday night, nor even whether the marriage was a happy one. Hoping I wasn't repeating that past mistake, I rummaged in the refrigerator for a wedge of Brie that Dwight had brought home from the market yesterday. An unopened sleeve of crackers and a bunch of grapes would have to sub for a casserole. I arranged the cheese and crackers on one of the pretty paper plates I found in the cupboard, placed the grapes in the middle, and covered everything with plastic wrap. When the gardenia plant arrived, I freshened up and rang for the elevator. The man on duty was still Sidney, who was starting to feel like an old friend by now.

He gave a smile of approval when I told him the flowers were from Kate. "That sounds like her. When my father died last year, she sent a beautiful wreath even though she hasn't lived here for going on five or six years."

I asked him which was the Lundigren apartment and if he knew whether or not Mrs. Lundigren was at home. "We heard she had to be hospitalized when they told her about her husband."

"Yeah. One of the porters said she came home around lunchtime today. Told me she was quite chatty in fact."

"Chatty? Kate said she had an anxiety disorder that made it hard for her to talk to people."

"Not today. Vlad says Denise talked to him more today than the whole time he's worked here. The friend that brought her home from the hospital told Vlad that the doctor gave Denise some pills that were better than three martinis."

When I got off the elevator, Sigrid and her team of detectives were conferring with a teenage boy in a far corner of the lobby.

She had her back to me and the others didn't seem to recognize me behind all the cellophane and ribbons. Sidney told me that the Lundigren apartment was around the corner, so I decided to mind my own business and stay on task. I did not want to risk being asked about Chloe Adams again.

"Mrs. Lundigren?" I said to the large heavyset woman who opened the door when I rang.

"No, I'm her friend Alice Rosen. Do come in. Denise is in the den."

I tried to say I didn't know the woman and was here only as an emissary of my sister-in-law, but it was useless. The woman was already disappearing down a hallway like a white rabbit, so I followed her through a small living room that looked like an illustration from *Better Homes and Gardens* into a room that was not quite as pretty but had a more lived-in air.

Denise Lundigren was nestled at the end of a couch upholstered in a flowery print. She had her feet tucked up under her and ruffled pink, red, and green pillows cushioned her back. She was small and pretty with dark hair and dark vivid eyes. I judged her to be in her early fifties. A large white cat sat purring on her lap and she gave me a tentative smile when I entered.

I set the gardenia plant and the cheese plate on the coffee table and introduced myself. "I'm Kate Honeycutt's sister-in-law," I said, using the name that would be more familiar to this woman, the name Kate still used for her professional work.

Denise Lundigren brightened. "Kate! She was here last spring. She brought me a crystal cat." A smile played on her lips as she stroked the white Persian. "Did you know Jake?"

I shook my head.

"They were so much in love. Just like Phil and me. And Jake was murdered, too, wasn't he?"

Tears ran down her cheeks and her friend nudged the box of tissues on the coffee table closer to the woman.

"Does her new husband love her?"

"Very much."

"She's so lucky. I'll never find anyone else like my Phil," she sobbed.

"Now, Denise, honey," said Mrs. Rosen. She moved onto the couch and cradled Mrs. Lundigren's head on her ample bosom.

"Look at me!" she wailed. "You know how I am, Alice. Nobody else is ever going to love me like he did."

I was alarmed, but the other woman just

312

made soothing noises and kept patting her back. Eventually Mrs. Lundigren quit crying, wiped her eyes, and blew her nose.

"Everyone says your husband was a good man," I said gently. "But everybody has enemies."

She sat upright with one hand on Mrs. Rosen's arm, the other on the cat. "Not Phil."

"He never had words with any of the staff?"

"Well, he did think Antoine might not be working out. Sometimes he stays after his shift is over and Phil's found him in places he's not supposed to be."

"What sort of places?"

She shrugged. "Upstairs in the halls or on the service landings. Sometimes down where people store their bikes and stuff."

"What about the residents?"

"Everybody liked him. Everybody except the people in 7-A. They said they were going to sue Phil, but he wasn't worried."

"Sue?" asked Mrs. Rosen. "Why would someone sue Phil?"

"Because he told the board all the things they've done. They said they were going to sue him for slander. Or was it libel?" She looked at me. "When Kate emailed Phil to say you were coming, she said you were a judge, so you must know which it is."

"Probably slander," I said. "Libel is usually written lies and slander is spoken lies."

"Phil never lied," she said flatly. "He couldn't."

"Did the police tell you how he died?"

She nodded. "Were you the one who found him?"

"Yes," I said and described Saturday night. The party. The unlatched door. Finding her husband on the balcony.

When I finished, Mrs. Lundigren said, "They told me someone could've followed him in or else someone was already there stealing some of Jordy's things and he saw them. Now maybe he'll believe me." Fresh tears trickled from her dark eyes. "Or he would if he was still alive. He thought it was me every time, even though I knew it wasn't."

She stared down at her cat and stroked him with gentle crooning noises.

Sidney had told me about her kleptomania. Embarrassed, I looked at her friend, who mouthed a word I couldn't understand.

"Go ahead and say it out loud, Alice," Mrs. Lundigren said angrily. She turned to me. "I'm a crazy person. Kleptomania. You know what that means."

I nodded.

"They say it's a sickness. *I* say I'm crazy. I don't even want the stuff. Phil knows — *knew* — I didn't. But I can't help myself. I try, but . . . do *you* think I'm crazy?"

"No," I said, as gently as I could.

"Phil says it really doesn't matter. We are what we are. But I'll tell you this. I'm not the only one who takes things."

"There's a real thief in the building?"

"Well, it's not all me! I didn't take anybody's jewelry, I don't care what they say."

She gave an impatient shake of her head, shifted the cat onto the couch, and leaned forward to undo the cellophane on the gardenia plant. As the florist had promised, it was covered in fat pale green buds. Two creamy white blossoms had already opened. Mrs. Lundigren took a deep sniff and smiled. "How did Kate know I love gardenias?"

Back upstairs, I switched on the lamps in the living room, poured myself a glass of Riesling, and curled up on the brown leather couch with my laptop to read up on kleptomania. Five o'clock came and went and it was nearly six before Dwight finally let himself in.

"How did the seminar go?" I asked.

"Fine. Did you know that there are cameras and police swarming all over the lobby and the basement door? The day man that they thought quit yesterday morning?"

"Antoine?" I said. "What about him?"

"They just found his body in one of the garbage bins."

CHAPTER 20

In the early seventies, with only horse-cars on the side avenues, it required an hour or more to go from down town to Forty-Second Street; and during snow storms there were often several days of suspended animation, except for foot-passengers.

— *The New New York,* 1909

Sigrid Harald — Monday evening

"He appears to have been stunned with a blow on the head and then strangled with his own necktie," Cohen said. The assistant ME stripped off his latex gloves and indicated to the others that he was finished with his examination of Antoine Clarke's body for now. "I've bagged his hands, but there are no lacerations on his neck and no obvious sign of someone else's skin under his nails."

"Time of death?" Sigrid asked, watching

as they tried to fit the young elevator man's contorted body into a body bag before strapping it onto the gurney.

"Won't know till I open him up. At least twenty-four hours, though."

"He's been missing since yesterday morning around nine o'clock."

"That fits. Rigor appears to be relaxing in the legs, but there's still a lot of stiffness in his torso, so he may well have died then. If someone can tell us they saw him eat a doughnut or a ham sandwich around that time, it would help us pinpoint it further."

Sigrid turned to Lowry and Albee. "First thing tomorrow morning, talk to the night elevator operator. Horvath," she told them. "See if he has anything else to say about when Clarke relieved him yesterday morning. And ask him what he knows about Corey Wall."

"You looking to tag the Wall boy with this, Lieutenant?" Elaine Albee asked.

"He was blackmailing Clarke and he disappeared at the exact same time. In the middle of a snowstorm. If he's not involved, why did he run?"

Which was exactly what Sigrid had asked Mrs. Wall when she and Hentz spoke to her a half hour earlier. They had put it more tactfully, of course, and the woman, still shocked by another violent death in the building, had not immediately realized that Corey might be involved. Her worry was that her son's disappearance meant he was in danger, too.

"I've called both of our daughters. One's at MIT, the other's at Stanford. Neither of them have heard from him."

The delayed discovery of the body meant that half of Manhattan could have passed through the basement since yesterday morning, and with the victim so neatly bagged for them, there was little for the crime scene unit to process.

Before letting the porters go, they had taken Vlad Ruzicka's dramatized statement as well as that of the other porter, one Hector Laureano, fifty-eight, employed there for eleven years.

Both seemed to be reeling from Antoine's death and both claimed not to have seen Antoine since quitting time on Friday. "He got off at four and we stay till five," Laureano said. He had not noticed the Wall boy with Antoine, and no, he really didn't know much about the day man at all. "He hasn't been here very long."

"What about Corey Wall?"

"He was just another kid," said Laureano. "Back when he was little, one of his sisters would bring him down to get their bikes and take him riding in the park. Haven't seen much of him since he got old enough to take trains and buses by himself."

Vlad Ruzicka, on the other hand, seemed to regret his lack of more exciting things to tell them. Watching his dramatic arm gestures as he acted out the little he did know, Sigrid was privately amused to remember that Hentz had called him Vlad the Regaler. Clearly the man wished he could hand them a head or two on a pike.

"I knew we had five of them wheely bins, but only four were here. I even checked all twelve landings. So I started looking back there in the storage area and there it was! Hiding behind a kayak and some skis."

His broad flat face expressed first the puzzlement he'd felt and then the surprise of his discovery.

"Swear to God I was starting to think it was Antoine killed Phil, that maybe he thought Phil was out to get him fired for something. Antoine needed this job even though he always acted like it wasn't good enough for him. Like he ought to've been a headwaiter in some fancy restaurant or something."

For a moment, the big bulky man became a mincing maître d' with his nose in the air and his eyes at half-mast as he looked down his nose at them.

When asked again about the last time he saw Clarke, he described how he had helped one of the residents get two heavy suitcases down to the street and into a cab on Friday. "As God is my witness, each bag weighed as least fifty pounds. 'What?' I asked her. 'You going for two months?' 'No,' she said. 'Two weeks.' And it wasn't even for a wedding."

After he had slammed the trunk lid on the cab and started down the sidewalk to the service entrance, he saw Antoine pull some bills from his wallet and give them to the Wall boy. "There was still plenty of daylight left, so I saw at least two bills, but I couldn't tell if they were fives or fifties."

"Did Corey give him anything in return?"

"Not that I saw." He pantomimed putting money in his pants pocket and giving it a satisfied pat. "Then he walked on up toward West End Avenue. Antoine passed me on the way to his train and I said I hoped he had a good weekend. 'Yeah, right,' he said and that was that. Who could know?" Ruzicka's face turned so mournful they almost expected to see tears. "Last words I ever heard him say."

It was now 7:15 and Sigrid was ready to

call it a day. Urbanska had left an hour ago to take the red flip-flop with Judge Knott's earring to the lab and to issue a be on the lookout for Corey Wall as a "person of interest." Lowry volunteered to check the car back into the motor pool for Hentz, and Albee went with him.

"Didn't you tell Buntrock you were playing tonight at some jazz club down in the Village?" Sigrid asked Hentz.

He gave her a wary nod.

"I'm headed home that way. If you want a lift, it'll give us a chance to discuss this case."

When he hesitated, she shrugged. "Or not. I have to go back upstairs. I must have left a glove in the lobby."

He followed her up the service steps. As she retrieved her glove from the couch, the front elevator doors opened for the Bryants, who seemed to be dressed for an evening out. Gone was the judge's disheveled look of this afternoon. Her sandy blonde hair fell smoothly around her face and she had given it a spritz of gold shine. A smoky blue eye shadow enhanced her clear blue eyes, and her lipstick was the same bright red as the cowl-necked sweater she had worn Saturday night. A dressier pair of gold earrings gleamed in the soft lights of the lobby.

There was a time when Sigrid would not have noticed what another woman was wearing or else would have been intimidated if the woman was as confidently attractive as this judge appeared to be. Although Grandmother Lattimore seemed to love her as much as her other granddaughters, she had bluntly voiced her doubts that such an ugly duckling could ever evolve into the swan every other Lattimore woman became, as if beauty were a birthright. Even when they were not classically beautiful, they carried themselves as if they were, and a willing world agreed.

"You're already too tall and your neck is too long, but you have nice eyes and they do say you're going to be real intelligent," her grandmother had said with a sigh when Sigrid was twelve or thirteen and nothing but skinny arms and legs.

It took Oscar Nauman to make her apply that intelligence to her looks, to realize that making the most of one's physical assets was not some arcane mathematical problem. For years, she had worn her fine dark hair pulled straight back into a utilitarian bun. Then, on an impulse, she had gotten it cut short so that it feathered across her forehead and softened her brow. After that, she read a couple of books, looked at some online tutorials, and experimented with light makeup that could and would enhance her high cheekbones and wide gray eyes. She learned that lip paint would last all day, and that some colors flattered her clear pale skin while others would make her look washed out. It was only an exercise in logic after all, she told herself, much like the puzzle rings she collected and put together when working through the intricacies of a homicide case.

Once she figured it out, she tossed half her wardrobe, invested in good makeup brushes, and gradually accepted that she could hold her own in that competition. She would never be as conventionally curvaceous and pretty as Elaine Albee or Lady Francesca Leeds, Nauman's former lover, or even this Deborah Knott, but knowing that he had found her as intriguing as any Dürer model was enough to give her a modicum of confidence.

"Lieutenant Harald! Sigrid," the judge said now, greeting her with a sympathetic smile. "Dwight told me about Antoine. How awful! After what Mrs. Lundigren told me this afternoon, I was sure he was the one who killed her husband. And now he's been killed himself?"

"Mrs. Lundigren? She talked to you?"

Hentz asked, bemused. He had no doubt that this woman could slather Southern charm around, but was charm enough to overcome Denise Lundigren's social anxiety disorder?

"Weird, isn't it? Everyone says she's shy with strangers, but her doctor must have given her one hell of a happy pill, because she wasn't a bit shy with me."

She saw her husband check his watch and she tucked her arm in his as he edged toward the door. "Sorry to rush off, Sigrid, but we're meeting your friend Elliott Buntrock for dinner down in the Village and we're going to be late if we don't keep moving."

"Elliott?" Sigrid asked, following them out to the sidewalk.

"The Village?" Hentz asked. He gestured to a late-model sedan parked at the snowy curb nearby. In the dim light, they saw an official NYPD sticker on the back fender. A card read NYPD OFFICIAL BUSINESS on the flipped-down sun visor, not that anyone needed to worry about tickets and tow trucks when so many illegally parked vehicles were still plowed under. "Lieutenant Harald's going our way," he said smoothly, "and she's offered me a lift."

Before Sigrid quite knew what was happening, they were waiting for her to unlock the car. Minutes later, she was headed down Eleventh Avenue with the other three chattering as if they had known each other for years.

Encouraged to tell them of her visit to Denise Lundigren, Deborah repeated what the woman had said about Antoine, how more things had disappeared from various apartments than what she had stolen, and how Phil Lundigren had found the elevator man in parts of the building where he had no business being after his shift was over. "She said he used to take cigarette breaks and then lied about it."

"That's probably how Corey Wall was able to hijack the elevator so many times," Hentz told Sigrid.

"Do people in the building know that Mrs. Lundigren is a klepto?" Deborah asked. "Don't they care?"

"For the most part, it sounds fairly benign," Sigrid said. "And something they were willing to put up with because Lundigren was such a sterling super. That's how that Mexican cat wound up in your apartment, though. Lundigren knew she'd cleaned there Friday morning. What he forgot was that she'd also cleaned for Luna DiSimone on Saturday morning."

Deborah, who was seated in front beside Sigrid, turned to look at Hentz, who sat behind Sigrid. "The other things that were stolen — is there any way Antoine could have gotten into those apartments?"

It was Sigrid who answered. "According to one of the porters, the locks on most of the service doors have never been changed."

"So who better than the man on the elevator to know when an apartment would be empty?" Deborah said excitedly.

Sigrid slowed to veer around a truck that had suddenly and with no warning decided to stop and double park in their lane. Till then she had caught several green lights in a row. The small delay meant that she had to speed up to get back into the flow, but a red light caught her in the next block. "Maybe Corey didn't hijack the elevator as often as Antoine Clarke claimed," she mused as she waited for the light to change.

Hentz saw where her thoughts were going. "Clarke could've slipped out of the elevator, onto the service landing, and been in and out of an apartment in minutes, then if anyone saw him, he could say that he was looking for the elevator."

Sigrid finished the thought for him. "Corey probably saw him, realized what was happening, and started blackmailing him."

327

"Corey was blackmailing Antoine?" Deborah asked. "Why?"

From the backseat, Dwight Bryant said, "Is the kid into drugs?"

Sigrid's eyes met his in the rearview mirror. Normally she would not have discussed a case with an outsider, but this murder had been committed in their apartment, he had helped take names Saturday night before reinforcements came, and he was, after all, an officer of the court, as was, of course, his wife. "Not drugs, Major. Poker. He's a gambler, a compulsive one from the sound of it. He's stolen so much from his family so that they've put locks on their bedroom doors and his parents have blocked his online access to poker sites, but his friend says he's still playing live games someplace in the area at least once a week."

"Ah," said Deborah, who nodded in understanding. "Therefore the need to blackmail Antoine instead of turning him in. After talking to Mrs. Lundigren, I thought maybe Antoine had killed her husband because Lundigren walked in on him while he was loading his pockets in our apartment. Could that still be the case?"

"Unless it was Corey Wall that Lundigren walked in on and the kid panicked," Sigrid said. "Clarke was in the building, if not in the apartment itself. It's possible that he was in the back hall and saw Corey slip out of the apartment through the service door."

"This could be a blackmailing standoff that left Clarke dead," Hentz said thoughtfully. "Corey was certainly at the party, so he could have seen that your door wasn't locked and decided to see what he could pick up to feed his gambling habit."

"That latch is getting worse, too," Deborah said. "Dwight, maybe you could take a look at it tomorrow? See if something could be tightened? I had to pull it to twice before I was sure it was locked."

An ambulance with siren wailing and lights flashing roared through the intersection at West 23rd and Sigrid had to brake sharply to avoid clipping its back bumper. A minute or two later, she turned onto West 14th. One of her rear tires hit a patch of ice at the curb and the car almost fishtailed into a delivery van in the next lane.

"Whoa!" Deborah said as Sigrid quickly corrected. "Good reflexes."

White-knuckled, Sigrid slowed as she tried to decide which of these branching streets would lead her to the West Village restaurant Buntrock had selected.

"He said for us to get off the train at Christopher and walk north on Seventh

Avenue," Bryant said as they all began peering through the windows.

"Must be near the club," Hentz said.

"There it is!" Deborah cried, pointing to a sign two doors off Seventh.

Sigrid signaled to turn. Miraculously, a car pulled out directly across the street from the restaurant and she slid her own car into the spot.

Helped along by rock salt and the day's weak sunshine, the street itself appeared almost completely ice-free, but dirty gray snow was still piled along the curb and had frozen back into ice so that Dwight's boots crunched on it when he got out to hold the door for Deborah.

As they were thanking Sigrid for the ride, Elliott Buntrock rounded the corner on foot and a big smile lit up his bony face.

"Perfect timing," he called, his open overcoat and scarf flapping in the wind like the wings of a giant heron. "I was afraid I was going to be late. Sigrid? Aren't you staying?"

She lowered her window. "Hello, Elliott. No, I'm just their gypsy cab."

"But why not? You have to eat. Unless you have other plans?" He gave a crafty smile. "Or is Roman cooking something special tonight?"

"Oh, God, you're right. He did mention medallions of calf's liver poached in wine. When I left this morning, he was trying to decide whether merlot or chardonnay would go better with the capers and the green beans."

Deborah, who did not like calf's liver or green beans, made a face. "You're joking, right? Who's Roman?"

"My housemate, and no, I'm not joking. He's an inventive cook, but some of his inventions are bombs."

"At least he cooks," Buntrock said with a half smile, which Sigrid returned.

"Elliott's seen my collection of take-out menus," she said, turning to the others. "You sure you don't mind if I join you?" It had suddenly occurred to her that there would be more than one source of some specific information at the table.

The Bryants assured her that she was quite welcome. Hentz, however, looked a bit apprehensive.

"And we can all go on to Smalls later and hear Sam play," Elliott said.

Sigrid was amused to see the look of discomfort deepen on Hentz's face. Not quite enough revenge for his laughter when Captain Fortesque had led the singing of

"Happy Birthday, dear Sigrid" last February, but it was a start.

CHAPTER 21

The stranger passing from restaurant to restaurant in up-town New York after seven in the evening would be very apt to conclude that most of the city had given up house-keeping and was taking its meals "out." . . . The constant irritation over servants has driven many thousands to seek . . . eating accommodations in hotels and restaurants.

— *The New New York,* 1909

Sigrid Harald — Monday night
On this slow Monday night in January, the hostess at the Thai restaurant was quite willing to change Buntrock's reservation for three to a round table for five at the rear of the long narrow room.

"Ignore the décor," Buntrock said, breezily dismissing the scuffed chairs, the crazed mirrors, and the red-and-gold wall hangings that had long since lost whatever crisp charm they might have begun with. "Wait till you taste their tom yum goong and the peanut sauce they serve with their pad thai."

Hentz and Bryant wanted to try the Thai beer, so Buntrock ordered two Singhas for them and a bottle of white wine for the table.

After an animated discussion, they decided to make their meal from a variety of appetizers that they could share rather than full entrees. When the drinks arrived, Buntrock made a graceful toast to the not-so-newlywed honeymooners, then said, "Any luck recovering that Streichert maquette, Sigrid?"

She shook her head and Deborah, who was seated across from her next to Buntrock, gave a gurgle of laughter. "I forgot to tell you, Dwight. I finally remembered where I've seen Cameron Broughton before."

He recognized that mischievous expression on her face, took a sip of his beer, and leaned back in his chair, prepared to be entertained.

"It was about three years ago," she told Sigrid. "I was holding court down on the coast, in Wilmington, and he was one of four men who pleaded guilty to a D&D."

"Oh?"

"The drunk part was no surprise. They'd spent the evening inside the Salty Dog Bar down on the Cape Fear River Walk. The disorderly part came when they took it outside, dropped their pants, and invited passing tourists to judge whose was the biggest."

Buntrock laughed. "You weren't asked to rule on that aspect, too, were you?"

Her easy laughter joined his. "No, but the reason I remembered was that Luna DiSimone tells me that he has a thing for penile humor." Trying to use decorous language more suited to a dinner table, Deborah repeated Luna's description of the Venetian figurines Broughton collected. "If he was in our apartment that night, I doubt if he could have resisted that maquette."

"You saying he killed Lundigren?" Dwight asked.

Deborah shook her head. "Not for a minute. Lundigren probably didn't know him and he certainly wouldn't have known the maquette wasn't Broughton's. I think the killer maybe dropped it on the floor, Broughton came in and saw it, thought it would make a good addition to his collection, and simply walked out with it — maybe slipped it in his overcoat pocket when he passed the coat rack out in the hall."

"I'll invite Mr. Broughton to come talk to us tomorrow," Hentz said.

"Good," said Sigrid, who had maneuvered to sit next to Dwight Bryant. While his wife and Buntrock listened to Hentz describe how playing piano in a noisy bar made him feel like wallpaper, Sigrid steered the conversation to his work as a deputy sheriff. At a pause, she casually said, "By the way, who is Chloe Adams?"

"Chloe Adams? She's —" He broke off suddenly and looked at his wife, who had evidently been listening to both conversations.

"Didn't I tell you when you asked me that earlier?" Deborah asked contritely. "I'm sorry. I thought I did. She's related to a lot of cleaning women around town and comes in when they need an extra pair of hands. I expect she's working for your grandmother now. Kate said Mrs. Lattimore had decided to go through the house and dump a lot of stuff that's been accumulating."

Sigrid nodded. "That's what her note said." She glanced over at Buntrock. "I know you were wondering where she got that maquette, but she didn't say. Just that she knew it was awful when she got it and that she had forgotten it was in the attic till she saw that magazine article."

"Streichert's granddaughter — the one that gave that interview? She lives in L.A.," Buntrock said, "but she's scheduled to speak at the 92nd Street Y in a couple of weeks. If you've found that thing by then and still want to give it back to her, I think I could arrange a meeting."

"Sorry," Sigrid said. "If it really is the murder weapon, we'll have to hang on to it till it goes to trial."

Their food arrived and the conversation turned to the weather, snow removal, and the trouble Deborah's nephew was in over a suggestive picture taken with his phone and posted on his Facebook page. She described the kids who had the three lockers around the nephew's locker and they batted around suggestions as to how a jealous and horny teenage boy might have worked the scam.

From there, talk moved on to memorable meals and travel. Buntrock was the only one who had been to Bangkok, and they were amused to hear that when he was there a few years back, he had bought a recording made by the king of Thailand. "Believe it or not, he was a pretty good jazz musician. Back in the thirties, he even sat in on some sessions with Benny Goodman and Lionel

Hampton."

"You're kidding," Deborah said.

Buntrock raised his right hand in a Boy Scout salute. "Word of honor. He played the tenor sax."

"The kings of Siam have come a long way since Yul Brynner," Sigrid said dryly.

Shortly after nine, Sam Hentz stood up and said he had to go. He tried to pay Buntrock for his share of the dinner, but was waved off. "You can buy me a drink later."

"It's a deal." He buttoned his overcoat and wound his scarf around his neck. "See you at the club, then."

When he was gone, Sigrid forked another dumpling onto her plate and turned a jaundiced gaze on her putative cousin. "Okay, so who is Chloe Adams? The truth this time, if you don't mind."

Before Deborah could protest, Sigrid held up a slender hand to stop her. "When a wife kicks her husband under the table, it generally means that he's about to say something she doesn't want him to."

Buntrock looked puzzled, but Dwight gave a rueful smile. "You got that right."

"So far as I know, domestic help doesn't come in on Sundays to clean, do they? Not in the South anyhow."

"Look," Deborah said quietly. "Let's talk about this later, okay?"

Buntrock put his fork down. "Shall I leave?"

"Why?" Sigrid asked. "You already know most of my secrets, Elliott, and I'm sure Major Bryant knows what this is about. True, Major?"

"You might as well tell her, shug."

Deborah was clearly conflicted. "All right," she said at last. "She made Kate promise not to tell any of you, but Chloe Adams is an LPN."

"As in licensed practical nurse?"

Deborah nodded.

Sigrid frowned. "What's wrong with my grandmother?"

"She's dying," Deborah said bluntly. "Her cancer's back."

"What?"

"I'm sorry."

Sigrid's frown deepened. "I don't understand. She had surgery and chemo six years ago, but at Thanksgiving she told us she was still clean."

"She lied. Kate says it came roaring back last summer and the doctors said more surgery would be useless."

"But chemo . . . radiation —"

"Chemo and radiation are precisely why

she hasn't told y'all. She's afraid you'll try to badger her into it. Her exact words to Kate were that she didn't want to spend the last year of her life bald and throwing up just so she could have an extra two months, and that's about all the doctors could promise her if she took the treatments."

"That sounds like Grandmother," Sigrid said as the implications sank in. "She wanted all of us there for Thanksgiving and one of my aunts kept saying she looked a little tired, but we thought it was because of too much company and overdoing on the dinner. She was supposed to go to my Denver aunt's for Christmas, but at the last minute she said she had a minor ear infection and didn't want to fly. That wasn't true either, was it?"

"I'm afraid not."

Sigrid sighed and gave a wry smile. "Poor Grandmother. She does know her daughters, though. Mother will understand, but both my aunts will be on the next plane when they hear about it. I can't blame her for not wanting a fight if her mind's made up. How long does she have?"

"I'm sorry. I really don't know. Maybe March or April?"

"So soon?" For a moment she looked bereft. "Then it really *is* too late for the aunts to do anything, isn't it?" She pushed her plate away and looked at her watch. "What time is it in New Zealand? I'd better let my mother know. She'll want to go down and spend some time with her. And she can help fend off the others."

"It's great that you'll have a chance to say goodbye to her while she's still in control of her life," Deborah said. Her voice wobbled and Dwight reached for her hand.

Sigrid frowned. "Deborah?"

"Sorry." Her blue eyes glistened with unshed tears. "My mother died the summer I turned eighteen. She had chemotherapy, radiation, the whole nine yards, and she was so miserably sick at the end. Weak and nauseated. And it only bought her a few extra weeks of life. I think Mrs. Lattimore's made a better choice."

Sigrid nodded. "Grandmother's always been a realist."

Buntrock poured the last of the wine into Sigrid's glass and handed it to her. She took a small sip, then set the glass back on the table and reached for her coat. "I'm sorry if this has ruined your dinner party, Elliott, but I'm going to take a pass on jazz. Tell Hentz I'll see him tomorrow."

"You didn't ruin a thing." He stood and held her coat for her. "Want me to drive you home?"

"Thanks but no thanks. Besides, you've had more wine than I did." She turned to the others. "Thanks for telling me, Deborah."

They watched her walk away and Elliott said, "I don't suppose you guys feel like hearing jazz tonight, either?"

"Sorry," Deborah said. "I really don't. Dwight? If you want to stay, I can get a cab back."

"We'll both get a cab back," Dwight said.

CHAPTER 22

Such criminals as these seem more cunning than brutal, but perhaps they are more dangerous for that very reason.
— *The New New York,* 1909

Sigrid Harald — Monday night (continued)
When Sigrid crossed the small shadowy courtyard from the gate to her front door, the streetlight on the corner picked out a blackened saucepan lying in the snow, its contents turned to charcoal. She let herself in to find Roman stacking the dishwasher. An odor of burned meat and vegetables permeated the entry hall and kitchen. Both the range hood and the guest bathroom off the hall had their exhaust fans running full blast.

"Did it again, hmm?" Sigrid said, hanging her coat and scarf in the hall closet.

"We really must install more smoke alarms," Roman said, a sheepish look on his face. "By the time I smelled smoke, the liver was burned to a crisp, and the beans! Well, you must have seen the pan? Completely ruined."

"The book's going well, then?" Her house-mate's rooms lay beyond the laundry and utility room. When he plugged into his iPod and lost himself in his writing, a dozen fire engines could roll past and he would hear nothing, certainly not a smoke alarm over in this part of the house.

"*Was* going well. *Was,* my dear, until I hit such a tremendous roadblock, and that's when I finally noticed the smoke. Too late to save even a morsel, I fear. Have you dined? I could whip up something."

"No, I've eaten, thank you. Elliott invited me to join him, along with that couple I told you about, the ones that know my grandmother."

"The visitors who found a body in that apartment Saturday night?" Roman pushed the start button on the dishwasher, untied the apron from his ample waist, and hung it on a peg in the pantry. "The nine o'clock news said that there's been a second murder in that same building. Is it true?"

"I'm afraid so."

"In a *garbage* bag?"

His fastidiousness made Sigrid smile. "It

was a clean garbage bag."

Which in turn drew a rueful smile from him. "I suppose that *did* sound a bit Lady Bracknell-ish. And I do know that murder isn't a sanitized drawing room comedy. All the same, my dear, *finally!* A homicide that isn't open and shut! I want to hear every detail."

He plucked two goblets from the cupboard, extracted a corkscrew from a nearby drawer, and led the way to the living room. "We shall have a glass of the merlot I marinated the liver in and you can tell me all about it. Perhaps something will trigger a solution to my roadblock."

"I thought your plot involved the poisoning of a dean at a woman's college," Sigrid protested. "The death of an apartment super and an elevator operator is nothing like that. Besides, it probably *is* open and shut. We're looking for one of the tenants, a teenage boy with a gambling problem who was blackmailing the last victim and who hasn't been seen since."

"One never knows," he said.

She accepted the wine he poured for her and settled onto the couch, not entirely reluctant to rehash the facts. Soon she would have to go to her computer and tell her mother the bad news. For the moment, though, she would relax and indulge his curiosity about her work.

Ever since he wound up in the middle of a murder in a children's dance theater, Roman's quirky logic had often cast a new light on her cases. Summing up the sequence of events would clarify things for her as well. So she began with Deborah Knott's phone call on Saturday and ended with finding the day man in one of those industrial-size trash bags, ready to be set out on the curb. Without mentioning Lundigren's true gender, she described his wife's kleptomania and psychological problems and her insistence that there was another thief in the building. "We'd begun to think he was both the other thief and the killer. Instead, he's another victim."

"And the boy you thought was the victim is now your prime suspect?"

"I'm afraid so."

"Not one of the other workmen in the building?"

"Sidney Jackson, the evening man, lives in Queens and was on duty during the party. He left before midnight and didn't return till he was called to come in Sunday morning. He lives alone, but he gave us the name of the all-night deli where he stopped on the way home and the name of the café where he was eating breakfast when the call came. The night man, Jani Horvath, was there on Saturday night before the super was killed and he was there when Antoine Clarke was killed. He's getting old and he says he immediately went to bed when Clarke relieved him. We haven't confirmed either alibi yet, and we don't have motives for them, although . . ."

"Although what?" Tramegra asked, pouncing on her hesitation.

"Horvath's in his sixties and he had the day shift until shortly after Clarke was hired, when they switched shifts. It was supposed to be a mutually agreeable change. We've been told that tips are better on the day shift, but that there's more work, more heavy lifting, and he has a bad back. Now I wonder whose idea it was to make the switch and whether Horvath really didn't mind giving up the extra tips."

"What about the super's wife?"

"She could have followed him upstairs and smashed him with that bronze sculpture, but she was in the hospital when Clarke was killed and it's a stretch to think we have two killers on our hands."

"Residents?"

"No love lost between the super and the people who live in the apartment directly overhead. In fact they're being evicted and blame the super. Unfortunately, they have a solid alibi for the time of the super's death. So far, Corey Wall's looking good for both murders. He needs money for gambling. He crashed the party and could have realized this was a good opportunity to loot a fresh apartment. Let's say Lundigren caught him there, threatened to have him arrested. The boy hits him with the sculpture and runs out the service door. Either Antoine sees him leave or somehow figures it out. Next morning, when he starts down to go sledding, Antoine lets him know that the tables are turned. It could be a Mexican standoff — 'You turn me in for stealing, I'll say you killed Phil' — or Antoine realizes that murder trumps larceny and tries to blackmail Corey, whereupon Corey kills him, panics, and stashes the body in one of those wheeled bins and hopes it won't be found till he's long gone. He's just a kid, so it wasn't well thought out. Both murders were probably unpremeditated impulses."

Tramegra frowned and topped off their glasses. "Not much mystery there," he objected.

"It's not one of your novels," Sigrid conceded. "But I've told you before, Roman. Real homicides are usually open and shut. Corey Wall will be picked up in the next few days. He'll be charged and he will eventually be found guilty. It's as simple as that. The only puzzle left is who took the sculpture, and we even have a possible for that."

Roman sniffed. "Maybe that's how *your* case will end. I've just realized that the killer in *my* case is the least likely person. The dean's secretary. She's been in almost every scene, but no one's paid her any attention because she's homely and timid. She was tired of the dean flirting with all the honor students and he ignored her so completely that it was both insulting *and* a constant ir-ritant."

Amused, Sigrid shook her head. "You got that out of our discussion?"

"The subconscious works in mysterious ways," he said airily. He poured the last of the wine into his own glass and rose. "I shall go write the chapter now while it's still perfectly clear in my head."

Ready to tackle personal matters, Sigrid sat down at the computer in her bedroom. As near as she could figure it, New Zealand was about sixteen hours ahead of New York, which probably meant that it was tomorrow afternoon there. Happily, there was a note from Anne that had been sent only minutes before, which might signal that her mother still had her laptop on. She immediately sent a message: "You there? We need to talk."

Back came: "We were just on our way out for drinks. Whassup?"

As concisely as possible, Sigrid repeated what Deborah Knott had told her and pressed the send button.

While she waited for a reply, Sigrid looked at her own calendar. The long leave of absence she had taken after Nauman's death had used up all of the time she had accumulated, but at the moment she had a new balance of thirty-four days.

And Grandmother's balance? Two months? Three?

By the time she had brushed her teeth and was ready for bed, there was a final message from Anne: "We'll see about changing our plane reservations first thing tomorrow."

CHAPTER 23

. . . the refuse from them makes the streets appear unkempt and uncared for.
— *The New New York,* 1909

Upon leaving Elliott, Dwight and I decided it would be just as easy, and certainly a lot cheaper and quicker, to walk over to Seventh Avenue and take the subway uptown. Even though it was cold, cold, cold, the wind had died down for the moment and walking was not too unpleasant as long as we held on to each other and avoided the worst of the ice.

The subway was half empty and we immediately found seats, but when we pulled into the Times Square stop several minutes later, Dwight suddenly grabbed my hand.

"C'mon," he said, and hurried me out of the train and up the steps into the neon exuberance of New York's theater district.

Most of the theaters are closed on Mondays, but those that were open were just letting out and the streets were thronged with people despite the bitter cold.

Dwight smiled down into my dazzled eyes and waved his hand to encompass the whole display. "I got 'em to turn everything on just for you."

"Oh, Major Bryant!" I laughed and stood on tiptoes to kiss him. "You shouldn't have!"

Grinning happily at my country bumpkin delight and pleased with himself for thinking of it, he stationed himself by a light pole right where Seventh and Broadway intersect at West 42nd Street and I leaned into his comfortable bulk to enjoy the blinking lights, the waterfalls of cascading LEDs, the riotous colors, the eye-popping whites. Brilliant blues and pure yellows chased each other up the front of buildings and erupted in a gush of green at the top. Reds and oranges blazed across the electric billboards. Garish razzamatazz brilliance dazzled my eyes and intoxicated my senses. Except for Dwight's strong arms around me, I would have gone reeling into the street, drunk with the explosion of flashing lights and color. It was Fourth of July fireworks without the bangs, a thousand overly decorated Christmas trees without the carols, and the perfect antidote for the sadness I felt for Sigrid and

352

Mrs. Lattimore.

"I want one of everything for our pond house," I told him when I had looked my fill.

"Dream on, kid." He acts appalled by my desire for neon bar signs, and maybe he's not pretending, but when we do get around to building some sort of screened structure next to the farm pond where we swim and fish in the summertime, I'm determined to wallpaper one side of it with the signs I've started collecting.

We found a place where we could sit with a cup of coffee and watch people passing who seemed oblivious to the lights that blazed overhead. Eventually, we threaded our way over to the bus stop and trundled up Broadway to Columbus Circle and on past Lincoln Center, ablaze in its own flood-lights.

We got off at our stop, and as we walked up the street to our building, I couldn't help noticing all the bags of garbage piled along the curb and remembered that Phil Lundigren had told us that first night that pickups were on Tuesday, Thursday, and Saturday mornings.

"If the porter hadn't found Antoine's body before it got loaded onto a garbage truck, it probably never would have been found," Dwight said. "Just wound up in a landfill somewhere."

Sidney was standing inside the lobby when we got there and he held the inner door open for us. He looked drawn and less dapper than when we'd first met. The night man was seated in one of the lobby chairs.

"Jani Horvath," Sidney said, introducing us.

Horvath was the oldest of the elevator men we had yet met, with thick white hair and an even thicker white mustache. He gave us a neutral look and nodded acknowledgment, but said nothing.

Once inside the elevator, I asked, "Any word on the missing Wall boy?"

"No, and his mother's going crazy," Sidney said heavily.

Once we were on our way up, Sidney told us that the building was buzzing with fear and speculation. Two men dead and a teenage boy missing?

"Half the people think Corey killed them both and the other half think one of the residents has turned into a homicidal maniac. They make me wait until they've unlocked their doors and got inside safely." He shook his head in uncertainty. "I'm not really nervous, but it does get pretty deserted here after eleven on a weeknight.

Jani's feeling it, too. That's why he's up in the lobby instead of down in the basement. He's not looking forward to his shift."

He stopped the elevator at the sixth floor and pulled back the brass gate. "If you don't mind me asking, I saw you two leave with those detectives . . . they don't really think Corey killed Antoine, do they?"

"They won't know till they talk to him," Dwight said.

"I hear he was blackmailing Antoine because Antoine killed Phil, but that's crazy. He's just a kid. I've known him since he was in his stroller. He's no killer."

"Then why'd he run?"

"Because he's scared?"

"If he's scared, why doesn't he go to the police? Or call his parents?"

Sidney's slender shoulders drooped. "Yeah. That's what I keep asking myself, too."

While Dwight brushed and flossed, I checked my email. There were routine messages from friends and colleagues and six or eight messages from the nieces and nephews. Emma wrote that their mother was taking it better than they had expected. Barbara totally believed Lee but had ruled that he couldn't post anything else on his Facebook page until it was shown who was responsible for that suggestive picture.

I clicked over to the site and saw that Lee had written in all caps: SUSPENDED UNTIL I FIND OUT WHO HACKED ME.

Ashley said she believed him, too, but she didn't want to go out with him again and had given him back his FFA jacket.

They had questioned Jamie Benton and Mark McLamb, who had the adjoining lockers, and the freshman girl who had the locker below his. They believed the girl when she claimed to have seen nothing — "She's a clueless freshman, for Pete's sake," wrote seventeen-year-old cousin Jessica, a junior — but they were convinced the two boys knew more than they were saying. They reported, only half facetiously, that they had even examined Lee's locker with a flashlight (à la *CSI*) and a magnifying glass (à la Sherlock Holmes) and found no sign of tampering with screwdriver or hacksaw.

A.K., eighteen and a senior, thought perhaps someone had switched locks, substituting his own for Lee's, but Lee insisted he had opened the lock with his own combination both before and after his lunch period and both times he had relocked it and twirled the dial on the lock.

One thing Lee did say was that he now

believed someone had opened his locker and gone through his things a time or two before. "I can't say how, but sometimes things look a little different. I thought I was getting absentminded, but maybe I wasn't."

The subject of their last email of the evening was "News Flash." Emma wrote that she'd just learned that Jamie Benton had asked Ashley out right before she and Lee started going together. "More tomorrow."

Dwight joined me on the bed and I passed my laptop over to him to let him check his mail while I went through my own bedtime routine.

When I returned, Dwight turned the screen around so I could read Cal's message.

"Aunt Kate took me over to Granddaddy's to see Bandit and then she let me bring him back with me. Trooper's mean to him and growls a lot. He hopes Saturday gets here fast." It was signed with a full line of X's and O's.

Kate had written, "Trooper does snarl every time he sees Bandit, but Cal's getting homesick for you two so I thought it would help to have his dog here. He's asleep now with his arms around Bandit."

"That was nice of her," I said. Truth to

tell, I was starting to miss Cal, too.

We turned off the lights and lay awake a few minutes trying to decide what we wanted to do next day. For Christmas, Dwight's mother had given us mock tickets to a Broadway play and a check large enough to buy real tickets, but we hadn't decided what we wanted to see. Comedy or drama?

"Nothing too heavy," Dwight said sleepily.

"Musical?" I asked.

He yawned. "Anything except *Mamma Mia!* Okay?"

"We could just go down to the TKTS booth and toss a dart at the list," I said, but he was gone.

I should have been sleepy, too. I *was* sleepy, but even though I nestled in next to Dwight, I couldn't seem to turn my brain off. I kept thinking about Lee and how someone seemed to be getting into his locker at will. If Emma was right, if the Benton boy was the one who did it, he might be afraid to admit it. Not only was Jenny Benton overprotective, she also had a wide streak of prudery. She would probably be horrified to think that her son had any idea what a girl's nude anatomy looked like. If he did it, was it because he was jealous of Lee or was it simply an adolescent joke?

Like Corey Wall taking the elevator when it was left unattended?

The digital clock beside the bed clicked from 11:45 to 11:46. When it hit 11:53, I slipped out of bed. No need to switch on any lamps; the reflected glow from outside was more than enough to let me navigate the rooms. I went out to the kitchen and opened the refrigerator, but I wasn't really hungry and none of the little boxes or packets tempted me. Instead, I poured myself half a glass of wine from the opened bottle on the counter and wandered back to the living room. Too cold to go out onto the balcony, but I stood by the French doors that let me see a small sliver of upper Broadway where traffic had dwindled to a few cars and cabs.

The street below me seemed almost as deserted as the lanes that crisscross the farm back home, yet even as I watched, a cab slowed to a stop in front of the building across the way. I moved to the dining room window for an unobstructed look and saw a couple emerge from the cab. The woman wore an evening cape and a long gown. With his back to me, I couldn't tell if the man was wearing a tux underneath his overcoat, but that was certainly a white silk scarf draped around his neck. Fred and Ginger home from a formal party?

I was amused by the juxtaposition of elegance and ugliness as he helped her from the cab. The space immediately out front was clear enough for her high heels and his patent leather shoes, but dirty snow still lined the curbs on either side of the polished glass door and large black bags of garbage were piled atop the snow by the service entrances of all the buildings from one end of the street to the other. I counted six bags from this building alone. Trying to multiply the garbage on this one street by the number of streets in the city numbed my brain. I sipped my wine and I wondered how many trucks it would take every day and what did they do with so much trash? Where was it all dumped? Or was it incinerated?

I vaguely remembered that when I'd lived here with Lev a million years ago, there had been controversy over landfills in the Brooklyn marshes, but surely they had long since reached capacity?

And why was I standing here in the middle of the night wondering about New York's garbage?

My glass was empty but I still wasn't sleepy. Okay, another half glass ought to do it, I decided.

When I returned to the window, I saw a

figure turn the corner onto Broadway. A moment later, the man on duty across the way stepped out onto the sidewalk and flexed his arms as if to get the stiffness out. He seemed to be waiting for something, and sure enough, down the block from West End Avenue came a slender dark-haired woman with a beagle on a leash. She paused to toss a small bag onto their pile of garbage, then the night man held the door for them and followed them back inside.

One thing about living in the country, you don't have to walk your dog and you don't have to pick up after it.

A cab moved slowly down the street, its headlights bouncing off the shiny trash bags and making the sidewalks sparkle as if dusted by glitter. Glassphalt. Made from recycled glass. Before I could start trying to estimate how much waste glass the city must generate, I finished my wine and went back to bed.

Just before I fell asleep, I found myself remembering Lee's comment that he thought someone had been in his locker before today. "I can't say how, but sometimes things look a little different," he had written.

Right. Thinking of how messy my own high school locker had been, I yawned and drifted off wondering how he could possibly tell.

It was still dark and the digital clock read 6:23 when I opened my eyes. I lay there quietly for a moment trying to grasp why I was awake. It was almost as if I had heard Lee's voice say, *"Things look a little different."*
Huh?
I closed my eyes and was almost asleep again when it finally registered.
Quietly, so as not to wake Dwight, I got up and went back to the living room. Without switching on any lights, I went straight to the window, looked out, and saw that I was right.
Last night, I had counted the garbage bags in front of this building's service entrance. I had then gone into the kitchen, poured myself a second glass of wine, and returned to this window to watch a cab come down the street. Its headlights had thrown the bags in sharp relief, enough to subliminally register a small change.
I carefully counted. Seven large black garbage bags were now heaped on the curb where before there had only been six.
My first impulse was to wake Dwight.
My second impulse was to call Sigrid Harald.

My third impulse, motivated by not wanting to appear melodramatic and stupid, was the one I acted on.

Even though I couldn't imagine why someone would lug another garbage bag out to the street in the middle of the night when there were no porters on duty, this *was* New York and what did I know? Maybe the person I'd seen disappearing around the corner earlier was a doctor responding to a late-night emergency, someone who suddenly realized he'd missed the evening garbage collection and decided to drop it off on his way out. And wouldn't I look like the village idiot if I woke Dwight or Sigrid because someone had added a bag of dirty diapers, vegetable peelings, and coffee grounds to the bags already there?

I stepped into my boots and slipped a parka on over my sweatshirt and warm-up pants. Out in the hall I started to ring for the elevator. Then I pictured Dwight leaning over my coffin to say, *"If you didn't want to feel stupid, what made you get into an elevator with the only employee still in the building? The one man who was known to be here when both Lundigren and Clarke were killed?"*

Too late then to say, *"Whoever heard of a killer in a walrus mustache?"*

So I opened the door to the service land-ing instead. I was briefly tempted to use the self-service back elevator. Sidney had told us that Jani Horvath usually slept during the long quiet hours of the night, but I didn't want to risk his hearing any mechani-cal rumbling. As quietly as possible, I crept down the stairs and past the first floor to the basement, where I eased open the automatic door into a dim and shadowy hallway that had only a security light to show me the way to the outer door. The instant I heard the door click shut behind me, I realized that I'd made a dumb mis-take. Sure enough, when I tried to open the door, it was securely locked.

Damn!

"This could be a problem," said my internal preacher.

"You think?" said the pragmatist, shaking his head at my stupidity.

No big deal. I would check out that seventh bag. If I was right, I could dash into the hotel down the street and call the police. If I was wrong, then I could wait till I saw someone approach the front door and slip in with them. Safety in numbers. This was New York. The City That Never Sleeps. Surely this building included early risers, morning joggers, coffee fiends. Dwight would never have to know how silly I'd been.

To my horror, I heard the front elevator descending to the basement.

I quickly retreated back around the corner and pressed myself against the wall.

The door swooshed open, followed by the sound of the brass gate being pulled back. Someone — Horvath? — shuffled across the hall. I risked a quick look and saw Horvath's white head and broad back disappear down a hall opposite the elevator doors. For one mad moment, I felt like pulling a Corey Wall and stealing the elevator.

"Yeah, right," jeered the pragmatist. *"An elevator with no buttons to push and an accordion gate to close first."*

Several minutes later from somewhere down that other hall came the sound of a flushing toilet, then footsteps back to the elevator. More door closings and the car rose again.

I realized I seemed to have stopped breathing and took huge breaths of air to calm myself.

When I reached the outer door, I carefully slipped one of my gloves between the door and the lock on the jamb so that I could get back in if I needed to.

There was a narrow areaway and a steep

ramp that led up to street level. At the top of the ramp was a gate made of steel bars, but it wasn't locked and I passed easily out onto the sidewalk. The air was bitter cold, and down on Broadway an ambulance went shrieking by. That way was east and I fancied that the sky looked lighter there.

From two blocks away, toward the river, I saw flashing lights and the roar of a heavy engine — a garbage truck making early morning pickups and coming this way.

I moved over to the pile of black bags and quickly ran my hands over the chilled plastic. Nothing odd about the first bag, but the second one atop the pile sent a frisson of horror through me as I realized that my hand had found a shoe, a shoe that felt as if it was attached to something.

"Mrs. Bryant? What are you doing? Did you lose something?"

I turned and was relieved to see a different brown uniform and friendly face.

"Thank God!"

I'm sure I was white as new-fallen snow, and he looked alarmed.

"You okay? You look like you've seen a ghost."

"In the bag!" I gibbered. "There's another body in that bag!"

"What?"

"Feel," I told him, guiding his hand over that foot.

He touched it and immediately jerked his hand back and stared at me in consternation. "Oh my God!"

"Do you have a phone?" I asked. "I forgot to bring mine."

"But Mr. Bryant — ?"

"No, he's still asleep. We've got to call Lieutenant Harald."

He slapped his own pockets and came up empty-handed. "There's a phone in the break room. Come on!"

He hurried toward the ramp and I followed him down and through the basement door. My glove fell to the ground and his foot sent it skidding across the floor inside, but I didn't stop to pick it up. The hall I'd seen Horvath go down earlier led to a sort of combination kitchen and common room with a set of tumbled bunk beds at the far end and a lavatory off to the side.

"Do you know Lieutenant Harald's number?" he asked, reaching for the wall phone. "Oh, never mind, I'll just call 911."

"I'll wait for them outside," I said. "Make sure the sanitation people don't take that bag."

I pulled up the hood of my parka and had taken one step toward the door when something slammed into my head.

Dazed, I fell to the floor. Before I could gather my senses, I felt myself being rolled over and over until my arms were pinned to my side. More rolling and I realized that he was wrapping duct tape around my body and over my face. I opened my mouth to scream and a wide strip of duct tape effectively silenced me. To my horror, even my nose was covered and breathing came hard.

I felt him grab me by the ankles and drag me across the floor. I bit into the tape that had folded itself upon my tongue when my screaming mouth closed. I was desperate for air and tried to writhe away from my attacker, but the struggle only made it worse. I was going to suffocate and there was nothing I could do about it.

Then merciful darkness took me.

CHAPTER 24

Occasionally there is an alley or small court that runs back or across the rear of the buildings, with its accumulation of rubbish and wretched out-houses where . . . thieves have their runways and hiding-places.

— The New New York, 1909

Dwight Bryant — Tuesday morning
Dwight turned in his sleep, reached for Deborah, and felt nothing but pillows. The window showed a dark sky, so he lay there half awake and listened for her to come back to bed. After a few moments, he realized that the only sounds he heard came from outside. A large truck was moving noisily down the street out front, but here in the apartment, all was quiet.

Puzzled, he rolled out of bed and looked into the bathroom.

Empty.

"Deb'rah?"

No answer and a quick look through the other rooms let him know she had gone out.

He glanced at his watch. Now where the hell could she be at 6:50 in the morning?

Another quick search showed that her parka and her boots were gone, which meant she had gone outside.

On the other hand, because she had not dropped her nightclothes on the bed as she usually did, he had to assume she had not dressed in street clothes, so she probably intended to duck out and be back before he missed her. But where?

He stepped out onto the balcony off the living room. The frigid early morning air nipped at his face. On the street below, a big sanitation truck with flashing yellow lights had stopped in front of this building and two men, well bundled against the cold, were collecting from either side of the street. A third man, one of this building's employees to judge by the brown uniform, was helping. Daylight had begun to lighten the dull gray sky, but from this height and at this angle, it was hard to make out features beneath their hats. As Dwight watched, the man slung what looked to be a rather heavy bag into the maw of the truck and then stood back, obscured by the other two men, with his hand on another bag as they cleared the curb of garbage. Disregarding them, Dwight leaned over the balcony and scanned the sidewalks.

No Deborah.

Down below, the man in the brown uniform swung his second heavy bag up into the back of the truck. Then, as the two sanitation workers followed the truck on down to the next pile of garbage, he disappeared through what was evidently a side entrance into this building.

Dwight quickly pulled on his boots and the wool slacks he had worn last night and grabbed up his wallet, keys, and phone, noting with exasperation that of course Deborah had left hers in the charger. One of these days he was going to chain that phone around her neck if she didn't start carrying it.

And start keeping it on.

Out in the hall, he rang for the elevator, and when it came, the operator with the walrus mustache gave a dour nod and pulled back the brass gate.

"Horvath, right?" Dwight asked as he stepped inside.

"Yeah?"

"You haven't seen my wife, have you?"

"The pretty lady that was with you last night?"

"Yes. Did you take her downstairs?"

Horvath shook his head. "Nope. You're the first from this floor since I came on duty." He closed the gate and the door and turned the brass handle so that they started down.

"You sure?"

"Positive, mister. Only been three people down so far and all of 'em were men." He paused as if to think. "And a dog."

"Could she have taken the service elevator?"

He shrugged. "I suppose. Would've heard it, though, and I didn't."

"And she didn't go out the front door?"

"Not that I saw, and I've been awake for at least an hour."

"Who else is on duty now?"

"Nobody. Just me till eight o'clock."

"But I saw someone in a brown uniform out on the sidewalk just now. He helped throw garbage bags in the truck."

"Not me, mister. Elevator men don't mess with garbage and the porters don't come on till eight."

The elevator stopped at the first floor and Horvath started to open the doors, but Dwight stopped him.

"Take me down to the basement."

"I'm telling you. There's nobody there," he protested. "I was down there not twenty minutes ago and I had the place to myself." Nevertheless, he closed the gate again and turned the brass handle another notch.

As soon as they reached the basement and the doors slid back, Dwight walked out into the dimly lit passageway and called, "Deb'rah? You here?"

No answer.

"Hey!" he called again. "Porter! Anybody here?"

Horvath watched impassively from inside the elevator.

Dwight spotted the outer door at the end of the passage and started toward it, flicking on light switches as he went. Something lay on the floor off to the side, and when he picked it up, he saw it was a glove, Deborah's glove.

His mind raced as he tried to figure out why she had come down to the basement and why she hadn't used the elevator.

He went back to Horvath and dangled the glove in front of the older man. "She *was* here. This is her glove. Who's the first porter on duty today?"

"Ruzicka and Laureano both come at eight," Horvath said again. "Although Laureano usually gets here a few minutes early."

"One of them sort of thin?"

"Laureano's on the thin side, but Ruzic-ka's built more like me."

Even from that height and even though he had not been paying that man much attention, Dwight knew that someone as hefty as Horvath would not have registered as thin.

He went back to the door and opened it to a freezing wind. Turning the deadbolt on the door so as to leave it ajar, he hurried up the ramp to the street. Still no sign of Deborah or of the man he'd seen come through this entrance. The garbage truck had crossed Broadway and was turning onto Amsterdam Avenue at the far end of the next block. He supposed he could chase it down, but to what point? Deborah had left the apartment before the truck got here and he was reluctant to leave the place where she had so recently dropped a glove.

Earlier, he had been irritated that she would go out without telling him. With two murders in this building and the teenage boy who could have killed them still on the loose, his irritation was turning into serious worry.

He pulled out his phone and ran through recent calls till he located Elliott Buntrock's number. When the man answered, his voice groggy with sleep, Dwight identified himself and apologized for waking him, "but I need Sigrid Harald's phone number."

Three minutes later, he was apologizing again. "Y'all hear anything on the Wall boy yet? Deb'rah's gone missing."

Without giving the lieutenant a chance to speak or offer reasonable alternatives, he explained his own reasoning for thinking that his wife could not have gone far, dressed as she was. "There was another guy here in a brown uniform. I saw him from the apartment balcony, out on the sidewalk, but the elevator man on night duty says he's the only worker here and nobody else is due till eight o'clock. I'm thinking that if there's an extra uniform around — What does the kid look like? On the skinny side? Something's pretty damn wrong here, Lieutenant, and I either get your help or I'm gonna start tearing this place apart room by room by myself."

"I'll be there in half an hour," Sigrid promised.

"And I'll be here in the basement," he told her. "If that bastard's hurt her —"

"Don't do anything rash, Major," she said. "I'm on my way."

Dwight turned to Horvath, who gave an involuntary step backward when he saw the big man's face.

"Honest, mister," he said fearfully. "I never saw her since last night. And nobody else is here. Honest. Just me."

"I need a flashlight," Dwight said grimly.

Horvath scuttled across the passageway, past a small laundry room, and down to the break room. Dwight followed. Two unmade bunk beds stood against the back wall at the far end of the long narrow room. The blankets were tumbled and the pillows lay haphazardly on both beds as if someone had pushed the covers all the way back against the wall and had made no effort to pull them smooth again. At this end were an old wooden table, several mismatched kitchen chairs, and a refrigerator. Along one wall lay a long counter that held a sink, a microwave, a toaster oven, and a television set. Off to the other side was a lavatory and a closet. An empty lavatory.

Ditto the closet.

When the white-haired elevator man handed him a powerful flashlight, Dwight used it to throw a beam of light under the bunk. Nothing. Back in the main landing area in front of the elevator, he gestured toward the end of the basement farthest from the outer door. The place was a warren of narrow halls and jumbled shadowy objects. "What's down there?"

"Storage. Every apartment has its own space. And there's a room for bicycles and kayaks and sleds."

With the flashlight probing everything he could see from where he stood, Dwight pointed the light at the recess that housed the service elevator. "Fire stairs?"

Horvath nodded. "You can't open the door to the stairwell from this side without a key, and Phil's the only one that had it. You have to go up to the second floor and walk down to open it from the other side. Same with the door in the lobby."

Farther down the wide passage, halfway between the niche for the service elevator and the outer door was another door. "What's that?"

"Goes to the boiler room," Horvath said.

Diagonally across the passage, close to the outer door, was another closed door. "And there?"

"That's the tool room. You know — snow blower, shovels, stepladders, leaf blower. That sort of stuff."

"Locked?"

Horvath shrugged.

Dwight strode down to the door and it opened easily. He found a light switch near at hand and used the flashlight to peer behind all the equipment.

The door to the furnace room was also unlocked, but the overhead bulb did little to brighten the cavern's dark recesses. A steel catwalk rimmed the near side of a deep concrete chamber that was at least twenty feet square and housed the boiler itself. Steel steps led down to it. The setup reminded Dwight of the boiler room in the bowels of the old Colleton County courthouse. Parts of the original steam boiler remained, but it had been patched and added onto so many times over the last eighty years that it looked like a Rube Goldberg creation. A variety of brass, copper, plastic, and iron pipes of different diameters jutted off in random directions, and an assortment of electrical cables connected the main boiler to mysterious-looking control boxes that could have spanned an era from vacuum tubes to computer chips for all Dwight knew. He had to take his hat off to the murdered super if that man had kept this monstrosity running for the last twenty years.

He played the light over the machinery and called Deborah's name.

No muffled cry. Just eerie silence except for a low hum from the machinery below.

The level on which he stood was neatly

jammed with steel scaffolding, metal extension ladders, and a miscellany of pipes that probably came in handy for keeping the boiler working. Cartons and bins held other supplies, including a large wooden box stacked with neatly folded canvas tarps, and Dwight's estimation of Phil Lundigren rose another notch. Too many workmen just threw their tarps in a pile. Lundigren evidently took pride in his work. This could have been a filthy cluttered space. Granted, it was not spit-polished, but the surfaces did not have a heavy layer of dust. The floor was swept clean and there were no loose bits of hardware to trip someone up.

He flashed the light behind the cartons and bins. Nothing moved.

Throughout his inspection, Horvath had hovered near the elevator. Now they were startled by the buzzer as one of the residents called for the elevator. The man seemed relieved to return to his regular duties.

Almost immediately, Dwight heard sirens out on the street and three uniformed cops barged through the basement's outer door.

"Major Bryant?" the lead officer asked. "Lieutenant Harald sent us. She should be here in a few minutes. She said your wife's missing from here?"

Dwight went through it again, hitting the

high spots: how she would not have gone far because she was probably wearing her parka over her nightclothes, how he had found her glove by the outer door, how there was a uniformed employee here earlier who had also vanished.

"I know you're worried, sir, but could it be that she just stepped out for a cup of coffee or something?"

The man sounded so reasonable that for the first time Dwight wondered if maybe he *was* overreacting. Deborah was gregarious. If one of the workers had come in early and she was on her way out for coffee, she might well have invited him to come along, her treat.

"The market around on Broadway opens at six," he said slowly. "And I think they do serve coffee."

"There now, you see? Bet you she's there right now. Why don't you go look since you know what she looks like and we'll keep searching here?"

Dwight reluctantly agreed. "I've covered the tool room, the boiler room, and the break room." He gestured to each in turn. "I haven't started on the storage area back there. Maybe you could — ?"

"Yessir!"

They unclipped flashlights from their utility belts, while Dwight hurried outside and up the ramp to the sidewalk. Even though he was almost running by the time he reached the corner, his eyes searched the sidewalks for Deborah's form. The Upper West Side was coming awake and starting another workday. Early commuters streamed past him, newspapers under their arms, cartons of coffee or tea in one hand, fare card in the other as they flowed toward the nearby subway station and down into the subterranean tunnels.

At the market, Dwight quartered the store like a birddog casting back and forth for a downed bobwhite. As he feared, Deborah was not there. Nor did he see anyone in a brown uniform.

As he returned to the apartment building, two more prowl cars pulled up with blue lights flashing to park next to the first two responders. Sigrid got out of one car, Detectives Sam Hentz and Jim Lowry emerged from the other, while three more uniformed officers joined them.

"Start at the beginning," Sigrid said before he could thank them for coming, so once more Dwight described waking up in the empty apartment, of determining what Deborah must be wearing, of hanging over the balcony to scan the sidewalks, of seeing a man in a brown uniform help the sanitation workers load the heavy bags from this building.

"But it wasn't the night man — Horvath — and he says he's the only employee on duty until eight o'clock, so who the hell was it and where is he now?"

Sigrid had gotten even quieter than usual as she concentrated on his words. Now she turned to Lowry and said, "Call Sanitation. Find out where that truck is and tell them to hold it."

"Oh, shit!" An iron band tightened around his chest as her meaning sank in and he remembered that Antoine Clarke's body would have been set out at the curb had that porter not hunted down the missing wheeled bin.

White-faced, he described how heavy the bags had seemed and how the slender man had swung the last one back and forth until he finally got enough arc to sling it up into the maw of the truck.

He read the look that passed between the three detectives and knew they were thinking the same thing.

"Describe him again, please," Sigrid said. "You said a hat and a brown uniform. Coveralls or jacket and slacks?"

"I didn't look that closely," Dwight admitted.

"But thin?"

"Yes."

"Black? White?"

"The light was bad, but I have an impression of light skin. Certainly not real dark."

"Any facial hair?"

"Not to notice. He —" He broke off as a slender young man entered the basement from the outside door. "What the hell? That's him!"

Before the others could stop him, he rushed forward and grabbed the newcomer by the collar of his brown uniform jacket. "What have you done with her, you bastard?"

Scared and bewildered, the new elevator man cowered and put up his hands to ward off the blow. "Done with who? When? I just got here."

"You've been here since six-thirty. You were out on the sidewalk. I saw you."

"Not me, man. What's going on?"

Hentz put a hand on Dwight's shoulder. "Calm down, Major."

"James Williams?" Sigrid asked. "The new elevator man?"

"Yes, ma'am. Just started yesterday."

"Okay," Dwight said, lowering his hackles.

"I get it." He released his hold. "Sorry."

Jim Williams straightened his jacket. "But for real, man, what's happening?"

Before Sigrid could tell him, her phone rang. She glanced at the screen and signaled for Hentz to finish explaining.

The uniformed cops returned from the back to report. "Nothing obvious, sir. We need keys to get into those storage bins and look behind stuff."

"Forget it," Hentz told Dwight. "The locks belong to the owners and even Lundigren didn't have duplicate keys."

He sent the three officers to check the nearer buildings to see if any of the night people on duty had watched the garbage pickups earlier and had noticed any activity from this building.

Sigrid ended her call. "That was Tillie," she told Hentz. "We're putting out an APB on Sidney Jackson."

"Sidney?" Dwight exclaimed. "The evening man?"

Sigrid nodded. "My sergeant got in early and started going through the pictures the party guests gave us. There's a clear shot, time-stamped, of Antoine Clarke opening the elevator cage at ten-ten and again at ten-fourteen, which means that Sidney Jackson doesn't have an alibi for at least part of the relevant period. That elevator was so crowded, I couldn't even swear myself who was working it when I got here Saturday night."

Hentz pursed his lips thoughtfully. "Like waiters and salesclerks."

"Invisible men," she agreed.

"Yeah, that could've been Sidney I saw out on the sidewalk," Dwight said. "He has the right build. Haven't they located that truck yet? Can you give me a car?"

"Easy, Major," Sigrid said, realizing that he had not noticed that Lowry had left after taking a call a few minutes ago. From the nod Lowry had given her, the truck had been located and stopped. "Soon as we know anything, you'll know."

The elevator descended and a weary Jani Horvath pulled back the cage just as two buzzes hit their ears. He spotted Williams, glanced at his call board, and said, "She's all yours, kid. Take her straight up to eight and work your way down."

"Yessir," an eager Williams said.

"Lieutenant?" one of the uniforms called from the outside door. "The night man across the street says he saw a woman and one of the men from here out by the garbage bags around six-thirty, give or take a few minutes."

A sick feeling washed over Dwight as he realized he had missed Deborah by less than twenty minutes.

"He say who the man was?" Sigrid asked.

"No, ma'am. Just that he saw them come back in, and then a couple of minutes later the guy came out by himself."

"Was he carrying anything? More garbage?"

"Sorry, ma'am," the young cop said. "He said the guy helped load some of the bags, but he didn't say if he brought one out with him."

Something in the lieutenant's look made him feel like a complete incompetent.

"I'll go back and ask him," he said hastily.

"You! Horvath," Dwight called as the night man headed for the break room.

"Yeah?"

"You said you came down here around six-thirty. You sure you didn't notice anything? Was the outside door open?"

He shook his white head. "Might've been a few minutes before six-thirty, and if that door was open, I'd've felt a draft, and I didn't."

Even as they spoke, the outer door opened again and the second porter, Hector Laureano, arrived.

"Hey, what's up?" he asked Horvath, following the older man into the break room.

The young cop was back almost immediately. "No, ma'am," he told Sigrid. "He came out empty-handed, stayed to help throw the bags in, and then went back in. Said he saw a big guy come out to the sidewalk a few minutes later and then go back in. No woman either time."

"Dammit!" Dwight exploded. "They're still here then! Horvath says Lundigren was the only one who could unlock the stairwell doors from this side. You have to go up to the second-floor service landing to get to the stairs and come down to open either the lobby door or this one. So he's done something with Deborah and he has to be hiding here somewhere."

"You said you found one of her gloves by the outer door," said Sigrid. "If she stuck it in the door to keep it from locking, maybe she did the same on that door. If so, Jackson could be anywhere in the building. Or he could have been waiting around the corner of the lobby till Horvath left and then walked out the front door."

Nevertheless, she sent the troops up on the service elevator to search the stairwell and the hallways. After giving them a description of Sidney Jackson, one man was put on the lobby door and another positioned at the outer door just in case he was still in the building.

Frustrated and unable to stand around doing nothing, Dwight had combed through the storage area himself, shining the flashlight from ceiling to floor, looking behind anything bigger than a wastebasket that wasn't locked in one of the cages.

As he passed by Hentz and Sigrid on his way to check out the front part of the basement again, he saw that Sigrid had her phone pressed to her ear again.

"They find the truck?" he asked.

Sigrid shook her head and stepped away to finish listening to what Jim Lowry had to report. No way was she going to tell Dwight Bryant that the truck had been found and that it carried a bag containing Corey Wall's body.

"I cut it open so that I didn't disturb the knot," Lowry said. "Looks like the poor kid was smashed on the head just like Lundigren. Probably happened around the time he went missing. No rigor anyhow. I've called for the crime scene unit, but we've gone down another layer of bags below that one and I'm pretty sure it's nothing but garbage."

"Good work, Lowry," she said. "Keep me

informed."

In a low voice, she told Sam Hentz what Lowry had found, but before he could comment, they heard Dwight call to them from the service elevator.

"Look here," he said and turned back one of the quilted plastic pads that hung from a series of hooks along the top edge of the elevator wall to protect the walls from getting banged by heavy furniture deliveries. "I noticed that one of the grommets wasn't on its hook, and when I reached up to put it back, the first one slid off and — well, look for yourselves."

He turned back the loosened pad and they saw a large blood spatter across the width of the pad.

Hentz stepped into the car and lifted the rear pad. More blood. Fairly fresh, too. None on the wall, though, which meant that someone had reversed the pads.

The floor of the elevator was fairly clean, but Dwight pointed his flash to the side wall where it joined the floor. "That grunge in the crack look like blood to y'all?"

"Call for a crime scene crew," she told Hentz, "and let's secure this elevator till they get here."

Dwight immediately brought over a chair that stood against the far wall and positioned it so that the door couldn't close.

"Major . . ." Sigrid began.

"You don't need to say it," Dwight said grimly. "I can see it's not fresh enough to be Deborah's blood. You reckon it's from that kid that went missing?"

"I'm afraid so."

"He came down to go sledding," Dwight said slowly, piecing together the likely scenario. "And he probably saw Sidney stuffing Antoine in a bag, so Sidney had to stop him, too. Only why you reckon Sidney killed Antoine?"

"Because Clarke could put him in your apartment at the same time Lundigren was killed. He must have seen people going in and out. Clarke was in early, planning to spend the night because of the predicted snow. Jackson could have told him he needed a bathroom break or something, and while Clarke ran the elevator, Jackson probably intended to duck in and grab those gold pillboxes, thinking their loss could be blamed on Denise Lundigren or some of the party guests. Just his bad luck that Lundigren picked that time to bring back that painted cat. Jackson probably panicked, grabbed up that brass maquette, and hit him as hard as he could. God knows what he hit the Wall kid with. We'll have the whole

390

basement processed. They'll turn it up if it's here."

As they spoke, the door to the stairwell was opened from the other side by one of the uniformed officers. "No sign of him here, Lieutenant. You want me to prop this door open?"

"Yes, please. What about the hallways?"

"That's gonna take a little longer. People are going to work, and so far, none of them have seen this Jackson guy today. There's a Mrs. Wall up on twelve who says she wants to speak to you."

Her cool gray eyes met Hentz's dark blue eyes.

"Want me to go?"

She shook her head. "Too soon. I want to talk to Lowry again."

Dwight looked around. "Was he that other detective? The one that called Sanitation? Where'd he go?" He took one look at their faces and his own face tightened. "He found the truck, didn't he?"

"She's not there, Major," Sigrid said. "The boy is, but she's not."

"Then where the hell is she?"

"If they're in the building, we'll find them. I promise."

He glared at her, then turned away.

"Where are you going?"

"To look for some rat holes. That bastard's worked in this building for almost twenty years. He's bound to know some we've missed."

As he strode away, Sigrid said, "Stay with him, Hentz. If he does find Jackson, we don't want another killing on our hands before we find out what he did with Judge Knott."

Chapter 25

Aside from the regular patrolmen there is the Sanitary Squad, that has to do with enforcing health regulation; the Traffic Squad, that regulates the traffic of the great thoroughfares; . . . the Boiler Squad, that examines engines, boilers, and engineers.

— *The New New York,* 1909

Dwight Bryant — Tuesday morning (continued)

"I thought you said you'd already searched here," Hentz said, following Dwight into the dim and cavernous boiler room.

"I didn't go down to the lower level." Dwight flipped the switch beside the door and frowned at the low-watt bulb that hung from a cord overhead. "I can't believe Lundigren kept that thing running with no more light than this."

He shined his flashlight on the steel steps

that led down to the steam boiler. Near the bottom was another wall switch, and this one turned on an array of fluorescent tubes concealed from above by the crossbeams to which the fixtures were attached.

While Hentz watched from the upper level, Dwight ducked under the many pipes and edged past the boiler into a recess in the wall beneath Hentz's feet.

"See anything?" Hentz called when Dwight disappeared from view.

"Looks like a barrel of rags back here." Dwight's voice bounced and echoed off the concrete walls and metal pipes.

He approached the chest-high barrel cautiously and gave it a shove that tipped it over and sent it clanging along the floor. "Nothing but rags," he called up to Hentz.

As he stooped to avoid the pipes that crisscrossed overhead, he heard an oddly familiar yet unidentifiable noise carried to his ears by an acoustical trick of the pipes. "Was that you?" he asked Hentz.

"Was what me?"

"I don't know. I thought heard something." He put his ear close to the return pipes but heard only the faint flow of water. As he started back around the boiler, he noticed a low flush door with a simple thumb latch. He stooped to open it and flashed the light inside a space that opened up higher at the back and seemed to terminate in a door secured with a heavy padlock. "Looks like it might have been the coal bin when the boiler was coal-fired," he said.

Again, he flashed the light all around and under the antiquated boiler, to no avail.

"I could've sworn this would be the sort of place he would hole up in," Dwight said.

As he came back up, he flicked off the bright lights till they were once again in near darkness, and his conviction was stronger than ever. That unexpected noise he had heard while below only strengthened it.

"You ever go deer hunting?" he asked Hentz.

"Huh?"

"Deer can't count, you know. They'll stay in the bushes and watch while four guys climb up into a deer stand." Dwight had gradually lowered his voice till Hentz could barely hear him. "When three guys climb back down and leave, the buck doesn't know there's still a man in the stand."

"Because deer can't count?" Hentz asked, humoring him.

"You got it, pal." Raising his voice to a normal conversational level, Dwight said, "No, we can cross the boiler room off. He's not here."

He opened the door for Hentz, gave the detective a significant look as the other man passed through, and in one fluid motion flipped off the light and slammed the door loudly.

Then he stood in the darkness and waited. Almost immediately, he heard a faint sigh, followed by that same rustling sound he'd noticed before.

It came again and he finally recognized it for what it was. His first impulse was to dig Jackson out of his hiding place and wring his scrawny neck. Instead, he opened the door and motioned Hentz back inside.

"He's over there," he told the detective. "Burrowed down deep in that bin full of tarps and drop cloths. I was sloppy when I checked it the first time. Didn't go down far enough."

Hentz walked over to the wooden bin and gave it a kick. "Come on out, Jackson. It's over."

They heard strangled noises as that pile of plastic tarps heaved and shifted till the night man surfaced and stood up. His face was contorted and they realized that he was crying like a guilty child who fears there's a whipping in his future.

"I didn't mean to!" Sidney Jackson sobbed when he hoisted himself over the edge of the bin. "They made me do it." He fumbled in his pocket for a handkerchief. "They made me! Phil! And Corey! Oh, God, Corey!" he wailed. "I knew him since he was a baby. I didn't want to hurt him. I didn't! I used to help take his stroller in and out. I let him pull the gate back for me when he was just a little kid. Why would I want to hurt him? Three minutes later — three lousy minutes! — and he'd still be alive." He wiped his streaming eyes and nose and tried to make them understand his hard luck.

"You think I wanted them dead? But they kept popping up. Every time I turned around, there they were — Phil, Corey, even Mrs. Bryant. Every damn time! I couldn't let them tell, could I? *Could* I?"

Sobbing as they led him out into the basement, he was a mixture of remorse and indignation. Grief for his victims mingled with petulance and self-pity for what he felt they had forced him to do. He collapsed onto the nearest chair and buried his face in his hands, blubbering and snuffling.

"Where is she?" Dwight snarled. "What have you done with my wife?"

"I didn't want to hurt her," Sidney sobbed, "but she was out there on the sidewalk when I got here to beat the garbage truck. She found Corey. She wanted me to

call 911. She was going to tell. What could I
do?"

CHAPTER 26

People when "cabined, cribbed, confined,"
cannot be very happy or comfortable.
— *The New New York,* 1909

I came to slowly, disoriented and hot. I was lying on my side in total darkness. Cautiously I wriggled my fingers and felt rough cloth. There was something familiar about it, but I couldn't make myself concentrate. More cloth touched my face and weighed on my body, which was probably why I was so warm. To my surprise, I could breathe. Not as deeply as my oxygen-deprived lungs wanted, but enough to keep me alive. My mouth and one nostril were completely covered with the duct tape, but as long as I lay quietly and took slow even breaths, I wouldn't suffocate.

Where the hell was I, though? Taped and swaddled, I had no clues. I could hear voices, muffled and far away. Should I try to draw attention to myself, or would that make Sidney come back and finish me off for good? Stupid, stupid, *stupid* not to have realized that he was the figure I saw disappear around the corner last night after setting the bag with Corey's body out by the curb.

He must have come back to make sure it got on the garbage truck without one of the sanitation workers noticing. Probably threw it in himself. Is that where he is now? Will he come back with a garbage bag for me?

I moved my head forward almost imperceptibly and felt a solid wall. Oh, God! Was I in a coffin? About to be buried alive? I gingerly tried to flex my legs backward. They were hampered by the weight of the cloth, but there seemed to be nothing solid behind me. Wherever I was, it wasn't a coffin.

Yet.

The muffled voices came closer. Two men?

I felt the surface where I lay give as something heavy pushed it down. Then light hit my eyes.

And I was not the one who screamed.

CHAPTER 27

Indeed, one hardly knows what New York would do if the police were not on hand to keep the lawless and the violent in restraint.

— *The New New York,* 1909

Frustrated and enraged, it was all Dwight could do not to grab Sidney Jackson by the scruff of his scrawny neck and shake him till he answered.

"Easy, Bryant," Sam Hentz said. "We found him, we'll find her."

"Hey, Lieutenant!" Vlad Ruzicka rushed down the hallway from the break room. "Come quick. She's in here! Jani almost sat on her! Hurry!"

Sigrid immediately started down the hall, but Dwight pushed his way past her. At the far end of the long room, they saw a startled Jani Horvath staring at what had been concealed behind the tumbled covers on the bottom bunk bed next to the wall. It looked like a silver-gray cocoon, a cocoon that wriggled. With the hood of her parka still over her head, Deborah lay bound in duct tape from her mouth to her toes. In his haste to get out to the curb before the sanitation workers discovered Corey's body, Jackson had evidently used a full roll of tape to keep her immobile while he made sure he was the one to toss Corey's body into the truck.

As Dwight gently turned her over, he was relieved to see blue eyes implore him and to realize abruptly why she wasn't struggling harder.

"Somebody get me some scissors," he called. Without waiting, he pushed back the strip that partially blocked her nose. "Better?"

She took a deep breath and nodded.

Scissors were produced and he carefully cut the tape on both sides of her face where it wound around the hood of her coat. She made impatient sounds that it was taking him too long. "Wait a minute, shug. You don't want me to cut your hair, do you?"

A moment later he had eased the tape off her lips and then cut enough to free her arms and legs. She looked like a mummy festooned with tattered wrappings, a beautiful mummy come back to life when he feared she was lost forever.

She insisted on standing, but moaned when he touched her head. "Ow! That hurts like the devil."

"Where?" Dwight pushed back the wool-lined hood and gently examined the spot she had touched. "You've got a goose egg there, but no blood."

"What the hell did he hit me with?"

"Whatever it was, you were lucky you had that hood on," Sigrid said.

She instructed one of the uniformed officers to take the Bryants to the nearest hospital and to wait until she was either released or kept overnight for observation. To her surprise, Deborah did not protest.

When they returned three hours later, patrol cars were still thick around the service entrance and a cop remained by the lobby door to check IDs.

"Mrs. Bryant!" the new elevator man exclaimed. "You're okay? Shouldn't you be in the hospital?"

Deborah gave him a dazzling smile and looked at the shiny new brass name tag pinned to his neat brown jacket. "I thought you were going to be Jim here."

"Yeah, I forgot to tell them, so go ahead

and say it."

She laughed. "Home, James, and don't spare the horses!"

CHAPTER 28

From 1860 to 1880, steam and hydraulic elevators were in use, but it was not until about 1888 that electric elevators came into vogue. . . . With the coming of the elevator the eight-story buildings began to pay better in their top floors than in their middle or lower ones. "High livers," so called, preferred the light and air up aloft. Everything began to rise with the elevator — buildings, prices, ambitions, expectations.

— *The New New York,* 1909

I've heard too many stories about stoics who insist they're fine, just fine, after a blow on the head, then twelve hours later they're dead from a blood clot or other complications.

Not me, baby. Life's too good to risk losing it because I might feel silly for taking up a doctor's time. I admit that I fought it the first time around when a crazy woman smacked me on the head last year, but the doctor who examined me then made me a believer when he described how one of my favorite actresses would still be making movies if she'd only seen a doctor after a minor skiing accident.

Dwight told me that I must have been wrapped up in those hot blankets motionless for about an hour, and that was serious enough for the doctor at the hospital to make me jump through several hoops, including a CT scan and a series of perception tests. My head was sore where I'd been hit, but I didn't have a headache, my reaction times were within normal parameters, and I could perfectly remember everything up to the moment I was whacked. The doctor finally theorized that I'd been stunned just enough to let Sidney Jackson swaddle me in tape and hide me in the lower bunk by pushing the blankets over me to look like an unmade bed.

"Between your lack of sleep, the adrenaline rush you must have had after finding that body in a bag, and your oxygen deprivation, you probably just transitioned from a daze into an exhausted sleep." He told me that I was a very lucky woman and discharged me with nothing more than a few samples of a mild pain reliever that he had on hand.

Once we were back in the apartment, Dwight wanted to coddle me. I myself wanted to go down to the basement and find out what was happening, but Sigrid had called him at the hospital while I was being examined and said she would be stopping by later, so Dwight convinced me I'd be in the way downstairs.

Just as well, because as we were getting off the elevator, James had handed me a small Tiffany Blue shopping bag. The handles had been tied together with a tag that had "For Apt. 6-A" crudely printed on it in black ink.

"It's been so busy today, I didn't see who stuck it there," he said, gesturing to a small pile of UPS and FedEx parcels in the corner, waiting for people to come home from work.

As soon as I felt the heft, I knew it was that piece of bronze erotica that Mrs. Lattimore had sent up to Sigrid's mother. I pulled the cords of the bag apart enough to peek inside and saw that it was swathed in white tissue.

"We'd better leave it for Sigrid's people to open," I told Dwight. "Though I'm willing to bet they won't find a single fingerprint or a single smidgen of DNA."

"None of Cameron Broughton's anyhow," Dwight agreed. Like me, he was convinced that it was Luna DiSimone's decorator who had taken it.

"You're probably right about Broughton," Sigrid said when she got there a little later. "I suppose we could link him to that flip-flop, but any good attorney would argue that your earring could have been dropped anywhere on this floor. And if he polished off his own fingerprints, then he polished off Jackson's. We might still find a trace of Lundigren's blood. Jackson admits that he panicked and grabbed up something heavy when Lundigren caught him rifling the apartment here. A man of impulse, our Sidney Jackson."

"Is he still blaming everybody else?" Dwight asked, as he opened a bottle of wine and filled our three glasses.

"Oh, yes. According to him, none of this would have happened if people had been where they were supposed to be. If Lundigren had come or gone five minutes earlier, if Corey hadn't come down to the basement at the precise moment he was disposing of Clarke's body, if Deborah hadn't come out just before the garbage trucks got here . . ."

We were seated around the coffee table in the living room. I suppose it was callous to ignore the reason a bath mat would be lying at an odd angle on the hardwood floor by the French doors, but truth to tell, I had almost quit noticing it. After a certain amount of time, an eyesore becomes something the eye passes over without really registering. I had finally changed out of my nightclothes and was seated at one end of the comfortable leather couch, ready to explore the plate of cheese and crackers Dwight had set out. I put a dab of Brie on a pita chip and popped it into my mouth, suddenly ravenous after missing breakfast and lunch. "So Denise wasn't the building's only thief?"

Sigrid was seated in a squishy leather club chair across the table from me and waved away the plate when I offered it, but accepted a glass of wine from Dwight.

"Jackson kept tabs on the whole building — who was home, who was out. Conditions for any one apartment had to be perfect." She sat her wineglass on the coffee table to tick them off on her thin fingers. "Denise Lundigren had to have cleaned there the same day that outside workmen were there, and the residents had to be out for the evening. Plus, the service doors had to have

409

one of the old locks on it. He'd helped carry in enough packages over the years to know which apartments had valuable little objects sitting around like those gold pillboxes."

"What about Antoine?"

"Jackson says Clarke figured it out right away and was willing to tell him what went on during his eight-to-four shift for a cut of the profits. Only he was greedy and wanted to hit every apartment that met Jackson's conditions, and Jackson didn't want to do it more than three or four times a year, so Clarke was starting to freelance for himself." Sigrid lifted her glass and took a swallow of wine. "Clarke drew the line at murder, though. He relieved Jackson during the party, but he'd gone to sleep before he heard that Lundigren had been killed. As soon as he heard the next morning, he called Jackson and accused him. Jackson knew it was either blackmail or exposure, and he couldn't afford either. He figured correctly that Horvath would go to bed before he got here and the porters don't work Sundays, so he thought he'd have plenty of time to dispose of Clarke before the man was missed, only here came the Wall boy down to get his sled and go have some fun in the snow."

Sigrid lapsed into contemplation of the

wineglass she held cradled in her hands and I figured she'd had a rough session with the boy's parents. That's always the hardest part for Dwight. I glanced at his face and he looked as if he was remembering some bad times of his own.

To break the mood, I said, "I know he hid that wheeled bin with Antoine's body, but what did he do with the Wall boy? Don't tell me he stashed him in one of those bunk beds, too?"

Sigrid shook her head. "Not with Horvath snoring away in one of them. No, he used the boiler room."

"Under the tarps?" Dwight asked.

She nodded.

"So the cavity was already there when he needed a bolthole."

"Right. He was no longer thinking clearly —"

"Hitting me and taping me up like a mummy was thinking clearly?" I asked indignantly.

Sigrid and Dwight both smiled.

"No, I guess not. I don't think he knew what he was going to do with you. The main thing was to get outside and sling Corey Wall's body onto the garbage truck before one of the sanitation workers tried to lift the bag. He no sooner got back inside than he heard the elevator descending, so that's when he dived into the boiler room and hid."

"Elevators," I mused, holding out my glass for a refill. "All that coming and going."

"Only up and down," Sigrid said. "Never in and out. Horvath told us that Antoine was jealous because Corey would be going off to college, working at a better job, making a richer life, while he was going to be an elevator operator all his life."

She swirled the wine in her glass. "In an odd way, I suppose the same went for Jackson, only he couldn't afford to lose this job at his age. Especially since he's still paying off the nursing home bills for his father."

Sigrid finished her wine and stood to go.

"Don't forget this," I said, handing her the little Tiffany bag. "If you ever find out why Mrs. Lattimore had it, I hope you'll tell us. Maybe we can get together if you're down next month."

"Maybe." She seemed almost shy for a moment as she thanked me again for telling her about her grandmother. "Mother's due in tomorrow night. I know she'll want to meet you."

"That would have been nice," I said, "but we've decided to cut our trip short and go home tomorrow morning."

(In the squad car on the way back to the apartment, we had agreed that we'd rather finish our honeymoon at home. With Cal.)

"I'm sorry your trip turned out like this," Sigrid said. "I hope it hasn't soured you on New York."

"It would take more than a murder investigation to sour me on this city," I said. "Only next time we'll bring our son with us. There's so much to show him."

"And I still want to hear Sam Hentz play the piano," Dwight said.

She smiled. "Me, too."

I gave her our Gilbert and Sullivan tickets, and as we walked her to the door, Sigrid paused with her hand on the knob. "Did your nephew figure out who used his cell phone and hijacked his Facebook page?"

I shrugged. "I haven't talked to the kids today, but I think I would have heard if they did."

"This may sound strange, but my housemate — he writes mystery novels, and something he said last night made me wonder."

"Oh?"

"You said that two other boys had the lockers next to his and a freshman girl had the one beneath his?"

413

"So?"

"I know that one of the boys might have done it because he was jealous of your nephew, but what if the freshman girl was jealous of the nephew's girlfriend? If he never paid her any attention, maybe he never noticed that she had watched him dial the combination on that lock. Old student locks aren't all that precise anyhow, are they?"

"Oh, Lord!" It was too logical not to be true. And remembering my own early teen years, who more likely to keep pawing through Lee's locker than a fourteen-year-old girl who had the hots for him? "The one person they all overlooked?"

Sigrid smiled. "The least likely suspect."

CHAPTER 29

From the high tower of the Singer or the
Metropolitan Building the eye travels
around the ring and sees waterways, land-
ways, bridgeways, railways, radiating and
crossing, leading outward and onward.
                    — *The New New York,* 1909

We spent the evening tidying up the apartment, emptying the refrigerator of everything that wouldn't make a picnic lunch on
the train, and packing our suitcases.

While I was busy elsewhere in the apartment, Dwight used a wood cleaner on that
bloodstain so that it really wasn't very
noticeable. Nevertheless, I wrote a note to
Jordy Lacour to explain that the police had
his missing gold-and-enamel pillboxes and
to tell him why there was an overly clean
spot on the floor near his French doors. We
left him a bottle of good brandy as a thank-
you for the use of his apartment.

I emailed the kids a group letter to ask if the culprit might be the freshman girl Jess had dismissed out of hand. Something in the picture's background had already made them start to wonder if it had been taken in a stall in one of the girls' restrooms. They had been ready to accuse Mark McLamb's girlfriend of helping Mark and Jamie Benton embarrass Lee, but thought the girl with the lower locker was much more likely since Lee hadn't even bothered to learn her name after bumping into her every day since school began back in September.

Cal had sounded ecstatic when we called to say we were coming back early. "Bandit's wagging his tail like crazy," he told us. "He's really, really glad." He paused, then said, "We're not gonna have to stay at Grandma's so you can finish your honeymoon, are we?"

"Absolutely not," I told him. "We've been missing you and Bandit way too much for that."

Next morning, as our southbound train broke free of the dark tunnel under the Hudson River and out into the first real sunlight we'd seen since leaving home, Dwight and I looked back across the snowy New Jersey landscape for a final view of Manhattan. We even caught a brief glimpse of the Statue of Liberty before Dwight settled into his seat with a contented sigh.

We both agreed that it would be good to get home.

"Yesterday?" he said. "When you told Lieutenant Harald that we'd be back? You said 'with our son.' "

"Did I?"

"Is that how you feel about Cal?"

Confused and unsure what he wanted my answer to be, I said, "I know that he'll never stop remembering that Jonna was his mother, but yeah, after a year, I sometimes forget he's not really my son, too."

"He should have been yours." Dwight drew me closer so that my head was tucked under his chin. "Whatever I'd felt for Jonna was gone long before Cal was born. I should have waited."

"No," I said. "If you'd waited, Cal wouldn't be here."

"Still . . ."

I reached up to touch his face and put my fingers across his lips to stop him. "Still, nothing."

He kissed my fingers and tightened his arm around me as the train lurched toward Newark. "All the same," he said, "I never told you this, but after the first few months, whenever Jonna and I made love, I used to pretend she was you. I knew it wasn't fair to her, but I couldn't help myself. It was you I made love to the night Cal was conceived."

I was flooded with such emotion that I couldn't speak.

He tilted my chin up so that he could look into my eyes, and just before we kissed, he said, "So in some psychic way, he really is your son."

My son?

Yes.

My thanks to those inveterate New Yorkers, Vicky Bijur and Susan Richman, for allowing me to take aspects of their Manhattan apartments and shape them to the needs of this book.

ABOUT THE AUTHOR

Margaret Maron grew up on a farm near Raleigh, North Carolina, but for many years lived in Brooklyn, New York. When she returned to her North Carolina roots with her artist-husband, Joe, she began a series based on her own background. The first book, *Bootlegger's Daughter,* became a *Washington Post* bestseller that swept the top mystery awards for its year and is among the 100 Favorite Mysteries of the Century as selected by the Independent Mystery Booksellers Association. Later Deborah Knott novels *Up Jumps the Devil* and *Storm Track* each won the Agatha Award for Best Novel. In 2008, Maron received the North Carolina Award for Literature, the state's highest civilian honor. To find out more abut the author, you can visit www.Marga retMaron.com.